BEACON STREET GIRLS

This book belongs to:

VERITAS AMICITIA GAUDIUM
truth friendship fun!

™

CR

promises, promises

First Edition

The characters and events in this book are fictitious.
Any similarity to real persons, living or dead, is coincidental and not
intended by the author. References to real people, events, establishments,
organizations, products, or locales are intended only to provide a sense
of authenticity, and are not to be construed as endorsements.

Series Editor: Roberta MacPhee
Art Direction: Pamela M. Esty
Book Design: Dina Barsky
Illustration: Pamela M. Esty
Cover photograph: Digital composition

Produced by B*tween Productions, Inc.
1666 Massachusetts Avenue, Suite 17
Lexington, MA 02420

ISBN: 0-9758511-2-8

CIP data is available at the Library of Congress
10 9 8 7 6 5 4 3 2 1

Printed in the U.S.A.

CR

Visit the Beacon Street Girls at: www.beaconstreetgirls.com

Isabel M.

Sometimes you just need to cool down ...

PART ONE

PROMISES TO KEEP

CHAPTER 1

ೞ

TICKLED PINK

"OH, OH ... I forgot. I've got some really interesting news!" Maeve exclaimed as she sank down in the middle of her sleeping bag, her giant, fuzzy pink slippers sticking out in front of her. "You're not going to believe it!"

"Lights out!" Mr. Ramsey called up the steep, ladder-like stairs to the Tower.

Charlotte jumped up to flip off the lights. "OK, Dad," she called down. "Good night!"

Charlotte's dad was pretty great about letting the Beacon Street Girls have sleepovers in the Tower as long as the girls kept the noise level down and cleaned up after themselves. He'd even helped the girls make individual pizzas this evening, and the aroma of homemade dough still lingered in the air.

The sleeping bags were arranged in a starburst pattern so their heads came together in the center of the room.

"Oops," squealed Charlotte as she tripped over Avery's legs on her way back to her sleeping bag, catching herself at the last moment before crash-landing right on top of her friend.

She stumbled to the sleeping bag, flopped on her stomach, and propped her chin in the palms of her two hands.

"Good catch," laughed Avery.

Charlotte shrugged. Her clumsiness was now just "pulling a Charlotte" to all her friends; her famous cafeteria disaster when the tablecloth got stuck in her zipper was hardly ever mentioned. Nope, she thought, she was just their friend ... clumsiness and all. It gave Charlotte a warm and cozy feeling.

Maeve lowered her voice now that the lights were out. "Seriously, I have totally important news," she repeated as the other four—Charlotte, Isabel, Katani, and Avery—inched closer to the middle so they could hear what Maeve had to say.

Charlotte pushed up at her glasses and squinted through the grainy darkness trying to focus. Maeve's animated expressions added so much to whatever story she was telling. Maeve could make a trip to the grocery store sound like an African safari.

"Anyway ..." Maeve paused dramatically. "Guess who's running for ..."

A tiny snort filled the momentary silence.

Avery was the first to giggle, but almost instantly, Isabel and Maeve joined in.

Before Maeve could say another word, a louder snort punctuated the silence.

"Charlotte! Is that you?" Katani asked.

No giggle this time. Katani's comment resulted in an out-and-out belly laugh from Avery. It was hard for the other BSG not to laugh when Avery did. They were all in hysterics now.

The next snort had them rolling on their sleeping bags.

"Charlotte!" Katani said.

"It's not me!" Charlotte said. She could feel her cheeks

turn pink. She knew the girls didn't really think it was her making that noise, but it was embarrassing just the same.

"But it's coming from your sleeping bag, Char." Maeve's observation was followed by the loudest snort yet.

"It's Marty!" Charlotte said, falling forward and laughing into her pillow. Marty, the Beacon Street Girls' mascot, was a wiggly, cuddly, always-getting-into-trouble-but-so-cute-he-gets-away-with-it, dog.

Ever since Marty came to live in the second-floor apartment of the stately Victorian home that Charlotte and her dad rented from their mysterious landlady, Miss Pierce, he had been a constant source of amusement for the BSG.

Marty's snores were the result of a full evening. First the "little dude" had greeted each BSG in ceremonial fashion, dancing around their legs and jumping up and licking their faces when they bent to pet him. Then he had supervised the making of the pizzas, dutifully snarfing up any dropped tidbits from the Ramseys' kitchen floor. He had begged his share of pizza crusts by sitting up, cocking his head to one side, and making pathetic, yet somehow irresistible, whimpering noises.

When Maeve had changed into her pink nightshirt and pink fuzzy slippers, Marty had gone wild! He lunged and pounced on the advancing fuzzies with every step she took, growling, nipping each slipper, and shaking it with intense ferocity if he happened to grab ahold of it.

No wonder he was exhausted. When the girls had finally rolled out their sleeping bags, he'd snuggled into a cute little ball at the end of Charlotte's sleeping bag and instantly fell asleep.

"How can such a little dog snore so loudly?" Isabel wondered.

Marty snort-snored and the five of them burst into

laughter all over again. It seemed the louder they laughed, the louder Marty snored.

"Does he always sound like that?" Isabel asked, her dark eyes wide with amusement.

Charlotte was laughing so hard she couldn't answer. She buried her head in her pillow and nodded her head.

The next snort-snore sent Avery rolling around on her sleeping bag, clutching her stomach, legs kicking wildly in the air.

"Shhhhh! You're going to wake him up," Katani told Avery.

"I don't see how he doesn't wake himself up," Maeve said.

As if he heard that comment, Marty lifted his little head, shifted his body so he was facing away from the girls and fell immediately back to sleep—this time without any snort-snores.

"Poor little puppy!" Avery said. "He's exhausted from protecting us from your slippers, Maeve."

"Who can blame him? Those things are as big as he is!" Charlotte said.

"Size has nothing to do with it. He just hates pink. Good boy!" Avery said as she reached over and petted the sleeping terrier.

Like Marty, Avery was a bundle of endless energy. Also like Marty, Avery was small—so much shorter than Katani, who looked like a contestant on *America's Next Top Model* in her satin blue pajamas.

"Leave it to you Katani," Charlotte said, "to look like a page out of a fashion magazine, even at a sleepover."

"The Kgirl has to keep up her image," Katani answered with a mock sigh. "You just never know when there might be paparazzi about."

"Now you sound like me," said Maeve, the budding actress of the group.

"No one could sound like you, Maeve," Katani replied matter of factly, while Charlotte, Avery, and Isabel chorused in laughter.

Maeve shrugged her shoulders. "What can I say? I'm one of a kind. Now ... do you all want to hear my news or what?"

In response, Avery threw a pillow at Maeve and the battle was on. Pillows went flying, Marty started barking, and the BSG laughed until the tears came rolling down their faces. The mayhem subsided when they heard footsteps on the stairs to the Tower.

"Do I hear a pillow fight in there?" Charlotte's father bellowed in a fake English accent, which also meant, "Please quiet down, I am trying to go to sleep."

"No, Dad. We're all done," Charlotte shouted as her voice shook with the giggles.

"Excellent news, Charlotte, I shall retire in peace now."

"Char, your dad is so funny," whispered Avery.

"Well, I know he thinks he's pretty funny," Charlotte responded. She paused, then added, "No ... he *is* funny." Her timing was perfect.

The BSG laughed in agreement. Mr. Ramsey was a pretty cool dad. He'd traveled all over the world, but he was a down-to-earth guy and pretty much let the girls do whatever they wanted in the Tower, as long as they didn't damage any property ... and they let him get some sleep!

"As I was saying," Maeve continued when the giggles died down. "I know who's running for seventh-grade class president."

"Duh! Who doesn't?" Avery said, hitting the side of her head with the heel of her hand. "Dillon Johnson."

Ms. Rodriguez, their homeroom teacher, had announced Friday morning that elections would be in three weeks. The news had started their Friday off with a bang of excitement that was still lingering on Saturday night. Charlotte was especially excited because this was a new experience for her. She and her father had lived all over the world and had only recently moved back to the United States. None of her other schools had held class elections.

Isabel pushed herself up on her elbows. "What's up with Pete announcing to the world in the middle of lunch that Dillon is running for class president? Didn't he hear Ms. R say that if you want to run you should email her by Monday morning? They want to post the candidates on the main bulletin board at the end of school on Monday."

"Pete Wexler isn't one to follow the rules," Avery reminded Isabel.

"But I still can't believe the way he did it!" Katani added. "I mean jumping up on the chair in the middle of the cafeteria and declaring that the seventh grade needed someone COOL to be president and that Dillon was the 'King of Cool.'"

"Well," Maeve said, tossing back her red hair, "he kinda is the King of Cool, but I'm not talking about Dillon. There's someone else running for class president."

"How do you know?" Avery asked.

"I found out when I stopped by to talk to Ms. R after school. I saw something on her desk."

"Whoa! Maeve! Were you snooping on Ms. R's desk?" Avery asked.

"I was SO not snooping, Avery Madden! I just happened to glance over. It was lying right on top! And it was all typed and formal looking. You couldn't miss it … it was huge," Maeve added dramatically.

The girls exchanged looks. Charlotte knew they were all thinking the same thing. Typed and formal looking? That could only be one person! Betsy Fitzgerald. Betsy was nice enough, but besides being a bit of a know-it-all, she had a tendency to make simple things complicated.

"Was it from Betsy Fitzgerald?" Charlotte asked.

"Can you believe it?!"

"Betsy Fitzgerald's running for class president?" Avery asked.

"So, who do you think you'll vote for?" Isabel asked. "Dillon or Betsy?"

"I'm really not excited about either of them," Katani said. "Probably the only reason Dillon is running is so that we can have more school dances. He loves to show off what a great dancer he is."

"He's got a one-track mind!" Avery said. "I think we should have gym nights instead."

"Who has a one-track mind?" queried Charlotte with a hint of amusement.

She was remembering how Avery was like a fish out of water at their first school dance earlier this year. Super-comfortable and totally coordinated on the soccer field, Avery had two left feet on the dance floor. So did Katani, but unlike Avery she loved dressing up. More importantly, Katani loved helping the rest of the BSG dress up, too. Katani was the Makeover Queen of the BSG—a regular Style Miracle Worker! However, to Katani's eternal frustration, Avery refused to let Katani talk her out of her favorite sweats!

"Maybe you should run for class president with an anti-dance platform, Avery," Charlotte suggested.

"Well, a pro-dance platform would best represent MY interests," Maeve said. "In fact, I can't wait for the election dance. Everyone dresses up fancy; they announce who won; and then we dance the night away. It's absolutely fantabulous," she added with a flourish.

The BSG grinned at that one. Not only was she a fabulous dancer, but Maeve had been the first Beacon Street Girl to go out on a date. Well, it was almost a date. Maeve and Dillon had gone to a Celtics basketball game with Dillon's dad and brother. Of course, Maeve wasn't supposed to be there, but that was a whole other story.

When Charlotte first met Maeve at the beginning of the school year, she had almost dismissed her as one of those "boy crazy" girls, but, as she got to know her better, she realized there was so much more to Maeve. Besides being eternally optimistic, Maeve was a bundle of fun, ready to drop anything to help out a friend. And, she was quite talented, too. Still, Charlotte wondered if Dillon became class president if that would make Maeve "First Girlfriend"? Of course, one almost-date does not a girlfriend make, so who knew.

"Give me a break," Avery said, rolling her eyes to the ceiling and flopping back on her sleeping bag.

"What's wrong with that?" Maeve asked. "I'd like more school dances."

"There are issues more important than school dances, Maeve," Avery told her.

"Avery's right," Katani said.

"You mean you'd rather have Betsy?" Maeve asked.

"Betsy Fitzgerald? Please!" Katani said.

"What's up with Betsy?" Isabel asked.

"That's a question I've never been able to figure out. What *is* up with Betsy?" Avery asked.

"She's not such a bad choice. Betsy is very organized," Charlotte pointed out.

"I'm organized," Katani said. "Betsy is obsessive. Besides, the class president should be more than organized."

"I don't know why you think Dillon's a bad candidate," Maeve chimed in. "He's very popular."

"Being popular has nothing to do with being a good leader!" Avery said. "In fact, to be a good leader you sometimes have to do things that aren't popular. That's why it's important that our class president know how to make good decisions."

"About what?" Maeve asked

"Oh, tons of things! Budgets, ecology. Stuff like that," Avery replied.

"Ave, I don't think kids really care about stuff like that," Maeve said.

"Well, I do," Avery answered emphatically.

"Me, too," added Katani as she and Avery high-fived each other.

There was a pause and it was suddenly very quiet. Not even a snort from Marty could be heard.

Isabel broke the silence. "Maybe YOU should run for class president, Avery."

"You've always dreamed of being president," Charlotte reminded her.

"President of the United States," Avery said.

"I thought you wanted to be a judge," interjected Maeve.

"Well, the President of the United States thing is not going to happen, Avery," Katani reminded her. "You have to be born in the United States to be President of the United States."

"Big Deal! So I'm adopted. I'm a citizen, just like you guys. So what if I spent the first four months of my life in Korea? I'm as American as ..."

"Apple pie ...?" Isabel suggested.

"Stop! You're making me hungry," Avery moaned.

"Still … rules are rules," Katani said.

"Well, like Ms. R pointed out at the beginning of the school year, rules are made to be challenged and changed! Arnold Schwarzenegger, the Governor of California, is already looking at changing that particular rule," Avery said huffily.

"*I'll be back … as President of the United States,*" Maeve said in her best Arnold accent. "*And I'll terminate anyone who gets in my way.*"

Maeve was definitely the performer of the group. Movies were her life. After all, she lived over the Movie House, and she could watch movies any time of day or night. Charlotte was convinced that someday she'd be on E! *True Hollywood Story* saying, "I knew Maeve Kaplan-Taylor when …" And perhaps, Charlotte fantasized, she'd also be on A&E's *Biography* telling the world about her junior high school days with Avery Madden, President of the United States. If anyone could convince someone to change a rule it would be Avery. She never gave up when she had a point to make.

"While Arnold's working on that minor detail … you might as well start getting some experience, Avery. Abigail Adams Junior High seems like the perfect place to start," Charlotte told her.

"Well … it did cross my mind … but … I can't."

"What do you mean you can't?" Katani pushed herself up, swung her legs in front of her in a cross-legged position, and leaned toward Avery. "Avery, all the things you said … about a leader being a team player and a good decision maker and being inspirational. That's YOU! You were describing yourself!"

"It could be any one of us," Avery said, looking around the group.

The girls looked into each other's eyes.

"Not me," said Maeve, who had learning problems. "I don't think people with reading problems make good leaders."

"That is completely not true, Maeve," Katani said quickly, rising to her friend's defense. "Remember your blanket project? You practically got everyone in the school involved in that one."

"Oh, yeah. I forgot about that," Maeve responded happily.

Charlotte wasn't sure if she had leadership potential either, though one day she hoped to be editor of their school newspaper, *The Sentinel*. Maybe when she grew up, she could write speeches for the president someday. Now, that would be fun—telling the President of the United States what to say, she thought.

"Katani's right," Isabel said enthusiastically. "You're a perfect candidate for class president, Avery. You have tons of energy and you aren't afraid to speak your mind. I like that in a president."

"I didn't say I don't WANT to run. I just can't. I promised my coach that I'd help with the soccer fundraiser which starts in a few weeks," Avery answered, secretly pleased that her friends were so enthusiastic.

"Avery, you have a passion to lead," Katani cried, more excited by the minute about the idea of Avery's candidacy. "Our class needs you! We need you!"

"But a leader is also someone who keeps the promises they make," Avery said. "I promised Coach Graber I would lead our team's fundraising efforts. I could never let my soccer team down. It just wouldn't be right."

"Couldn't you do both?" Isabel asked hopefully.

Avery hung her head. "My mom just had a big talk with me about like not getting 'overextended' and stuff."

"But that just leaves us with Betsy and Dillon," Katani

said. "The seventh-grade class deserves someone who will represent our interests better than those two."

Charlotte glanced at Maeve, who looked like she was about to say something, but changed her mind. The BSG knew that you never wanted to question Katani when she was on a roll. It was better to talk to her when she was all calmed down. She was much more willing to listen over a cup of hot chocolate at Montoya's Bakery.

The subject switched to Avery's soccer tournament and the game tomorrow. Soon the group quieted, and one by one, the Beacon Street Girls fell asleep.

WHO ELSE?

Long after their conversation had died down and the steady breathing of her four friends filled the Tower, Katani's head was still whirling. No way could she vote for either Dillon or Betsy. Avery was right! Popularity was so overrated. Katani liked what Avery had to say about budgets and decisions. Those were important things that even kids should know about. Yup, she thought to herself, Avery would be a great class president!

As Katani lay awake thinking of things—issues the class president could take on—Avery, her face smushed down in the pillow, started snoring like a three-hundred-pound gorilla. Katani wondered how such a big noise could come out of such a small body.

Finally, Avery turned over, mumbled in her sleep and kicked her legs until she freed them from her sleeping bag. The snoring stopped. Thank goodness, Katani thought. Maybe she'd be able to get some sleep now. But for the next hour, Katani thought of nothing but the upcoming election. Somehow she just had to convince Avery to run.

Charlotte's Journal

I just love Tower sleepovers! Last night Mr. Marté's snoring was the big entertainment ... now they know what I have to put up with every night! Dad's homemade pizza dough was a hit, too. Everyone brought toppings and we each made our own individual pizzas. Maeve and I smothered ours in four types of cheeses. Isabel brought a huge bag of pepperoni to share. Katani brought lots of veggies—mushrooms, onions, green peppers, and black olives—she and I were the only ones who liked the olives. She didn't just toss them on her pizza. She arranged them in the most beautiful design. Leave it to the Kgirl to have a pizza that looks like it could be in a magazine.

Avery brought spinach for her pizza. Sounded pretty gross to me, but I had a taste and it wasn't bad at all. Maeve refused to try it. She said, "Spinach on pizza is a food crime."

In the morning, I woke up before the others and decided to climb on my window seat to write. (Serious writers have to practice all the time!)

When I looked across the room, I could see the full moon setting in the west, perfectly framed in Maeve's window. It was the color of a huge Florida orange, and it seemed to just hang in the western sky over the lights of the cars on the Massachusetts Turnpike. I wished Isabel was awake for it. She loves the color orange so much. She would've flipped over this.

I like that my window faces east—I guess because I've always loved sunrises. They aren't the same as sunsets at all. No matter where I've lived—Africa, Australia, Europe—sunrises have always meant new possibilities ... new adventures. (Ever see a lion walking toward you at dawn?)

This morning when I glanced around the Tower to each window—mine, Katani's, Maeve's, and Avery's—it was painfully obvious that SOMETHING WAS MISSING. I don't know why it never occurred to me, or to any of us, before.

Isabel doesn't have her own place in the Tower: no window of her own, no window seat, no name in lights. It doesn't feel right ... and it's not fair. She is one of the BSG now.

I don't know how to fix this. I don't even know how to bring it up without upsetting the others. Katani might have some real problems with this. She already has to share her room with her sister Kelley; I know she won't be excited about losing some of her space in the Tower.

How can we add space for Isabel without taking away space from the rest of us? Solution desperately needed.

CHAPTER 2

ॐ

ON SECOND THOUGHT ...

"MOM ... I'm home!" Avery hollered as she raced through the front door. She dropped her duffle bag inside the door and trotted into the kitchen, where she found her mom going over a list for another upcoming charity event. Avery thought her mother might have given up on stuff like that after the whole guinea-pig-in-the-salad-bowl disaster a month or so ago. But her mother had said it was her calling to raise money for charities. It was what she was good at, so she might as well keep at it. She had a point, thought Avery. But what if Coach G knew about the guinea pig disaster? Maybe he'd change his mind about wanting her to take charge of the soccer fundraiser, Avery thought hopefully.

"What's up?" Avery asked, as she rocketed past her mom and went straight to the refrigerator.

"I'm just putting together my calendar for next week," Mrs. Madden said, looking up from the paperwork spread on the table in front of her. "Did you have fun at Charlotte's?"

"It was awesome! I made a spinach pizza for dinner, but Maeve thought it was too gross for words!" The mention of food set Avery's stomach rumbling again. Mr. Ramsey had made pancakes for the girls this morning, but that felt like hours ago. Avery grabbed a bean burrito from the freezer, shoved it in the microwave, and pushed *start*. Then she grabbed the phone, punched in Coach Graber's number, and opened the refrigerator again looking for something to go with the burrito.

"Avery, dear, please close the fridge. I swear when you're home that refrigerator door is open more than it's closed," Mrs. Madden said in an amused tone.

Avery took one last look at everything inside and shut the door just as Coach Graber's answering machine clicked on. As the message played, she wondered if it would be possible to talk her mother into buying one of those refrigerators with the see-through doors so snackaholics like herself could scan the contents quickly.

Coach Graber's answering machine beeped. Avery swallowed hard and started her message. "Coach G, this is Avery. I was ... uh ... just calling to ask about the fundraiser. I mean, I'm still planning on doing it and everything, but ... well ... uh ... something's come up at school, and I need to know if this fundraiser's going to take like a lot of time and stuff. Guess we can talk about it later."

Mrs. Madden put down the calendar, took off her reading glasses, and looked directly at Avery. "What was all that about?"

Avery felt as if a police spotlight had been shined on her. "Well, Ms. Rodriguez announced that class elections are coming up ... and we were all talking at Charlotte's last night that ... well ... I've always wanted to be president of something and ... my friends ... all thought that maybe a good place to start would be ..."

"Avery Koh Madden. You have basketball AND soccer AND you promised to be in charge of the soccer club fundraiser. And don't forget about your schoolwork! Do you think you have time to run for class president?"

"I know, but …"

"Avery, you have so much going on right now, you have to be careful that you don't get overextended. I think you would have to give something up, sweetheart."

"I know, but the girls—they think I'm perfect for the position and … I've always wanted …"

"I agree that you would be wonderful, but unless you give up one of your other commitments, you can't run for class president. That's way too much. You will be too exhausted."

"I won't. I have a ton of energy."

"Avery," her mother admonished as she stood and put her arm around Avery's shoulders. "I know you. This is too much. I am going to have to say NO on this one."

Avery's mind flashed from basketball to soccer to the soccer club fundraiser. She thought of saying that she would gladly give up some of her schoolwork, but she knew that wouldn't win any points with her mom.

The microwave dinged and she grabbed the warm burrito, wrapped it in a napkin, and headed upstairs.

"Avery … please don't leave your bag in the foyer," her mom called from the kitchen.

Avery snarfed down a chunk of her burrito as she turned on her computer. Great, a message from Maeve. Then she remembered her bag. She rocketed back downstairs, grabbed her duffle, shot back upstairs, and tossed it in the direction of her bed. Before she had a chance to respond to Maeve, there was another message from Isabel.

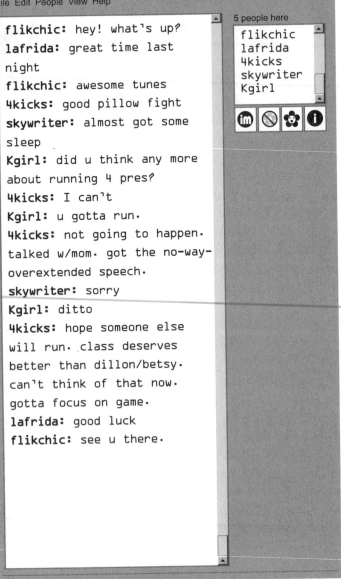

Chat Room: BSG

File Edit People View Help

5 people here

flikchic
lafrida
4kicks
skywriter
Kgirl

flikchic: hey! what's up?
lafrida: great time last night
flikchic: awesome tunes
4kicks: good pillow fight
skywriter: almost got some sleep
Kgirl: did u think any more about running 4 pres?
4kicks: I can't
Kgirl: u gotta run.
4kicks: not going to happen. talked w/mom. got the no-way-overextended speech.
skywriter: sorry
Kgirl: ditto
4kicks: hope someone else will run. class deserves better than dillon/betsy. can't think of that now. gotta focus on game.
lafrida: good luck
flikchic: see u there.

RUN! RUN! AS FAST AS YOU CAN!

Katani signed off the computer and started to put her room in order. She always set aside time on Sunday after church to clean her room and plan the upcoming week. Katani's bedroom looked like something out of *Pottery Barn Teen*.

Katani shared her room with her sister Kelley. Even though she loved Kelley dearly, Katani thought sharing a room with her mildly autistic sister was a major annoyance. If Katani left anything lying around, Kelley might walk off with it—especially Katani's nail polish. So it was very important for Katani to keep her side of the room straightened up so Kelley wasn't tempted.

Katani made the best use of every space—like her desk. She loved all the shelves and cubbies above her desk. Her desk accessories were brushed with stainless steel. The magazine holders and pencil holders were made from wire mesh. The muted silver complemented the blue plastic stacking boxes which held everything from nail polish to paper clips. She had six in all, each a wonderful shade of blue. She used cardstock in her signature sunflower yellow to label the boxes. It was the perfect accent. Yellow always made her smile. Sometimes Katani thought she should live in Miami, Florida. Lots of yellow there and great fashion, too!

Katani finished organizing her desk and plopped on her bed. Loud noises always freaked Kelley out, so Katani put on her earphones, plugged them into her CD player, and cranked up the volume.

She grabbed a mini yellow pad and started writing. Before she knew it, she'd come up with a terrific list of why Avery should run for president of the seventh-grade class.

Why Avery Should Run for Class President:

1. *Good decision maker*
2. *Makes quick decisions*
3. *Makes fair decisions*
4. *Leadership experience—organized soccer players to help younger players*
5. *Says what she thinks ... ouch! (but honesty is good)*
6. *Very practical*
7. *Not easily swayed. Sticks to what she thinks is best ... even if it's not popular*

Katani flipped to the next sheet of paper to start a second list, "How to Convince Avery to Run For Class President," when Kelley wandered into the room with her favorite stuffed animal, Mr. Bear.

"Whatcha doing, Katani?" Kelley asked.

"I'm trying to figure out how to convince Avery to run for seventh-grade class president."

"Why?"

"Because class president is important and the two people who are running wouldn't be as good as Avery."

"What's number one on the list? Number one! Number one!" Kelley asked.

"Good decision maker," Katani said.

"What's number two on the list? Number two! Number two!" Kelley asked as she danced around the room to her own tune.

Katani dutifully read through the list as Kelley called out the numbers. "That's all," Katani said when she reached number seven.

"YOU should be president, Katani," Kelley said loudly.

"President Katani ... President Katani."

"Kel, that's really sweet but Avery is the one who has always wanted to be president. It's just that she thinks she's too busy. I'm trying to convince her that busy or not, she should run."

Kelley shook her head and crossed her arms in front of her. "President Katani. President of the Abigail Adams Junior High School. Best darn school in the world."

Kelley sounded just like their Grandma Ruby, the principal of Abigail Adams Junior High. Katani wanted to laugh out loud, but she didn't dare. Kelley would get mad and then it would be a big scene.

But Kelley's words made Katani blink. Where did Kelley ever get that idea?

"I don't think so," Katani said, but even as she said it, Katani felt something bubbling inside her.

Kelley pointed to the pad. "You WANT to run for president," Kelley repeated before she left the room, loudly singing, "Run! Run! As fast as you can! Can't catch me, I'm the Gingerbread Man! Vote for President Katani!"

Katani looked at the list in front of her—good decision maker, leadership experience, says what she feels—just replace soccer team captain with Talent Show stage manager and the list could be about her. Katani realized Kelley was right. She'd been stirred up ever since they had started talking about the elections last night. Was it more than just wanting to have a good candidate? Or was it because she really wanted the job?

How did Kelley do it? Katani wondered. There were days when Katani thought her sister didn't have a clue as to what was going on, and other days when Katani thought Kelley was part mind reader. Sometimes, she seemed to know what Katani wanted before Katani even realized it was what she wanted.

With a tingling realization, Katani suddenly knew that she wanted to be president of the seventh-grade class.

Wow! What a shocker!

Katani jumped up and started pacing around her room. This was Avery's lifelong dream. How could she just swoop in and take over? But if Avery couldn't run, shouldn't someone take up the cause? "It's not like I'd be doing it for myself," Katani reasoned out loud. She'd be doing it for the whole class—Avery, too. But Katani wasn't sure if Avery or the other BSG would see it that way.

Katani was still toying with the idea when she arrived at the soccer fields in Corey Hill Park later that afternoon. The tune that Kelley had been singing all morning was stuck in her head, "Run! Run! As fast as you can! Can't catch me, I'm the Gingerbread Man!"

As she waited for the other BSG, she applied pale pink lip gloss and adjusted her multi-colored knitted cap as Isabel walked toward her.

"Cool cap," Isabel said.

"Thanks!" she said, twirling around for Isabel to see. Katani had knitted the cap herself in alternating stripes of bright violet, in-your-face kelly green, and her signature sunflower yellow. It was the perfect complement to her bright violet hoodie. "Kgirl, that is the coolest yellow," Isabel enthused, pointing to the bright yellow stripe in Katani's hat. "It reminds me of the color in Van Gogh's sunflower paintings," she added.

"Yeah, isn't it awesome? I couldn't believe it when I found the yarn," said Katani.

"You have to teach me to knit sometime. I want to make

a bunch of cool scarves this winter. Maybe something in Valencia orange and sage green," Isabel added, carried away with the colorful vision in her head.

"No problem. Scarves are easy to knit. I know ... I should teach all the BSG how to knit. We could do scarves for Maeve's shelter. The kids would love it," exclaimed Katani.

"Great! We could call ourselves the BSG knitwits," laughed Isabel.

Isabel and Katani chatted for a few more minutes about violet and yellow—how it was such an awesome color combination. The other BSG sometimes thought they were a little obsessive about the topic, so Isabel and Katani decided to keep their "colorful conversations" just between the two of them.

As soon as Maeve and Charlotte joined them, they headed to the top of the bleachers. It was the last round-robin soccer tournament of the season.

Katani loved to watch Avery play. Avery was the youngest player on the Brookline U-14 team. Today she was playing left midfield, racing up and down the field playing offense and defense. Avery had great soccer instincts, full of endless energy and motion. Even when the ball was on the other side of the field, Avery never stopped cutting to get open or running back to mark the opposing players. Not great at sports herself, Katani enjoyed watching her friend play.

"Whoa! Did you see that shot on goal?" Charlotte nudged Katani and pointed. Charlotte wished she was on Avery's team, but played on the U-12 team.

Katani shook her head. Today, she was having too hard a time concentrating on the game; she was so preoccupied by the upcoming class election. She just couldn't shake what Kelley had said about the list ... "These are Katani things."

But how would Avery feel if she decided to run? Avery could be sooo competitive …

"OOOhh," the crowd let out a collective groan, but the Brookline fans and the other BSG were standing and cheering loudly.

"What happened?" Katani asked, her attention jarred back to the game.

"Avery just stole the ball from #7 on the red team!" Maeve said. "Wow! If Avery hadn't gotten there, #7 probably would have scored. Anyone want some hot chocolate from the concession stand?"

"Yes, please," answered Charlotte.

"That sounds good. I'll help you. Come on, Maeve," Isabel volunteered. "Want some too, Katani?"

Katani nodded.

Isabel and Maeve got up, slid past the fans sitting in the bleachers to their left, and trotted down the bleacher steps.

As soon as they left, Katani and Charlotte turned their attention back to the game. On the field, the ball sailed toward the sideline and into the crowd of spectators.

"Char, I need some advice," Katani said as the players on the field waited for someone to retrieve the ball and throw it in. "About running for class president."

There, it was out. That was the first time that Katani had said it out loud. The words rang in her ears and gave her goose bumps. She was both proud and embarrassed at the same time.

Charlotte didn't say anything at first, but Katani could tell she was surprised by the idea. Charlotte took her eyes off the field and looked directly at Katani. "But what about Avery?" she asked.

Katani looked away from Charlotte and watched Avery as she dribbled the ball past midfield and passed it forward to her teammate Amanda Cruz, who was playing left wing. "I'd never run if Avery was running ... but since she can't ..."

Charlotte and Katani both watched intently as Amanda dodged two defenders and took a shot on goal. When the goalie dove for the ball and made a great save, the crowd cheered and jumped to their feet.

Katani was silent, waiting for Charlotte to answer. "Well?" she finally asked. "What d'ya think?"

"You're right. Avery made it clear in her IM that her mom said no way," Charlotte said.

"You know I'd never run if Avery was running; I'd never do that to a friend," Katani repeated. "It's just that all the things we talked about last night got me thinking about leadership and the class budget. I have so many ideas! And the more I thought about it, the more I realized that I could do a good job."

This time Charlotte didn't hesitate. "Katani, you'd be great! You did so well as the manager for the Talent Show. You're very good with budgets. You're as organized as Betsy. I think the seventh-grade class would be lucky to have you for class president."

"You don't think Avery will be mad?"

"Are you kidding?" Charlotte said. "How many times did she say, 'Maybe someone else will run?' She'll be thrilled to have a quality candidate to vote for. To represent the seventh-grade class. To represent her! This way, her voice will be heard, too."

They both laughed. There was no way Avery's voice would ever not be heard.

Katani took a deep breath, let it out slowly, and smiled for the first time since she started this conversation. She spied Isabel and Maeve weaving in and out of the crowd as they returned, each carrying two cups of hot chocolate.

"Thanks, Charlotte. You're the best! Let's keep this between us, OK? I'll tell everyone myself tomorrow." She gave Charlotte a quick hug before turning her attention back to the game, just as Maeve and Isabel returned to their seats.

Even though Avery's team was winning, Katani couldn't wait until it was over so she could go home and email Ms. Rodriguez that she, Katani Ida Summers, was going to run for president of the seventh-grade class. The very thought sent a wave of excitement through her. With the Beacon Street Girls behind her, she knew that she had a good chance—no, a GREAT chance—of making it! Kelley was right. President Katani had a certain ring to it.

UNDER THE WIRE!

Avery didn't have a chance to get Coach Graber alone after the game so she didn't know if he'd gotten her phone message. She'd just email him later. Besides, she was so caught up in the after-game celebration and pizza that she kind of forgot.

When Avery finally got home, she took a quick shower and went to her room.

Between the soccer games and the BSG sleepover, her room had become a pit stop. In fact, that was a great way to describe her room—it was a pit. Even though she had two walk-in closets, almost every piece of clothing she had worn in the last week was on the floor. On top of that, all her soccer equipment was piled up—and it wasn't pretty.

Her mom used to try and get Avery to clean it up every day, but now all she did was walk by and shake her head. Avery's clutter made her "neat freak" mom a little uneasy, but Mom and daughter both agreed that if Avery promised to pick up once a week, Mom would ignore "the pit." The arrangement worked for both of them.

It was clear that Avery had plenty to clean up today to get ready for the week ahead, but she decided to spend some quality time with her pet snake, Walter, first.

"Hey Walter," she said, tapping the glass. Walter was coiled up inside his hide box. She kept the aquarium in her other closet because Carla, the housekeeper, freaked whenever she saw the snake. Avery would gladly have traded Walter for a furry companion if her mom wasn't so allergic to everything with fur. Watching Maeve's guinea pigs a few weeks back had been fun, but what she really wanted was to have Marty full-time. Her mother's allergies made that impossible.

Still, Walter had his plusses. Avery loved the way he stuck out his tongue at her. When she picked him up, Walter coiled around her arm and raised his head, his little black tongue going in and out at regular intervals. He was getting ready to shed his skin again. She could tell because his eyes were getting milky.

Avery wished she could shed some of her own responsibilities, but she didn't know which ones she would shed. She liked—no LOVED—doing all those things. She hung her head, wishing there was a magic solution to this dilemma.

There was a tap at the door, and Avery's oldest brother, Tim, who was in college, stuck his head in. "I'm going to shove off ... back to school. Great game today."

"Good night. Oh, and thanks for coming to the game."

"Hey! You look like your best friend just died. What's up?"

"Nothing. I mean, nothing that I can do anything about."

"Talk to me, kid," Tim said, coming in the door, and picking up a Nerf ball off the floor. Pushing a pile of clothes out of the way with his foot, he sat down on the floor next to Avery.

"How's the snake doing?" Tim asked, tossing the Nerf at Avery's head.

"Better watch out, I'll sic Walter on you."

Tim grimaced. He was not a big fan of snakes. Neither was her other brother Scott.

"So what's going on, shorty? You look kind of glum," Tim continued.

"Seventh-grade class elections ... I want to run for class president, but ..."

"Go for it! You've always been interested in stuff like that."

"That's just it. I want to run, but Mom says I can't. She doesn't want me to get 'overextended.'"

"Got a lot going on?"

"Basketball, soccer, and the soccer club fundraiser. I told Coach Graber I'd be in charge of it."

"Whoa! What are you—the Energizer Bunny? It's no wonder she said chill!"

"But she said I could run if I gave up something else. The problem is I don't want to give up anything else. Well, I'd give up the fundraising thing but ... I promised Coach G. I'd rather give up schoolwork."

Tim laughed. "That'll work. I can see Mom really going for that!"

"Yeah ... I know."

"So no President Madden!"

"I guess not."

"Tough break, kid. And I think you had it in you," Tim said, tousling her hair, careful to avoid contact with Walter. "Well, gotta go. Maybe next year for President Avery."

As he got up to leave, Tim bounced the Nerf ball off her head.

Avery put Walter back in his aquarium and made sure the wire cover was securely in place. Then she checked on her other pet, the Frogster, who was sitting on his rock staring into space. The Frogster was into relaxation. Or as her friend Nikki liked to say, he was "chillaxing."

Suddenly, Avery felt really tired. It had been such a busy weekend. Maybe she would go to bed early, and clean up in the morning. She grabbed her favorite pjs and got ready for bed.

The lights had been out for a half hour before she shot up and turned her computer back on. She couldn't sleep. All she could think about was running for class president. Why had she forgotten to talk to Coach G after the game? She decided to make a last-ditch effort to ask Coach exactly how much time the soccer club fundraiser would take. Maybe it wasn't as much as she thought. She sent him an email asking how much time was involved and exactly when he would need her. With that out of the way, she was finally able to fall asleep.

As soon as she woke up, Avery rushed to her computer to see if Coach Graber had responded. She clicked on the newest email in her inbox.

```
To: 4kicks
From: Coach Graber
Subject: Soccer Club Fundraiser


Avery—
Glad you emailed. I've been meaning to call
you for days and forgot to talk to you after
the game yesterday. I have a big project at
work so we're going to have to postpone the
soccer fundraiser until late spring. Hope
```

```
that works for you. I'll keep you posted.
Coach G.
```

"Yes!" Avery cheered as she raised both arms in the air. Ms. R had said to email her before class on Monday, hadn't she? Immediately, Avery tapped out an email. She could barely contain her excitement. After their talk the other night, she knew she could count on her friends to support her. At least she knew she had four votes. That was a great start.

CHAPTER 3

☙

AND THE RACE BEGINS

"YOUR STYLE of one-frame cartoons is perfect for the layout of the paper," Jennifer Robinson, editor-in-chief of the Abigail Adams Junior High School newspaper said to Isabel when she called her at home. "We want something edgy that reflects current issues at school. Are you up for that?"

Isabel, of course, had said yes—who wouldn't want to be on the staff of *The Sentinel*?! But Isabel had tossed and turned all night, wondering if she'd be able to follow through. What if she couldn't do it? She loved drawing cartoons, but usually hers featured cute little birds and what she thought of as "everyday kid smarts." What if she couldn't come up with "edgy"? Edgy was for kids like Anna and Joline. She was more … *cute*.

Jennifer's words echoed in Isabel's head as she got dressed this morning. "Something edgy that reflects current issues at school." Isabel wanted to do this, but felt like she needed advice to get started on the right foot.

When she told her mother about being asked to draw cartoons for the paper, her mother had been excited and proud of her. Isabel didn't want her to see that she was nervous about whether she could be edgy. Plus, edgy to a mother meant a belly shirt!

"Wait up!" Isabel called out when she caught sight of Charlotte's vintage denim jacket half way down the hall. Charlotte didn't hear her and continued on. Isabel ran after her weaving in and out of the students in the seventh-grade hall.

"Charlotte!" she called again. Charlotte turned and stopped when she saw Isabel. "Charlotte, I'm so glad I caught up with you. I desperately need your advice. I got a call from Jennifer last night. She wants me to be on *The Sentinel* ... as the *official* cartoonist. I'm so excited ... but, I don't know if I can do it. I'm so nervous ... cartoons on demand ... edgy cartoons on demand ... maybe it's too hard."

"Oh, Isabel, you can do it!" Charlotte said as she hugged her. "Your cartoons are so awesome! I wish I could draw like you. My doodles are almost as bad as Avery's."

"No way, Charlotte. Your drawings are good. They're like the kind you see in travel books."

"Thanks, Isabel. I feel flattered hearing that from such a great artist as yourself," Charlotte grinned as Isabel gave her a playful punch on the arm.

"I am so glad you recognize genius," Isabel added in a snobby accent.

Charlotte and Isabel continued to walk slowly down the hall, their classmates hurrying past them on either side. "But, seriously, Charlotte, I was up all night trying to think of ideas. Cartoon ideas come so easy to me when I don't have to think of any. Now that I know I need two cartoons by the end of the next week, I'm completely and totally blank. It's like I can't think of anything."

They had stopped at Charlotte's locker, and she was busily

working her combination. Charlotte paused. She wanted to say something encouraging to Isabel who was sounding really nervous.

"I think the best thing to do, Isabel, is to listen to what everyone's talking about," Charlotte said as she jerked her locker door open. "Maybe it will spark some ideas."

"OK, I can do that," Isabel answered, leaning back against the locker next to Charlotte's.

She closed her eyes for a moment and focused on the hall talk around her. Isabel trusted Charlotte. Charlotte understood things that other people didn't. Maybe, thought Isabel, it was because her friend was really smart and had been all over the world.

Charlotte hung up her jacket and took out her books for her morning classes while Isabel tuned in to snatches of conversations as kids passed in the hall. As soon as she was finished in her locker, Charlotte slammed her locker door and leaned back to join Isabel in eavesdropping.

"... Dillon as president ..."

"... class president ..."

"... Betsy Fitzgerald is running for treasurer."

"... would make a great secretary ..."

"What's that?" Charlotte asked, pointing to the neon green sticker on Josh Trentini's shirt.

Four more classmates passed wearing the green stickers somewhere on their shirts. Isabel stopped the next person wearing one, who happened to be Josh's identical twin, Billy. "What's your sticker say?"

Charlotte and Isabel both stared at the sticker on his collar.

"Yurt Alert?" Charlotte and Isabel asked at the same time.

"Yeah, Henry Yurt is running for class president," Billy Trentini said before he continued down the hall.

"Hmmm. I think I see a theme. Class elections?" Isabel asked.

"I think you have a winner with Henry Yurt," said Charlotte. "The Yurtmeister should make for some very *interesting* cartoons."

Charlotte, Isabel, Katani, and Maeve arrived at homeroom simultaneously, just as the bell rang. Avery was already in her seat and smiling. Isabel figured yesterday's victory had soothed Avery's disappointment over not being able to run for class president.

"Let's take our seats," Ms. Rodriguez said. "We have a lot to go over this morning."

Ms. R usually kept homeroom relaxed and easygoing. On Mondays, she often gave the students a chance to talk about what had happened over the weekend. But not today. Today, she asked them all to take their assignment books out. Quickly, she went over a whole list of upcoming events at school, ending with a reminder that the slate for the upcoming election would be posted on the main bulletin board at the end of the school day.

"I'm pleased to say we have a full slate of candidates. I'm looking forward to an exciting campaign," she said as the bell rang. "Don't forget to turn in your book reports," she reminded them all.

As everyone pushed out the door and headed to first period, Isabel thought how Monday had a particular feel to it … rushed and harried. Immediately, an image popped into her head. A robin on Monday morning. Something about the early Monday morning worm. Now that would make a great cartoon. Isabel smiled to herself, and then she shook the thought away. She was supposed to be contemplating the seventh-grade election. But, nothing had popped into her head about that.

Cartoons on demand … maybe she wasn't ready to be Abigail Adams Junior High's resident cartoonist just yet, Isabel thought nervously. She'd better ask the other BSG if they had any suggestions.

Isabel was the last to arrive to the BSG lunch table. She pulled out the chair between Charlotte and Maeve. Katani and Avery were sitting on the other side of the table. Both of them watched her as she sat down. No one had started eating except Avery, who was well into her favorite turkey wrap that was stuffed with Craisins and carrots and cranberry sauce.

Isabel thought everybody in the lunchroom seemed jittery today … even the Beacon Street Girls. As soon as Isabel sat down, Katani glanced over at Charlotte. Charlotte smiled at Katani and nodded to her as if encouraging her to go ahead. What was going on?

"Guess what!" Katani and Avery said at the same time.

"Go ahead," Katani said, slumping back in her chair.

"No … you go ahead," Avery said, rolling her eyes.

Katani and Avery looked at each other and motioned for the other one to go first. Exasperated, they both turned to face Isabel, Maeve, and Charlotte, and said at the same time, "I'm running for class president."

They turned to look at each other again.

"What?" Katani asked. "What did you say?"

"I said I'm running for class president!" Avery announced excitedly. "Coach G put off the fundraiser until spring. So now I can run. Isn't that great?"

Avery glanced around the table. "Hey," she said. "I expected whoops and cheers, but all I'm getting are goofy looks. What's going on?"

Avery turned to Katani, who looked like she had

swallowed a canary. "I thought you said you didn't want to run?" Katani said.

"I NEVER said I DIDN'T want to run. I said I COULDN'T run because I had too much to do. My mom said if I cut one thing that I could run. Now because the fundraiser thing was pushed back ... I can run. Isn't that great?"

No one said anything. Isabel appeared confused, Maeve stared at the ceiling, and Charlotte looked nauseous.

"Uhhh ... what did YOU say, Katani?" Avery asked.

Katani looked at her shoes.

"What did you say?" Avery asked again.

"I said the same thing you did. I'm running for class president too," Katani said.

"You're running for class president? What's up with that? I didn't know you were even interested, Katani!"

"Well, the more we talked about class president, the more important it seemed. We talked about it at the game yesterday, and Charlotte said she thought it would be a good idea."

Isabel and Maeve looked at Charlotte, who looked like a deer in headlights.

"I thought you decided not to run, Avery ... and Katani is a leader ... like you," Charlotte finally squeaked out.

No one knew what to say. The Beacon Street Girls' lunch table was an island of quiet in a lunchroom sea of chaos. Isabel looked to Maeve, usually so good at filling in the silence, then at Charlotte, who looked totally miserable.

They all seemed frozen in that awkward moment and then Avery started eating again as if nothing had happened.

"I'll withdraw," Katani said finally, picking at the food in front of her. Her eyes were down, as if she dared not look at anyone else in the group. Isabel thought it was the closest she had ever seen Katani to crying.

How could Avery keep eating at a time like this? wondered Maeve.

CHAPTER 4

છ

TWO TOO MANY

AVERY took another bite from her wrap. "That's crazy," Avery said as she continued chewing. "We can both run."

Katani glanced over at Avery. "What?"

~~Avery took another bite of her wrap. "Why not?"~~

"How's that going to work?" Isabel asked.

Avery looked across the table at Isabel, Maeve, and Charlotte, who were staring at her like she was an exhibit in *Ripley's Believe It or Not!* "Why is everyone making such a big deal about this?" Avery asked. "Coach says that good competition brings out the best in everyone. The better your competitors, the more inspired the play. It'll be like that, Katani. I can't think of a better competitor."

"This isn't a soccer game, Ave," Katani protested.

"Duh!" Avery said, slapping her forehead with the heel of her hand.

"You're really running ... like for real?" Maeve asked.

"Yes, Maeve, for real!" Avery shouted. "Is there any way to FAKE run for class president?"

"I mean, you're not just TALKING about it ... you've told

Ms. R and everything?"

"I HAVE," Avery said. "I don't know about Katani!"

"I SAID I was running. What did you think that meant?" Katani responded somewhat angrily.

Avery shrugged. "I don't know. I didn't know you were even interested in running for class president."

Katani opened her mouth, but before she could say more, Betsy Fitzgerald stopped by their table. She leaned low so the people at the tables on either side couldn't hear and said, "Did you hear? Henry Yurt is running for class president."

"Yeah, we know." Avery answered. Betsy Fitzgerald always had an annoying way of stating the obvious.

"I'm running for treasurer..."

"We thought you were going to run for president, too," Isabel blurted. "Why did you switch?"

"When I found out that no one was running for treasurer, I couldn't believe it! The treasurer position is very important."

Avery noticed how Betsy looked each one of the Beacon Street Girls in the face as if she had to convince them of this. "I checked in with Ms. Rodriguez this morning before class to make sure she'd found the note I left for her on Friday. When she pointed out that no one was running for treasurer, I decided to go for it. Laura Doyle and Sammy Andropovitch are going to help with my campaign."

"Campaign?" Katani queried, sounding annoyed. "But no one is running against you!"

"Well, yes ... that's true, but I promised Laura and Sammy they could be my staff after the election." Avery thought she made it sound as if they would be horribly, horribly disappointed if she didn't make them earn this honor. "I know I'm running unopposed—so the election is only a formality—but it doesn't hurt to emphasize the importance of the office to the class in general."

Betsy paused as if waiting for someone to agree with her. When no one did, she went on to another topic. "So with Dillon and Henry running, it looks like we'll have a guy for class president."

"Not necessarily," Isabel said, looking at Avery and Katani.

"I'm running," Katani said.

"And, I'm running," Avery said.

"You're BOTH running?"

Avery thought Betsy's eyeballs might pop out and roll across the lunchroom floor. She almost laughed out loud.

"Let me get this straight. You're both running?"

Katani and Avery nodded.

"Against each other?"

"Well, I wouldn't exactly put it that way," Katani huffed.

"What other way is there?"

Avery continued to eat. Katani stared up at Betsy. Everyone else was quiet.

"I suppose either one of you would be better than the ..." —Betsy scanned the lunchroom so she could see exactly where Dillon and Henry were before she continued—"the alternatives. But really ... Katani, Avery ... one of you should think about dropping out. Otherwise, you'll be dividing the vote and ... well, we could end up with a less-qualified choice." She gave them both knowing looks before she moved on.

The silence was deafening. Betsy's logic had got them all thinking. Maeve couldn't stand it anymore. "Avery's right! Of course it can work. I remember a movie about two friends who ran for office ..."

"Maeve, this is real life," Katani said sharply.

"I know that," Maeve said quickly, miffed by Katani's tone. "But I find movies inspirational. Anyway, hmmm ... I can't remember the title ..."

"Does it have a happy ending?" Isabel asked hopefully.

Maeve tilted her head to one side and chewed on her lip. "I can't remember that either."

Katani sighed in annoyance.

Uh-oh, thought Charlotte. This election could get a little kludgy.

As Maeve was probing her movie memory, Dillon dropped by, leaned on the table, and said with a dazzling smile, "Good afternoon, dudettes. I'm Dillon Johnson, and I'd like to be your class president."

"Well, I'd like to be YOUR class president and so would Katani," Avery said as she wadded up her lunch bag.

"Too bad you aren't running."

"Too bad *we* are running," Avery retorted.

Dillon shot a puzzled look first at Katani and then at Avery. When it sunk in that they were serious, he laughed. "Yeah, that'll work. Two of the BSG running. Good luck!" he called over his shoulder as he headed off to the next table.

Dillon's departure left the Beacon Street Girls' table in silence ... again.

"Look, Avery ..." Katani said, staring at the table. "I'm not sure this is a good idea. What if one of us wins?"

"I don't know why everyone is making a big deal out of nothing. I've competed against friends on the field and on the court and it's never been a problem. How is this any different?"

No one said anything.

"You mean what Dillon said?" Avery asked.

"Well, Betsy also said ..." Isabel started.

"Whoa! I can't believe it! You guys are going to listen to Betsy and Dillon? The other night all you could talk about was how they didn't represent how you thought."

Avery looked across the table at Isabel, Charlotte, and Maeve, then turned to face Katani. "Come on, Katani. You of all people aren't going to let Dillon Johnson talk you out of running for president, are you? Of course he'd like to see one or both of us drop out. That would mean more votes for him! Trust me. It'll be alright."

With that, Avery compressed her lunch bag into a more compact ball shape and got up from the table. "Avery for three!" she shouted as she launched the lunch bag ball toward the garbage can in the corner.

It was a perfect shot.

TAKE ME TO YOUR LEADER

Maeve was trying to follow Mr. Moore's lecture on bugs, but it was B-O-R-I-N-G with a capital B. He was drawing bug parts on the board and naming them. Maeve was trying to figure out when in her life it would be important for her to know that the middle part of a bug is called the thorax. Just talking about bugs made her feel like there was something crawling up her leg. She had to stop typing notes on her laptop now and then to brush off her leg just in case.

Finally, Mr. Moore stopped talking. Maeve heaved a sigh of relief. All that bug talk had made her head buzz, Maeve smiled to herself. Bugs and buzz—good joke.

They were supposed to spend the rest of the hour reading Chapter 5 in their science textbooks, but Maeve couldn't concentrate. She kept thinking about the scene in the lunchroom today. Katani and Avery were both running for class president! How could that possibly work? she wondered.

As her mind wandered, Maeve wracked her brain. OK, what was that movie? She knew it was an older movie, but not black and white. The two main characters had been guys—friends—who were running against each other in an election. She couldn't even remember the actors' names.

At lunch, Isabel had asked if it had had a happy ending, and honestly, Maeve couldn't remember. But, it must've had a happy ending. She loved happy endings. At this point, Maeve was starting to wonder if she really had seen such a movie. If there wasn't a movie like that, there should be! And, if she had anything to say about it, it would have a happy ending. Suddenly, Maeve agreed with Avery. Why couldn't this work out?

By the looks on their faces as they left the lunchroom, Isabel, Charlotte, and Katani weren't so sure. They all looked kind of shell-shocked.

It would be hard, almost impossible really, to decide which BSG to vote for, Maeve reasoned. Avery and Katani were both qualified. How could she choose between her best friends like that? Maybe this was going to be a difficult election after all.

To make matters worse, after lunch when she was on her way to her locker, she ran into Dillon.

"Yo, Maeve, got a minute?"

Maeve almost laughed out loud. Dillon thought he was so cool sometimes.

"What's up D?" she asked.

"I need a favor. Can you come over to my house and help me make posters for my campaign? I can't even draw a straight line," he said sheepishly.

Maeve was flattered. After all, Dillon was one of the most popular boys in the seventh grade and she did like him. He was so cute and he never got mad at her about the whole Celtics game date thing when she lied to her parents about where she was.

❀

She was about to say yes, until he mentioned that Pete Wexler would be there, too. Maeve groaned inwardly. Pete Wexler was such a tease. He always made fun of her red hair. Once, in kindergarten, he had said that her hair looked like Bozo the Clown's. She had never really forgiven him for that.

So she said to Dillon, "Oh, I'm sorry, I can't … math tutoring."

She was surprised when Dillon's face fell.

"OK … I guess I'll see you later then," and he took off.

Maeve hoped he wasn't annoyed with her.

The BSG had made such a big deal the other night about Dillon not being a leader. She didn't think of Dillon "that way" any more, but he was still good-looking and fun to be around. Kids really liked him; weren't those the signs of a leader, too? she wondered.

Anyway, Maeve was thankful she was meeting with her tutor this afternoon. That way, she could say no to Dillon without feeling guilty … and she could avoid Pete Wexler.

Maeve looked up at the clock. She had five minutes left of science class. Just enough time to type a note to herself.

Maeve's Note to Self:
1. Look on my favorite movie sites for a movie about friends who run for office.
2. Stop by Irving's and pick up some Swedish Fish.
3. Go window shopping at Think Pink! It's not just a store—it's a state of mind!
4. Race home and meet tutor (so cute).

The bell rang as Isabel pushed into the halls with all the other students. She gathered her books at her locker and put on her coat. But instead of going out the door at the end of the seventh-grade hall, she seemed pulled the other way, toward the office. There was already a crowd gathered as Ms. Rodriguez and Mr. Danson came out with a large sheet of paper and pinned it to the main bulletin board outside the front office. Everyone craned their necks trying to get a peek.

When Ms. R and Mr. Danson finally retreated, the crowd pushed forward and it was impossible to see anything. As Isabel waited for the crowd to sift out, Jennifer came up behind her. "That's what I like to see!"

"What?"

"*The Sentinel* staff on top of current affairs."

"Is that why you're here?" Isabel asked.

"Yeah. I was going to ask Charlotte to cover the seventh-grade election, but the truth is I really love political stuff. I covered the eighth- and ninth-grade elections last month. It'll be interesting to see if the seventh-grade elections will be different this year. The class advisors—Ms. Rodriguez and who's the other one?"

"Mr. Danson."

"Oh, OK, the social studies teacher. Anyway, they decided to have the elections a month later to give the seventh-grade class time to adjust to junior high, and to get to know each other first."

By then, the students in front of them had drifted away and Isabel and Jennifer found themselves staring at the board. Immediately, Jennifer pulled a notebook from her backpack and began writing down names.

✿

Slate of Candidates for The Seventh-Grade Class Election

Presidential Candidates
Dillon Johnson
Avery Madden
Katani Summers
Henry Yurt

Vice-Presidential Candidates
Jessica Bentley
Robert Worley

Secretary Candidates
Trisha Alvarini
Yuko Osawa

Treasurer Candidate
Betsy Fitzgerald

Isabel copied down the names of the students running for each office. She wouldn't have been surprised to find only three names under presidential candidate. Isabel had hoped that Katani or maybe even Avery would have hunted down Ms. Rodriguez before the end of school and asked to drop out of the election. Now that their names were posted for the entire school to see, Isabel knew neither girl would drop out. Katani and Avery were both proud. And both competitive. Yup, she sighed to herself, it was going to be an interesting election … maybe even a scary one.

"Hmmm. Henry Yurt. That's Haley Yurt's little brother, right?" Jennifer asked.

"I don't know. I'm just getting to know the seventh graders. I don't know many of the older kids."

"Haley's an eighth grader. It's kind of funny that her brother is running for president after the stink his sister made after last year's elections."

"What happened?"

"She made a big fuss about how class elections are really stupid and nothing more than a popularity contest."

"Did she run?"

"No … that's the weird thing. She wasn't even running. She's just kind of negative. You know the type. Never has anything nice to say about anyone else. Thinks everything is boring and stupid."

"Hmmm. That's weird. That doesn't sound like Henry at all. He always has a smile on his face. He's kind of the class clown."

"Well, maybe he's running for class president as a joke to tick off his sister," Jennifer said as she looked at her watch. "Yikes! Gotta get going. Remember Isabel, the paper is coming out the day before the elections. Deadline for articles is the Monday before the elections, but since your cartoons won't need any editing, you can have a "drop-dead" deadline of Wednesday morning. We go to press right after school on Wednesday."

"Got it." That gives me two and a half weeks, Isabel thought. Maybe I'll be OK.

Then Jennifer called from down the hall. "EDGY!"

Isabel felt a huge twinge of anxiety again about her ability to draw something edgy. In fact, she was beginning to feel more than a little uncertain about the whole election. Everyone had been so upset today at lunch. But, at least the BSG had a way of working things out. The cartoon thing, though, had her really stressed. Had she bit off more than she could handle?

❀

Avery's Blog

Check it out. I'm running for class president! There are four of us: Dillon Johnson, Henry Yurt, my friend Katani Summers, and me. The election is in three weeks. Katani said she wasn't going to run because she has some squirrelly idea that friends shouldn't compete with friends. My soccer coach says the better your competitor—the better the game. I compete against friends all the time. So I don't see the problem. I think it will be fun.

My favorite competition quote:
"Besides winning, the most fun thing is getting out there and mixing it up with friends; it's the competition."
—Al Unser, Jr., race car driver

Survey says:
What is your favorite way to compete with friends?
a. trivia games
b. one-on-one games (tennis, bowling, golf, etc.)
c. cards/board games
d. team sports

Results from the last survey:
What do you like to do at the beach?:
a) Swim (42%)
b) Build a Sand Castle (41%)
c) Play ball or Frisbee (12%)
d) Fly a kite (3%)
e) Lie there and bake (2%)

CHAPTER 5

ଓ

POSTER MANIA

ISABEL couldn't believe the change in the seventh-grade hall from yesterday to today. There were posters everywhere; not only for the presidential race, but also for vice president, class secretary, and treasurer. Most were handmade. But not Betsy's. Her posters looked professionally printed.

Dominating either end of the seventh-grade hall were toxic green banners. "Yurt Alert" was written in sloppy black letters. There were smiley faces on each end.

"Can you believe this?" Isabel asked when she caught up with Charlotte.

"Looks like you'll have plenty of material to choose from for your political cartoons."

"Yeah … but I don't know anything about political cartoons. I'm not sure where to start. I don't want to get it all wrong."

"I know, you should look at *Doonesbury*. My father loves that cartoon. Maybe you'll get some ideas from reading stuff like that. Did you have class elections in Michigan?"

"Yes … but it was pretty low key. Kids here are intense."

"I think that's because we live near Boston. Remember the Puritans and all that. They were very serious people and really hardworking, and had tons of town meetings and councils. I think people here are still like that a little. I'm just glad that I'm not running for office. See you later."

Katani, Maeve, Avery, and Charlotte all had lockers near their homeroom. But because Isabel had joined the school year late, she was almost in the eighth-grade hall.

"Yurt Alert?" Isabel heard one eighth-grader ask another. "Haley Yurt is running for office? What a joke!"

"No, that's her brother ... he's running for seventh-grade class president."

Isabel jerked her locker open and started putting books in and pulling other books out. Suddenly, Katani was at her shoulder.

"Look at this! When did they have time to do all this?" Katani asked.

"It's unbelievable!" Isabel agreed.

"This is what I get for deciding at the last minute. Listen, I'm going to need help putting posters together and you've got the best lettering. Do you think you could help me after school?"

"Sure," Isabel said.

Katani looked around at all the posters. "If there's room to hang any more posters! They must have been working on these all weekend while I was deciding whether to run or not. I'm so far behind. I'll never catch up!"

"Wanna meet in the art room?" Isabel offered. She could see how worried Katani was.

Katani nodded. "Yeah, that makes sense. Thanks!"

Isabel wasn't used to Katani looking frazzled. She usually looked so totally confident and together. Isabel's heart went out to her. "Look, it's OK not to have the first posters up. The election is three weeks away, not tomorrow. We'll be able to get them up soon. We'll start right after school, OK?"

"OK. But I don't have any materials-poster boards, markers, all that stuff."

"Don't worry. We'll brainstorm slogans and make a list of what we need so we can start on them as soon as possible."

Isabel paged open her spiral notebook and wrote in huge letters: HELP KATANI WITH POSTERS TODAY AFTER SCHOOL. She showed the note to Katani. "See you then."

Katani took a deep breath. "Thanks! You're a lifesaver. See you in homeroom." And she started down the hall to Ms. Rodriguez's classroom.

Isabel felt a warm feeling spread as she gathered books from her locker for morning classes. When she first came to Abigail Adams, Katani had been downright cold to her. But somehow they had managed to make the friendship work. Isabel was flattered that the independent Katani had asked her for help. She ripped the reminder from her notebook and placed it on top of her pile of books. She'd put it in her assignment book later when she got to homeroom.

Just as she shut her locker, she heard someone call her name. She looked out at the sea of heads bobbing by, but didn't see anyone, so she started down the hall.

"Isabel! Isabel!" She heard again,

Avery popped out of the wall of people. "Great! I caught you! Listen, you gotta help me! I need posters pronto! Look at this!" She pointed to the posters hanging on either side of the hall. "Can you believe it? You'll help me, won't you? I thought we could get started on them right after school."

Isabel felt her cheeks redden. "After school today?"

"You don't have anything going on, do you?"

"I ... uh, well ... I sorta have another commitment."

Avery's eyes followed her to the reminder note on top of Isabel's books.

"You're helping, Katani?" Avery asked.

"How about tomorrow? Sorry. It's not that I don't want to help you," Isabel said, feeling helpless. "Maybe Maeve can help you."

"Whatever," she said and disappeared down the hall.

First Come, First Served

As they walked to the lunchroom, Charlotte listened to Isabel relay the whole poster incident.

Poor Isabel! It was so hard to be put on the spot like that! Having to choose between two friends! Charlotte was almost grateful that she had *Sentinel* meetings after school this week so she wouldn't find herself in the same dilemma. "Oh, Isabel ... what'd you say?" Charlotte asked.

"There wasn't much I could say, except sorry. I did tell Avery that she could ask Maeve. Listen, I'm going to get a salad today ... meet you at the milk station?"

Charlotte made her way to the hot lunch line. Avery ran up, bumped into her, and grabbed her arm. Startled, Charlotte dropped the plastic lunch tray. Yikes, klutz attack, she muttered under her breath. Of course, the tray clattered to the floor, sending silverware shooting under the kids' feet in front of her.

"Hey ... I'm glad I caught you," Avery said, as Charlotte dropped to her knees to retrieve the silverware, which kept getting kicked further away as kids shuffled forward in line.

Charlotte turned pink with embarrassment, but Avery acted like nothing was going on. She dropped on her knees and crawled along with Charlotte. "I need posters! Can you help?" Avery said.

Charlotte reached for a fork just as Robert Worley moved forward again, and it rocketed across the lunchroom floor. Avery shot after it like she was being timed, grabbed it, and raced back. She handed it back to Charlotte. "Well, can you help me?" she asked.

"Sorry, I can't help with posters anytime after school this week because we have meetings for *The Sentinel*. But I'll be happy to help you with slogan ideas," Charlotte said as the lunch lady spooned mac & cheese onto her tray. American junk food really was tasty, she thought as her mouth watered.

"Great," Avery said, spewing out a couple of sunflower kernels in the process. "Excuse me," she said and swallowed hard. "And my speech? Will you be able to help me with my speech? I've got lots of ideas, but I need someone like you to help me put the words together so I'll really wow everyone."

Charlotte looked across to the salad line. Her eyes met Isabel's. Isabel gave her a sympathetic look. "Well, uh … sure," Charlotte said as reached for a bowl of applesauce and added it to her tray. "I guess I can do that."

"You're the best. I knew I could depend on you!" Avery said, and then trotted off to their lunch table.

Charlotte met up with Isabel at the milk station.

"Posters?" Isabel asked.

"No … slogans and speech."

No sooner did the words leave her lips than Katani walked up to her. "Charlotte, I need to talk to you before you get to the lunch table."

"What is it?" Charlotte asked.

"Isabel is helping me with posters, and I really need you to help me with my speech."

"Uh … of course."

"I knew I could count on you," Katani said as she turned. "See you at the table."

Isabel didn't say anything, but looked at Charlotte with wide eyes.

Charlotte blushed.

"Well, it's not like they both asked me to help them today after school."

"Maybe I should have offered to help Avery after dinner tonight," Isabel said as they wove their way through the crowded cafeteria toward the BSG table.

It was so quiet at the BSG table that Charlotte wondered whether things would ever get back to normal. She felt a little scared inside. Yesterday had been awkward, but nothing compared to the tension in the air today. Everyone ate quietly, stealing glances at one another. Charlotte tried to lead the conversation in another direction—any direction other than class elections. She tried talking about the upcoming football game, but her heart really wasn't into it. When Isabel got up to get a cookie, she found her chance to bring up something important.

"I was thinking after Saturday night in the Tower ..." Charlotte started.

The thought of that night in the Tower made everyone squirm a little.

Charlotte plodded on anyway. "You know, we all have our own private little space, our own window, our own window seat, but Isabel doesn't. She's one of us now, and she needs her own special space."

"Whatever," Avery said. "I don't have time to think about stuff like that right now. I have a few other things on my mind."

Charlotte nodded. "I understand," she said.

Charlotte snuck a glance at Katani who looked slightly annoyed, then looked up and saw Isabel heading back to the lunch table. "All I'm saying is, think about it, OK? Isabel deserves her own space in the Tower."

Maeve and Charlotte looked at each other as Katani and Avery stood up and bolted in opposite directions. Charlotte shook her head. Weirdness was definitely setting in, she thought. She could feel it right down to her toes!

LAST CHOICE

The bell rang, and Maeve joined the throng of kids in the hall as she headed for her locker at the end of that long, long Tuesday. She was glad Charlotte's locker was right next to hers ... she hadn't had a chance to talk to her since lunch.

"I thought today would never end, Char. The only way I could get through class was to think that I'd be stopping for a Swedish Fish fix on my way to Hebrew school," Maeve said.

"Mmmm. You know, I would die for some Swedish Fish right now, too, but I have a *Sentinel* meeting."

"Avery asked me to help her with her posters today after school. I was so flattered that she would turn to me first ... I would have done it in a heartbeat, but you know how it is with all the after-school things I have! Tomorrow I have tutoring, and Thursday I have hip hop class."

"I know what you mean," Charlotte sighed. "Avery asked me to help with her slogans and speech and then five seconds later Katani asked me too."

"They both asked you?"

"Yeah."

"What did you say?"

"I said I would ..."

"Do both?"

"Well … the speech is still a few weeks away. I should have time to help them with the right wording and all."

"I guess so." Maeve thought it was only natural that both Katani and Avery would have asked Charlotte to help with their speeches. Charlotte had such a way with words. With Maeve's dyslexia … it was tough for her to get words down on paper. The laptop helped, but it was still a struggle. "I should have had you write my acceptance speech for the award I won. I really blew that!" Maeve had blanked out when accepting her Junior Community Service Award last month. She felt really bad that she'd forgotten to thank the BSG, so she'd had a private ceremony for them later in the Tower.

"The speech you gave to all of us in the Tower was perfect. No way to improve on that!" Charlotte said.

The thought of the Tower made Maeve think of today at lunch. "Hey! I'm so glad you said something at lunch about the Tower and Isabel. You're absolutely right. She should have a space of her own."

"I didn't want to say anything in front of Isabel, but I know how she must feel. Moving here, leaving her father behind in Michigan, having to live by her Aunt Lourdes' rules. It must be tough; her Aunt Lourdes can be really strict and old-fashioned, you know."

"It's so unfair! I couldn't stop thinking about it. We should just divide the room into five equal slices."

"It's a room, not a pie, Maeve. Besides, I'm not sure how everyone else would feel about that," Charlotte said as she slipped on her vintage denim jacket.

"It's the only way to be fair. Each of the BSG should get the same exact amount of space."

"How are we going to divide four windows between five people?"

Maeve scrunched her lips together in concentration. "There has to be an answer!" she said.

Charlotte caught Maeve's eyes and nodded down the hall. Maeve turned to see Isabel coming their way.

"Isabel! There you are! Where are you going?" Maeve asked.

"Oh, I promised Katani I would help her with posters in the art room. I felt so bad when Avery asked me to help her today and I already said I'd help Katani. I suggested she ask you. Are you helping her?"

"Oh, uh ..." Maeve's cheeks reddened when she realized she hadn't been Avery's first choice after all. "Yes, she asked me, but I have Hebrew school." Maeve's feelings were really hurt. It seemed like she was never anyone's first choice when it came to projects.

"This is only the first day of campaigning," Isabel commented.

"It's too complicated having two of the BSG running for class president," Charlotte said.

"They should have thought of that," Maeve said crossly as she shut her locker door and walked away.

"What's up with her?" Isabel asked

Charlotte just shook her head. She knew Maeve felt bad about being Avery's second choice. But, it seemed unfair to Maeve to tell Isabel that.

CHAPTER 6

CR

EVERYONE HAS ISSUES

WHEN she got to school the next day, Avery was painfully aware that she was the only candidate who didn't have any posters. She looked at the other candidates' posters as she headed down the hall on her way to lunch. Avery noticed that Katani only had two signs—one on her locker door and one on the door to a seventh-grade room. They were printed on the computer and didn't say much, just "Katani for Class President."

Avery hit the side of her head with the heel of her hand. Why hadn't she thought of doing that? It would have been a good temporary solution until she made real posters. Well, she might start out soft, but she would finish strong.

Avery didn't know exactly what she wanted to put on her posters anyway. More posters had gone up and she needed to think about how to be original. Dillon had a dozen that said, "Vote Dillon! He's One in a Million." Henry Yurt was sticking with "Smile! It's a Yurt Alert!"

Avery was not surprised when she got to the cafeteria to find Laura and Sammy standing in front of the doors handing out flyers for Betsy. Laura thrust one into her hands. "A vote for Fitzgerald is a vote for progress," she said to Avery.

"As if we had any other choice," Avery muttered.

Laura didn't hear Avery's comment because she was busily handing another flyer to another seventh grader.

Avery snaked through the crowded lunchroom to the BSG table.

"Did you see this?" she asked, throwing Betsy's flyer on the table before she sat down.

"Yup, got one," Maeve said, tossing her copy on top of Avery's in the center of the table.

"We all did," said Katani, dropping hers in the center as well.

"This is pretty intense—'More honors classes,' 'A better homework corner,'" Isabel read from her copy.

"Look at the bottom. She also wants Abigail Adams student government leaders to have day-long exchanges with student government leaders at other junior highs. Guess I don't have to worry about that one," Maeve said.

"And don't forget the last of her ideas right here at the bottom of the flyer … she wants the class budget to go toward hiring guest speakers or taking field trips to museums, and she wants a student internship program with local businesses," Charlotte said.

"Wow, that's impressive!" Maeve said. Still smarting from Avery's snub, a little part of her wanted Avery to feel bad.

"A big YAWN if you ask me," Avery said. "Let the teachers worry about stuff like that. The whole point of student government is to deal with things that really affect us—the kids. Besides, no business is going to have kids our age working for them. Our attention spans are too short!" laughed Avery.

Maeve had regretted her enthusiasm for Betsy's ideas the minute she had spoken. She was relieved that Avery didn't seem to have even noticed her comment.

"And then there's Henry Yurt. Did you see his banner in between the locker rooms?" Charlotte asked.

"Musta missed it," Avery said.

"I don't see how! It was that toxic green—maybe he dyed a bunch of old bed sheets. I have no idea where he found dye that color. It's hideous!" Katani said.

"Hideous and huge!" Maeve added. "It hangs ceiling to floor between the boys' and girls' locker rooms. He must have used one of those wide markers on it because it was covered with a bunch of crazy ideas," Maeve said.

"Yeah ... he wants to make school more fun. He has lots of different ideas," Charlotte said.

"Like what?" Avery asked nervously. Making school more fun was something all the kids could get into ... including herself.

"Like ... a day when everyone walks backwards," Charlotte said.

"Hmm. That sounds really practical," Katani said sarcastically, obviously unimpressed.

"A Pajama Day," Isabel added, intrigued with the possibilities.

"Finally! The world will get to see my pink fuzzies!" Maeve said happily.

"And what was the last one?" Isabel asked.

"How could you forget? It was the best!" Maeve said.

"Oh, yeah! Green hair day," Charlotte said, giggling.

"What's with that boy and the color green?" Katani wondered.

"I hate green hair," Isabel piped in.

"Excuse me, but it's not easy being green," Maeve said in a voice that made her sound like she was in a Muppets commercial.

They burst out laughing as Dillon walked up to their table.

"Glad you girls still have a sense of humor," he said. "Actually, I'm kinda surprised you're all sitting at the same table."

"Why wouldn't we?" Avery asked.

"Well, with the election and all ..." Dillon raised his eyebrows.

They watched Dillon as he moved to the next table, smiling broadly and patting everyone on the back.

"Hey Dillon," someone shouted to him from a table across the aisle. "We want bigger chocolate chip cookies!"

"You got it!" Dillon called back, giving them the thumbs up, and flashing a Cool Guy Smiley grin.

The BSG table watched in silence.

"Speaking of Dillon," Charlotte finally said, breaking the silence. "Did you see his campaign issues?" She held up a small blue sheet of paper with bold, black printing for everyone to see.

"Where did you get that?" Katani asked.

"From a pile in the library. It's a survey." Charlotte held up the paper and read off to the group.

Which Would You Like?

Check off which issues are most important to you:

— Homemade chocolate chip cookies in study halls
— New sports uniforms
— School dances every week with better music

(maybe even a DJ)

— A class trip to NYC

— Other _____

Please deliver to locker #184 and Vote Dillon—He's One in a Million.

"Does he think the seventh-grade budget is endless?" Katani asked. "We'd need thousands of dollars to pay for all that!"

"He didn't promise to do all those things," Maeve said.

"No, he just promises whatever people want to hear," Katani shot back at her.

"I'm not worried about him," Avery said, tilting back in her chair and throwing her Hackey Sack up in the air and catching it.

"You should be," Katani said, leaning across the table toward Avery. "I am! Sounds like he's promising exactly what most kids want to hear."

"What issues are you running on, Katani?" Isabel asked.

"Well, I think ..." Katani started. She looked around the table. Her eyes locked on Avery's. "I don't know if we should talk about this now."

"What's that supposed to mean?" Avery asked.

"It means I don't think it's a good idea to talk about this right now. Maybe we should be talking about something else."

"You think I'm going to take your ideas?" Avery asked, sitting forward and putting her hackey sack on the table.

"I didn't say that," Katani said, pushing back from the table and crossing her arms in front of her.

"Then why won't you talk?" Avery asked.

"Well, I will if you will," Katani challenged.

"If I will what?" Avery asked.

"Tell us what issues you're running on!" Katani raised her chin as if daring Avery to do it.

Avery was stunned. "I … I have lots of different ideas." It was true. Avery had spent the night writing down ideas. Unfortunately, nothing had jumped out at her as the main idea that she should focus on.

"Like what?" Katani asked. It was definitely more of a challenge than a question.

"Like …" Avery faltered, looking around the room for a clue and grabbing the milk carton from in front of Charlotte. "Like having nutrition information for the school menu published each week."

"Oh, so Dillon is running on a pro-cookie campaign and you're the anti-cookie campaign?" Katani asked with a snide chuckle.

"I didn't say that …"

"Look," Charlotte said. "Maybe Katani is right. Maybe talking about the campaign should be off-limits at lunch."

"Fine with me," Katani said as the bell rang and the room sprang to life around them.

"Fine with me," Avery echoed, but her answer was lost in the noise of the lunchroom as chairs scraped the floor and everyone rushed toward the exits. Avery grabbed her Hackey Sack and threw it up in the air.

It wasn't that she didn't have an issue. Avery had too many issues. Too many things she thought were important: not having ethnicity boxes on standardized tests, mandatory afternoon snacks so blood sugar didn't drop, recess after lunch each day, etc. Real issues. Important issues. In fact, there were too many ideas for one poster. And the more Avery thought of which issue to concentrate on, the more confused she felt.

She was completely freaked out. This should be easy for her. She shouldn't have to think so hard. Everyone knew she was the one who wanted to be President of the United States. Everyone expected her to have great ideas and a real plan for achieving them.

Avery couldn't help looking up at the posters on the walls of the seventh-grade hall as she went to her locker. She'd thought that "Avery for President" would be enough, but running a campaign was more complicated than she'd ever considered. The longer it took her to decide on her issues and get her posters up, the more pressure there was to be spectacular and out of the ordinary.

And the more she tried to squeeze an "out-of-the-ordinary" idea from her brain, the more paralyzed and uninspired she felt. Avery looked at one of Betsy Fitzgerald's glossy posters and felt panicky. For the first time since she had sent the email to Ms. R, Avery wondered if she might be in over her head.

CAMPAIGN 101

Katani spent her study hall that afternoon putting the finishing touches on her campaign plan. She had no idea campaigning would be this sophisticated when she and Isabel had made the temporary signs. Dillon had his "One in a Million" slogan and Henry had his crazy "Yurt Alert!" Even Betsy had a flyer listing her ideas, and she was running unopposed.

One vice presidential candidate stole a line from the Avis Rent-a-Car commercial—Jessica Bentley for Vice President. #2 tries harder.

Both vice presidents were emphasizing how they were good helpers. Only the class secretary candidates didn't seem to have any issues or slogans.

Katani didn't want to be gimmicky, that would be too cheesy. But she wanted to do something that would make her campaign stand out. She was still steaming that Avery had tried to force her to share her campaign issues. It wasn't that she was hiding anything. It was just that Avery hadn't made any of her posters yet. What if Avery decided to use the same ideas? If she did, then when Katani put up her main set of posters, she would look as if she were copying Avery instead of the other way around. Not that she thought Avery would really do that on purpose, but it was better to be careful. Things were definitely getting murky.

Kgirl List:

1. *Ask Isabel to help me with more posters.*
2. *Put something on the posters that will make them stand out. Feathers? Glitter?*
3. *Ask Charlotte and Maeve to help with a poll ... or maybe do something via the Internet.*

Katani paused with her pen in midair. Should she ask Charlotte and Maeve to do a face-to-face poll with a clipboard, or should she do it via Internet? Better yet, she could do an impromptu poll after school today. She would stand at the door and ask kids as they walked out. It was still early in the election, but she had to know what page everyone was on.

SURVEY SAYS ...

Katani stood outside the seventh-grade entrance of the school and waited for stragglers.

She checked her watch. She had hoped to poll half the class, but she was far from successful. She had only spoken to twenty-nine. She decided to ask one more person before she collected Kelley and headed home. One more person would be one third of the students.

Loren Tayagi pushed through the seventh-grade door. Katani asked in an even tone, "Excuse me ... if the election were today, who would you vote for?" She showed him the clipboard where she had the candidates' names listed in large letters.

Johnson
Yurt
Summers
Madden
Or Undecided.

"Point if you like," she added.

Loren shrugged. "It's private," he said and trotted down the steps.

Katani sighed as she added one more slash mark to the undecided column. A lot of the students had said they were undecided. But then, it was early in the campaign. She hadn't kept track of boy vs. girl answers, but it seemed to her that most of the boys were for Dillon ... though a couple had said, "the Yurtmeister."

She counted up the slash marks and wrote the totals next to each name. She quickly figured the percentages and scribbled those beside the totals.

Johnson 5 (17%)
Yurt 2 (7%)
Summers 4 (13%)
Madden 3 (10%)
Undecided 16 (53%)

Katani couldn't believe that Charlotte and Isabel had both said undecided! And Maeve! She wouldn't give a clear answer. She had said, "You gotta be kidding me! I'm late!" So Katani hadn't counted her answer at all.

Maybe Charlotte and Isabel had said "undecided" because they were together, and they didn't want to reveal their votes in front of the other BSG.

Katani was sure Charlotte and Isabel would vote for her. After all, Charlotte was the one who had talked her into running in the first place, and Isabel was helping her with the posters.

Maybe she should change Charlotte and Isabel's answers from undecided to Summers—that would give Katani a one-vote lead over Dillon, which she figured was a more accurate result. Maybe Charlotte and Isabel didn't want to say anything in front of Maeve because they knew she was supporting Avery. Somehow, Katani would have to find out. Running for office was giving her a headache.

❀

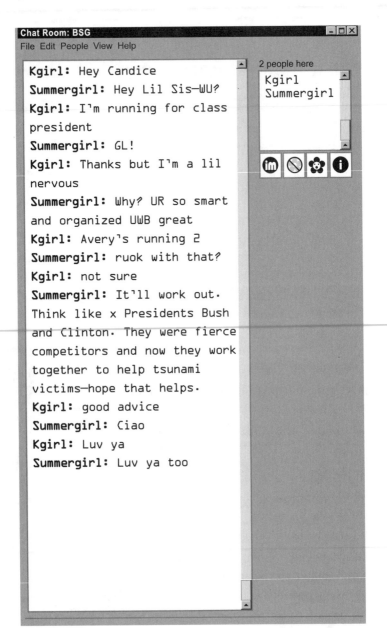

Chat Room: BSG

File Edit People View Help

> **Kgirl:** Hey Candice
> **Summergirl:** Hey Lil Sis—WU?
> **Kgirl:** I'm running for class president
> **Summergirl:** GL!
> **Kgirl:** Thanks but I'm a lil nervous
> **Summergirl:** Why? UR so smart and organized UWB great
> **Kgirl:** Avery's running 2
> **Summergirl:** ruok with that?
> **Kgirl:** not sure
> **Summergirl:** It'll work out. Think like x Presidents Bush and Clinton. They were fierce competitors and now they work together to help tsunami victims—hope that helps.
> **Kgirl:** good advice
> **Summergirl:** Ciao
> **Kgirl:** Luv ya
> **Summergirl:** Luv ya too

2 people here

Kgirl
Summergirl

CHAPTER 7

❧

PIECING IT TOGETHER

AVERY glanced at her watch. 6:55 A.M. She shifted her weight from her left to her right foot and then jumped up and down impatiently. Charlotte should be here any minute.

Charlotte had agreed to meet Avery at Montoya's before school so they could discuss slogans. Avery had to get her posters done and up. She looked up Beacon Street toward Summit Avenue, and when she looked back, she saw Charlotte running toward her.

"What happened to you?" Avery said when Charlotte was in earshot.

"Sorry! Marty didn't want to come in after his morning walk. He was squirrel hunting," she panted. They both laughed. Marty wasn't much bigger than a squirrel himself.

"Let's go in. I'm hungry," Charlotte said.

Avery launched into her list of ideas for her presidency as soon as they stepped into the bakery. She was still talking when they sat down at a table with their hot chocolates and mini-muffins.

For once, Avery let her food sit and just talked. She had

❁

a huge list of ideas to get through before she could start in on her breakfast. Charlotte sipped on hot chocolate and nibbled on her muffins while Avery rambled on.

"Wow, Avery! You really do have a lot of ideas," Charlotte said when Avery finally paused to take a bite of muffin.

"I KNOW! Too many for one poster. Too many for one speech. Am I right?" Avery asked, a thin chocolate mustache etched on her upper lip.

Charlotte nodded and pointed at her own upper lip to let Avery know about her mustache.

"Finally, this morning it came to me. It was so easy I don't know why I didn't think of it sooner," Avery said as she grabbed a napkin and wiped off her chocolate mustache.

"What?" Charlotte asked.

"I mean, I want to let students know that I'm open to their ideas—after all, a president is supposed to be all about them—the people—projects they want to do—but when I looked at all my ideas, the ones I felt the strongest about were the environmental issues."

Avery took a crumpled piece of notebook paper out of her backpack, unfolded it, and tried to smooth it out so Charlotte could read it. In case she couldn't, Avery said them out loud. "Paper recycling, an anti-school-litter campaign ..."

"I hate litter," Charlotte said.

"Me, too! It's so nasty looking. I thought we could pick up litter around the school and maybe along Beacon Street. Maybe we could get one of those Adopt-a-Street signs, 'This area kept litter-free by the seventh-grade class at Abigail Adams Junior High.' Wouldn't that look great?"

Charlotte nodded enthusiastically. "I love that," she enthused.

"We can use the money from aluminum can recycling to

raise money for environmental causes. And we could grow this year-by-year. I mean, more projects. More fundraisers. And eventually, by ninth grade, I thought our class could start a cat rescue program. So how do I put this on a poster?" Avery asked breathlessly.

"Wow," Charlotte said. "These are great ideas ... too great for one little poster."

"That's why you're here. I need a writer to help me sum it all up in just a few words. Something like—'Vote for Avery, *the Green Candidate.*'"

"I think Henry has established himself as the green candidate."

"Doh!" Avery said, smacking her forehead with her hand. "Duh! Of course. How else do you say environmental without saying green? How about the three Rs: reduce, reuse, recycle? Can we use that somehow? How about: 'Avery: Your 3 R candidate?'" Avery asked.

"I'm not sure if everyone knows about the three Rs—I've never heard that before," Charlotte said.

"You're kidding me," Avery said.

"Remember, I haven't lived in the United States since I was four years old," Charlotte said.

"Maybe I should just focus on recycling. But how do I put that into a cool slogan?" Avery asked as she ripped the napkin into a thousand pieces.

Charlotte grabbed the pad of paper. She had never seen Avery so hyper. "I think better on paper," she said as she bent over the pad and started scribbling notes.

Avery's leg started jiggling. She tried to read what Charlotte was writing down, but Charlotte's handwriting was too cramped and tiny. Before Charlotte even had a chance to finish, Avery blurted out, "I got it! Vote Avery! For the Best Junior High Ever!"

"Well …" Charlotte said, scrunching up her nose. "It doesn't have anything to do with the environment or even recycling."

"But … I like it," Avery said, flipping the pad of paper back around and printing the slogan in big letters at the bottom.

"It does have Avery-like enthusiasm," Charlotte said, relieved.

The bell over Montoya's door jingled as it opened. Avery looked up to see Katani and Maeve coming through the door.

"Oh, no!" Avery said, scrunching down in her seat. "Don't turn around, Charlotte! Keep your head down. Look that way and maybe they won't see us."

But Charlotte had looked over her shoulder when the bell jingled. "Avery, they've already seen us, and they are our best friends," she said angrily.

Avery blinked. Charlotte never got mad.

Avery peeked around Charlotte as Katani and Maeve stopped at the counter to order.

"I know, but I've got to get this done this morning before school so I can start on the posters right after school. I'm the only candidate that doesn't have any posters up."

"We can still think all day," Charlotte said.

"Shhh! Here they come!" Avery said when Katani and Maeve turned from the counter and headed their way.

Charlotte sighed. This was not fun anymore … and to her surprise, she actually felt a twinge of annoyance toward Avery and Katani.

Suddenly, Avery sprang into action, flipping over the sheets of paper on the table as quickly as she could.

"Avery! What are you doing?" Charlotte asked in a loud whisper.

"I don't want to give away my game plan."

"I think Katani has plans of her own …"

Avery stopped and considered this. "Do you know what they are?" she asked, as Katani and Maeve sat at a table two tables away.

"Well, sorta …"

"Are they better than mine?"

"Avery, they're … different," said Charlotte, feeling weird that the BSG were at separate tables.

"Like what kind of different? Good different? Bad different?"

"Just different. Look, I don't feel comfortable talking about this with you."

"What are you saying?"

"I'm saying we don't have much time, and we need to get some slogans for you and not talk about Katani's ideas."

Avery considered this and decided Charlotte was probably right. She flipped over the papers, scooted her chair closer to Charlotte, and hunched over the papers on the table. She continued to talk to Charlotte about her campaign ideas in low, hushed tones. It was like they were huddling up in the final seconds of a basketball game, whispering so that the other team didn't hear their game plan.

Avery looked up and saw Katani looking at her. Katani forced a smile. But Avery didn't smile back. She just couldn't.

Minutes later, Katani got up, and without saying good-bye to everyone, left. Charlotte thought Katani had tears in her eyes.

"Where's she going?" Avery asked.

"School, Avery. We need to get going, too."

Avery looked at her watch and yelped. "I gotta go! I was supposed to meet Ms. R before homeroom." Avery jumped

✿

up so fast that she bumped the table. The dishes rattled. She scooped the papers from the table, stuffed them in her backpack, and zipped out the door.

☙

Charlotte breathed a small sigh of relief as soon as Avery disappeared out the door. She looked over at Maeve, who looked equally relieved.

"Wanna walk to school together?" Charlotte asked.

Maeve nodded. "Helping Avery with her campaign?" she asked as they slipped out the door and headed toward school.

Charlotte nodded. "We were trying to come up with campaign slogans. Were you helping Katani?"

"She asked," Maeve said. "My schedule's so full! I felt bad because Katani helped bail me out with the blanket project. I promised I'd try to help her if I could."

"Did she ask you to help her with posters tonight?"

"No, she wants to run another poll, and she wants me to man one side of the lunchroom door while she does the other."

"Are you going to do it?"

"Well, I would if I could," Maeve answered, "but I have to babysit Sam after school."

Charlotte glanced sympathetically over at Maeve. Maeve's little brother could be a handful sometimes with his obsession about all things military. Once when Charlotte had spent the night at Maeve's, Sam had conducted a "raid" and pelted the girls with water balloons while they slept. Maeve got so mad at him she screamed that she was going to turn him into a Popsicle and put him into the freezer.

"I can't wait until this election is over ... I feel so torn," Charlotte said.

"You don't know the half of it! Dillon called last night. He asked me to help write a song for him."

"Write a song?!"

"Well, technically he asked me to rewrite lyrics to an existing song."

"What?"

"Let me start over. Dillon called to ask if he could borrow my portable karaoke machine. He wanted to know what CDs I had. After I read him the list, he really liked the song 'If I Had a Million Dollars.' He thought it was perfect for his campaign and wanted me to help him come up with new lyrics for the song ... well, kind of a spoof. You know, using some of the lyrics, but changing them for his campaign. 'If I had a million votes, I'd be class president!'"

Charlotte smiled. "That's kinda cute."

"Oh! There's more!" Maeve said with a dazzling smile. "He's printing off a bunch of fake million-dollar bills with his face in the middle and wanted to know if I would help pass them out during lunch while he sings the song."

"Are you going to help him?"

"I don't know. I mean, even if Dillon isn't my romantic destiny, I still like him."

Charlotte smiled to herself. Maeve was so dramatic, and such a romantic.

"I mean," continued Maeve. "Dillon is a fun guy, and I could see him being a good president."

"Did you tell Katani that?"

"Are you kidding? I mean, she would think I was a traitor or something. Promise you won't tell Avery either."

"They'll both go crazy when they find out."

"Could be worse," Maeve said as they went through the seventh-grade entrance of Abigail Adams Junior High.

"How?" Charlotte asked.

Maeve nodded in the direction of Laura and Sammy, who were listening intently as Betsy gave them directions for the day. "We could be one of Betsy's clones."

"Never!" Charlotte said. Maeve always knew how to make her laugh.

"Have you given any more thought to how Isabel can have a space in the Tower?" Maeve asked.

"No. Do you have any ideas?"

"I thought maybe she could share the corner between the two of us," Maeve said as they approached their lockers. "You know, half of your wall and half of my wall."

"Huh? Well … maybe," Charlotte said. She didn't know how to tell Maeve she didn't like that idea at all! That wall and window were so special to her. She had moved a lot in her life and it was nice to be able to call one special spot her own. Besides, Charlotte didn't think it was fair that she and Maeve should be the only ones to sacrifice. What about Katani and Avery? If they each gave up half a wall, Isabel ended up with two halves, or a whole wall, and she and Maeve would end up with only a half a wall each. How was that fair? Things were getting really confusing.

Before she could figure out how to say any of this, the bell rang, and they rushed inside Ms. Rodriguez's class for homeroom.

FEATHERS AND SEQUINS

"I can't wait to show you what I brought for the posters," Isabel said as she and Katani made their way to the art room at the end of the school day. "I went through my scrap basket and found all sorts of interesting trinkets."

"I can't wait to see them!" Katani had her campaign file

box in one hand and was pulling her wheelie bag behind her with the other. "I bought the foam board yesterday and cut it last night, so it's all ready to go."

Isabel had spent lots of time in the art room, and once inside, she headed for the table next to the windows. It was her favorite spot. She loved the soft light of New England in the fall. She watched expectantly as Katani unzipped her wheelie bag.

"I thought bright jewel tones would be the most eye catching," Katani said as she unpacked stacks of foam board. "I have three tones: emerald green, golden yellow, and royal purple."

"I love these colors," Isabel said, reaching over and pulling a golden yellow foam board from the stack. "But, these are an odd size. Did you cut them down to fit into your wheelie?"

"Actually, no. It just worked out that way. The only places that didn't have many posters were the bathrooms—eeyew, don't want to put any posters in THERE!—and above the lockers. Not exactly eye level."

"Good point," Isabel agreed.

"Then I noticed that the spaces between the lockers and the classroom doors are usually empty and right at eye-level. It's a tall, narrow space—eighteen inches by six inches. We'll have to make more, but they'll have more impact."

"You are unbelievable Katani; you went and measured everything," Isabel said, pulling the plastic grocery bag of goodies from her backpack.

"I just can't help myself," Katani laughed.

"Well, I think you'll be happy. What I brought matches well with your colors," Isabel said as she pulled little Ziplock bags filled with feathers and sequins from the bag. "I thought if we used fabric, sequins, and feathers, it would be more eye-catching."

"Ohh—like collage! Isabel, that's such a cool idea!"

"I thought it would make your posters stand out from the others."

"Awesome."

"But with the small size and the addition of feathers and sequins, we're going to have to keep it simple and short. I was thinking each would say 'Katani for President,' of course, and then we'll add one little tagline to each like—'Feather our budget' and 'Earn more to do more'—you know, stuff that'll emphasize how you'll get us more money," she grinned.

"Great!" Katani shook her head happily. "I brought black paint pens. Do you want to letter or glue?"

"Glue," Isabel said, fishing a small hot glue gun from her bag and plugging it in. "I love my glue gun," she added gleefully.

"You are definitely an oddball artist type," Katani said affectionately. And then she added, "But a prepared one."

"I know," Isabel answered proudly.

The two friends got down to work in earnest. Isabel and Katani were sorting out all the materials and setting up an assembly line to efficiently piece together the posters, when Avery crashed through the art studio door. She was kicking a big box of supplies in front of her and dragging a bag of supplies behind her.

No Drips, No Runs, No Errors

Avery was used to carting around sports equipment. Art supplies were a little out of her league. Soccer balls, field hockey sticks, and skateboards were a little heavier, but poster boards were a different challenge. When the wind had caught the broad side of the poster boards, she'd practically gone airborne! The short trip between her mom's SUV and the front door of the school took twice as long as it should have with the wind that morning. Every step was a struggle. Her mom had wanted to help her, but Avery told her that was too uncool. So Avery had struggled on her own.

Her mother had taken her shopping the night before, and Avery had bought poster boards, paintbrushes, and paint. If the Yurtmeister hadn't attached himself to neon green, the choice would have been easy. Avery was running on environmental issues. Green would have been the perfect color. Instead, she had picked up a huge container of orange poster paint. She didn't want to be confused with Henry Yurt, and besides, the orange was on sale.

Orange? Green? It really wasn't that important. Color, Avery told herself, wasn't going to win or lose the election for her. Kids wouldn't be that stupid, she thought matter of factly.

Avery couldn't help glancing over to the table by the window. What were Isabel and Katani doing? Were those feathers? What was that sparkly stuff? Was Katani running for president or putting on a fashion show?

Avery unscrewed the lid from the paint jar and pulled the sheet of paper from her pocket. She read the slogan she had written:

Vote for Avery
For the Best Junior High Ever!

Avery had also decided to make a few that said, "Avery the Green Candidate," even though she was using orange paint. Avery stuck her brush in the paint.

"Whoa! This stuff is awfully watery," Avery said as she dripped paint across the poster board. She did her best to

✿

wipe it off with a paper towel and try again. She painted on the letters of the first line, but the paint was so thin and drippy that if it had been red, it would have looked like the title to a horror movie. Avery noticed that the letters were a little crooked and running downhill. She would be more careful on the next poster. She'd started the second line too close to the center and had to crowd the letters on to fit.

Avery thought she'd better push up the sleeves of her sweatshirt before she continued. She laid her paintbrush on the paint jar so she wouldn't get paint on the poster board. Even though she was extra careful, the paintbrush flipped out of the lid and fell onto the blank poster board.

"Is it supposed to be this watery?" Avery mumbled to herself. She tried to prop the wet paintbrush on the jar lid, but it kept flipping out. Each time, it made a new splotch mark on the poster board. Exasperated, Avery gave up and laid the paintbrush directly on the poster board.

When she moved the paint jar off the poster board and onto the table, the lid slid from her hand and hit the floor. Orange paint splattered out in a halo around where the lid had landed face down on the tile floor.

As she bent down to pick up the lid, Avery's bunched up sleeve caught the corner of the poster board. The poster board flipped up, launching the fully loaded paintbrush across the room. It landed in the middle of the table where Katani and Isabel were working. Droplets of orange paint flew everywhere.

"Whoa!" Avery gasped.

"Ahh!" Katani screamed. "Avery! What are you doing?"

"Sorry," Avery muttered.

"You almost ruined my posters!"

"I said I was sorry!" Avery shouted back. Avery didn't

know what the big deal was—ruined and almost ruined were two very different things.

Isabel picked up the paintbrush and brought it back to Avery's table.

"It's so runny," Avery said.

"Did you shake up the jar before you started?" Isabel asked.

"Oops," Avery said.

Isabel snorted with laughter. Avery could be so funny sometimes, and she really was the absolute worst artist she had ever seen. Marty could do a better job than Avery.

She looked over at Avery's first poster. "Avery, you better use a pencil and a ruler to draw a light guideline so the letters don't run downhill and ..."

"Hey ..."

Avery and Isabel turned to see Katani standing with her hands on her hips. "Isabel, who are you here to help? We have a schedule. I'm never going to get these posters put up if you spend all your time over there!"

"Chill, Katani," Avery said. Katani crossed her arms and stared at her, looking at this moment very much like her Grandma Ruby, principal of Abigail Adams Junior High.

"It's OK, Isabel. I'll be just fine," Avery said haughtily. "Go back to your cutting and gluing. I'm running for class president, not entering an art contest."

Katani pursed her lips together and gave Avery the famous Kgirl look. Avery thought Katani might want to reconsider her career plans—only teachers and policemen gave that kind of look.

"I was only trying to help," Avery heard Isabel say when she returned to the table by the window.

"But you said you would help me! I'm depending on

you. Look at this! She got orange paint on my purple foam board," Katani complained.

"She didn't do it on purpose. Besides, we can just shift this over and glue this on top of that. It'll be OK. You won't be able to tell."

Katani let out a pained sigh. Avery didn't think she sounded too convinced. Katani was so picky, picky about stuff that didn't really matter, Avery thought.

Avery found a yardstick and a pencil and started drawing lines on the blank poster boards. She was almost finished when Betsy Fitzgerald stormed into the room.

"OK," Betsy shouted. Avery jumped and spun around nearly knocking over the open jar of orange poster paint with the end of the yardstick.

"Who did it? Which one of you stole my posters?" Betsy demanded.

"What?" Avery asked. She could tell that Betsy was close to tears. This was a first. Avery'd never seen Betsy Fitzgerald upset before.

"You heard me! Who took down my posters? I hung three at the entrance of the seventh-grade hall—one on each side and one on the overhead beam. All three are gone!"

"Why are you asking us?" Katani asked defensively.

"SOMEONE took them down. They were there at the end of school, and then I went to the library to do a little research, and when I came back down the hall, they were …" The words caught in her throat. "GONE!"

"I'm so sorry, Betsy," Isabel said. "That's really horrible. How many did you make?"

"Twelve all together."

"Twelve," Avery said in disbelief. How could anyone make twelve posters? In spite of herself, Avery was impressed.

"Do you have any left?" Isabel asked.

"I'm not sure," Betsy said, quieter and calmer now.

"Do you want me to help you check?" Isabel offered.

"No. Thanks, Isabel. I can do it on my own. Sorry if I made it sound like you'd taken them, it's just that ..." Betsy stopped, tears coming to her eyes.

"That's OK," Isabel said, walking over to Betsy and putting her hand on her arm.

"Don't worry about it, Betsy," Avery yelled over to her. "Everybody's seen your posters already."

Katani looked down and mumbled that she was sorry Betsy's posters were gone. Avery kept right on painting. Personally, she wasn't sure if she would ever understand Betsy Fitzgerald. She was so intense about everything.

CHAPTER 8

ભ

TRUE COLORS

"SO, KATANI, how's the election going?" Katani's dad asked as the two of them pulled out of the driveway in his truck.

Katani squirmed. She did not want to get into a discussion about the election with her father. How could she explain to him all the trouble she and Avery were having? He would never understand. Maybe if she stared out the window he would think she hadn't heard him.

No such luck.

"Katani?" her dad raised his voice. "Are you off in another world? I wanted to know how the election campaign was going?"

"It's fine, Dad," she answered, hoping a short answer would satisfy him, but knowing that it probably wouldn't.

"How is it going with Avery running too?"

Katani could feel her face flush. If Candice told her dad about Avery, she would never forgive her sister.

"Did Candice tell you Avery was running?" Katani asked her dad sharply.

"Nooo, Candice did not tell me," he chuckled as he

turned the corner into the school. "I was at the school fixing some wiring in the science lab and I saw the posters."

"Well, don't tell Mom about it, 'cause I don't want to have a big, long discussion about competition and staying true to your values and friendship and all that," Katani blurted out to her father.

"Things getting a little rough between you and your pal?" her father looked at his daughter sympathetically.

Katani almost felt like crying and sharing the whole horrible election mess with her dad. But she didn't have time, and it was way too complicated anyway.

"It's fine, Dad. Really, it's fine," she said as she jumped out of the car.

"Thanks for the ride," Katani said as she pulled her wheelie bag from her father's van and slammed the door. She really didn't want her dad to think she was upset. She had taken the remaining foam boards home last night and finished them. She'd talked her dad into dropping her off at school today on his way to work. Of course, her grandmother would have brought her early to school, but that would have upset Kelley's routine. Just a few minutes early or late could throw her into a tailspin that could last the rest of the week.

Poor Kelley, Katani sympathized. It must be hard sometimes to be so different. She wondered if Kelley dreamt about what she wanted to be when she grew up. She would have to ask Kelley about that sometime.

Katani hurried to put her poncho and books in her locker so she could start hanging the posters. At home, she had tested hanging the foam board with masking tape. It hadn't worked too well. So, she convinced her father to get duct tape. The rolled loop of duct tape was strong enough to hold the posters and would come right off when they were finished. She could even save it to use another time. "Whoever invented duct tape," Katani marveled, "was a certified genius."

Katani congratulated herself on choosing foam boards and on Isabel's innovative idea to use collage. The boards were a little heavier, but they looked very sharp! It was worth the extra expense. By making lots of small ones that fit beside the classroom doors and hung at eye-level, she had increased her exposure. Her posters would really stand out.

Katani had only five more signs to hang up by the time her grandmother and Kelley came down the hall.

"My goodness," Mrs. Fields said. "You certainly have made a bright impression on the hall. What slogans did you come up with?"

Katani read off the first, "Feather the budget."

"I'M KELLEY SUMMERS AND I APPROVE OF THIS MESSAGE," Kelley shouted.

Mrs. Fields smiled at her granddaughter. "I do as well."

As Katani read off the remaining slogans, Kelley shouted the tagline she had picked up from the many political commercials on TV.

Each time she said it, Katani felt like cracking up.

"It's a good effort," Mrs. Fields said. "I wish you luck with your campaign."

As Kelley walked with her grandmother toward her locker she pointed at every poster she saw hanging on the wall. When it was a Katani poster, she would say the now all-too-familiar line. When it was any other poster, Kelley would say, "I'm Kelley Summers and I DON'T approve of THIS message."

Katani smiled. There were times when having Kelley around made her feel so good. But then Katani realized that if the hall had been filled with her classmates instead of empty as it was now, Kelley's shouts of approval and disapproval might make her feel embarrassed. If only everyone could see Kelley as she did!

After Katani hung the last poster, she walked back down the hall and scrutinized each one to make sure it was hanging straight and there were no hot glue stringies hanging around.

Katani glanced up to see one of Avery's posters hanging overhead. This one read, "Avery the GREEN candidate," which was funny since it was in big, orange letters. What a drippy mess! She wouldn't be surprised to find Avery totally covered in orange paint today. In spite of her sense of competition, Katani giggled. Avery's artistic talents, or the lack of them, were really something else. Her posters looked like a third grader did them. And the really funny thing, thought Katani, was that Avery probably didn't even care. Suddenly, she missed her spunky friend.

However, Katani was still a little annoyed with Isabel for rushing to Avery's rescue when she had promised to help her! And then, she'd taken off to help Betsy count her posters as soon as they were finished cleaning up. What was that about? Like Betsy, the most organized person in the world, who wasn't running against anyone, needed help?

Katani caught sight of another of Avery's posters hanging above the lockers and rolled her eyes … it looked so sloppy!

Katani saw one of Betsy's glossy posters and remembered how upset she'd been when she burst into the art studio yesterday. Betsy'd had her posters professionally printed. She didn't blame Betsy for being upset. Katani would be really angry if any of her posters were missing. However, it wasn't as if Betsy had put all the time and effort that Katani and Isabel had put into the foam boards.

When she reached the end of the hall, Katani was surprised but thankful that Henry Yurt had taken down his vile green banner that hung between the seventh-grade hall and the eighth-grade hall. The hall looked much better without it. Still, it was strange. Why would he take his banner down weeks before the election? Katani wondered.

"Hey, Katani," Maeve said, coming up behind her. "Your posters are fabulous! The colors! The sequins! The feathers! It's so … fabulous!"

"Isabel helped," Katani said wanting to share the credit. She really wouldn't have been able to do them without Isabel's help.

"Wow! You two are so creative! I've never seen campaign posters quite like those! Such style! So sophisticated! The colors are simply smashing," Maeve gushed enthusiastically just as Avery walked up behind her.

"Yeah, that's why people vote for candidates. It's because of the colors they choose for their campaign posters," Avery said, rolling her eyes.

"That's funny from someone who calls herself the 'green' candidate," Katani said.

"In this case, green is an issue, not a color," Avery retorted. Katani rolled her eyes, but inside she admired Avery's quick-witted comment. Avery really was a natural politician. The thought that maybe Avery could win this election suddenly made Katani nervous.

"Speaking of green …" Maeve said, pointing up. "What happened to Henry's banner?"

Katani shrugged. "Guess he took it down."

"That's funny … I saw it when I left last night, and I haven't seen him yet this morning," Avery said.

"Did you hear that someone stole Betsy's posters yesterday?" Katani asked Maeve. "The three that were right here between the seventh-grade hall and the eighth-grade hall."

"No, really … what happened to Yurt's banner?" Avery asked. "It was hanging here at the beginning of the hall right where your posters are now, Katani."

"Yeah, Avery's right," Maeve said. "I kinda miss it."

Kids were milling around, disappointed that the banner wasn't there, which Katani totally didn't get!

"How could anyone miss that toxic green monstrosity? It was so tacky!" she said.

"It was gone when you hung your posters up?" Avery asked.

"How could I put my posters up if the banner was there?" Katani asked.

"I'm just asking!" Avery said.

"Asking or accusing?" Katani wanted to know.

"Lighten up, Katani. I never said you took the banner down," Avery said, exasperated with her sensitive friend. "But it's gone, and your posters are there. It's a little mysterious …"

Henry Yurt came rushing down the hall at that moment— a vision in a purple bow tie and red suspenders. He'd been wearing bow ties and suspenders every day since he announced that he was running for class president. Katani wondered if he planned to wear bow ties and suspenders every day if he were elected. If he did, Katani was convinced this was yet another good reason for her classmates NOT to vote for Henry and to vote for her instead! Really, who wanted a president that acted like a cartoon character?

"Hey, Henry," said Maeve.

"Good morning, worthy opponents and lovely ladies,"

Henry said, flashing a big politician grin at the girls.

"What's with the bow ties and suspenders, Henry?" asked Avery.

"It's my campaign uniform," said Henry. "I was inspired by Harry S. Truman, 33rd President of the United States. He's my Grandpa Bob's favorite president. He said Harry Truman was honest and fair. He liked to wear bow ties, and he was little, just like me!"

"What do you think about his Cold War policies?" asked Betsy.

Henry kept talking as if Betsy didn't say anything.

"Grandpa Bob was in the Navy in World War II. That's when Truman became president …"

All of a sudden, Henry Yurt stopped talking. He had finally noticed that his green banner was gone.

He stood there for a moment with his mouth open, but nothing came out. Katani thought that maybe this was the first time she'd ever seen Henry Yurt without a smile on his face. Finally he managed to stammer, "Wh-where's my banner?"

Betsy put her hand on her hip. "Missing! Just like three of my posters," she said.

"Someone STOLE my banner?" Henry asked.

"AND my three posters," Betsy added.

A woeful look passed over Henry's face. He swallowed hard and then tried to smile. "Hmm! I didn't realize how popular I am. I guess my campaign materials have already become collectors' items," he said.

Always trying to make everything into a joke, Katani thought. But she didn't laugh. No one else did either.

No one said anything else about Katani's posters hanging where Henry's banner used to be. Avery sure made it seem like she was the one who took the banner down. Well, maybe

Avery would be willing to touch Henry Yurt's toxic green monstrosity, but Katani wouldn't sink that low.

ᙇ

The lunchroom was buzzing when Katani arrived at the BSG table. Somehow between homeroom and lunch, a few more posters went missing.

"Did you hear?" Maeve asked. "More posters are gone. I think this is getting creepy. Maybe we've got a serial poster thief around here."

"Two more of Henry's and one of Dillon's," Charlotte said.

"Who could be doing it? Who's wandering around the halls during class time?" Isabel asked.

"Not that many people have passes during class," Katani said.

"Only the kids that go to Speech," Charlotte said.

Speech! Katani hadn't thought of that. Charlotte was right. And now that she thought of it, Katani realized that the speech classroom was right where the seventh-grade hall stopped and the eighth-grade hall began. Right where the first posters disappeared. Katani only knew one person who took speech ... every day. Every morning.

Before she could think about this any more, Anna and Joline drifted up to the BSG table.

"So ... this candidate business is getting kinda nasty, huh? Really dog-eat-dog." Anna smirked at this comment and looked knowingly to Joline. "How fitting."

Joline giggled at Anna's joke. They shared knowing looks.

"How tragic that candidates have to stoop to stealing other candidates' posters in order to get ahead," Anna continued. "Personally, I can't understand that kind of behavior," she added for good measure.

Katani looked around the table. Isabel looked down at her salad. Charlotte seemed totally interested in her tuna fish sandwich. Maeve glared at Anna, and Avery kept on eating as if nothing was happening.

Katani was about to open her mouth, because wasn't it just a couple of weeks ago that Anna and Joline pulled a fast one at the Abigail Adams Talent Show and stuck the dancing hippo tape in the Hip Hop Honeys' act? They almost ruined the show with that one. She couldn't believe how hypocritical they were. But Isabel spoke first.

"You think one of the candidates is doing this?" Isabel asked. "What makes you think that?"

"To get the advantage, of course," Anna said.

"But who would do that?" Isabel asked.

"Well, I've noticed that neither of you has lost any posters yet," Anna said, looking at Avery and Katani.

"I just got mine up today," Avery said, before she tossed a handful of sunflower kernels into her mouth.

"So you think by taking other people's posters down, you'll get equal time?" Anna asked Avery.

"I didn't say anything about taking any posters down. I just said I put posters up!" Avery said.

"Banners then?" Anna asked.

"That's more your style, Anna!" Avery quipped as she slurped down the rest of her milk.

Anna turned then to look at Katani and raised an eyebrow. Joline, chief assistant to Anna, mimicked her leader's moves. All except the eyebrow raise. Neither said anything, but Katani knew what they were insinuating.

Katani was furious. How dare Anna and Joline hint that she would be so devious as to take other posters down! "We're not interested in any of your warped theories, Anna."

"It's not a theory, Katani. Posters ARE missing. Every presidential candidate has posters missing—except for two."

Then she turned on her heel and left, Joline following after her.

"You know, if somebody ever ran a 'mean girl of the month' contest, I would nominate those two. They are so annoying," Maeve whispered loudly after the Queens of Mean.

Katani felt like she had been punched in the stomach. She hadn't taken any posters down, but what if someone else she knew had? What if someone who wanted her to be president, who didn't "approve of" some of the other candidates and who had speech class every day, every morning ... What if THAT someone had taken the posters down?

A DOSE OF PINK

After school and before her hip hop class, Maeve headed for Razzberry Pink's shop, Think Pink!, on Harvard Street. She needed a good dose of pink today. Something to lift her spirits. The atmosphere had been downright tense in the lunchroom today. Maeve wasn't sure which was worse, Anna and Joline—the Queens of Mean—hinting that Avery or Katani had been snatching rival campaign posters off the walls, OR the intensely competitive energy that filled the room every time Avery and Katani were together. It was horrible! Maeve knew a quick side trip to Think Pink! would make her feel so much better.

Charlotte had run into Ms. Pink in the park a few weeks before when Marty instantly fell in love with Razzberry's pink poodle, La Fanny. That was when the group found out about Think Pink! And, it had quickly become one of Maeve's favorite shops.

Maeve pushed through the door and took a big breath.

How was it that it even smelled pink? What was that scent? Strawberry or cotton candy? Whatever it was, it smelled delicious!

The walls were painted with broad vertical stripes of every shade of pink imaginable. There were pale pinks, deep pinks and neon bright pinks. Along the edges of the wall, strings of pink lights lit up the room. There were pink flamingo lights and pink globe lights. Overhead, a dazzling array of pink umbrellas pointed down from the ceiling. In the center of the room hung an impressive pink chandelier.

And that was just the décor. Think Pink! was crammed with all kinds of delightful, interesting, and desirable merchandise that was all pink, of course! There were pink notebooks, pink pens, and an assortment of pink stationery and note cards. There were bins of pink candies and shelves filled with pink jams, jellies, and sauces. Pink candles. Pink glassware. Pink fashion accessories—purses, hats, earrings, scarves, and necklaces. Ms. Pink even had a bookshelf with titles of books that all included the word pink. Titles like: *Murder of the Pink Elephant* and *Priscilla and the Pink Planet*. Naturally, the covers of the books came in a wide variety of pink shades. It might have been too much, but Ms. Pink had placed beautiful green palm trees throughout the store. The effect was one of a lovely pink forest.

Maeve took in another deep breath and smiled. She thought perhaps this was a store decorated and stocked just for her. Of course, it would be a problem for anyone who didn't like pink … someone like Avery, for example.

"How are we today?" asked Ms. Magenta, the salesgirl. "May I help you find something to put you in the pink?" All of Think Pink!'s staff wore outrageous pink outfits and had the store name printed on their name tags.

Maeve wanted to find out how old you had to be to work at Think Pink! As soon as she could, she was applying for a job. She'd already picked out her Think Pink! name—Ms. Blushing Rose. She smiled at Ms. Magenta as if she were Blushing Rose and already worked here. "I've come to visit that feather boa again! I'm saving up for it. One of these days, it's going to be mine."

"Go ahead and try it on again," Ms. Magenta said. She took the boa from the shoulders of the one mannequin in the store and draped it over Maeve's shoulders.

Made from a combination of dark pink feathers interspersed with silver tinsels, Maeve thought this feather boa was the most beautiful thing she'd ever seen. She ran her hands down the length of the boa, then tossed one of the long ends over her shoulder.

"Breathtaking," Ms. Magenta said, clapping her hands together.

When Maeve put on the feather boa, she felt so special—like she was an Academy Award winner or something. If Maeve were running for class president, she would be known as the pink candidate! She would wear this boa in the hall everyday to remind everyone to think pink and act pink. She took a practice stroll down the middle aisle of the store as if it were the red carpet at some movie premiere. When she turned to walk back, she saw a flyer on the checkout counter.

"What's this?" she asked.

"Oh, the contest. Ms. Pink just announced it," Ms. Magenta said. "Take a flyer."

"'My Pet Looks Perfect in Pink,'" Maeve read. "What a great idea! I can just see how cute Marty would be in pink!"

"It's for a wonderful cause, too. All the entry fees benefit the local shelter. You know how fond Ms. Pink is of animals,"

Ms. Magenta added.

"I love a good cause," Maeve said twirling one final time with the boa.

"Well, be sure to tell your friends."

Maeve hung the feather boa back on the mannequin. "Bye for now. I should be able to afford it in a couple of weeks."

"Toodles! Stop by any time," Ms. Magenta called after her. "And don't forget! Think Pink!"

As Maeve rushed off toward the dance studio, she reread the contest flyer. This is perfect, she thought. The BSG could use something fun and frivolous to distract them right now. Marty would look so cute in pink! This was something they could all do together! Even Avery would be excited. She was crazy about animal shelters.

CROSSING THE LINE

"It will all work out. It will all work out," Charlotte said to herself as she plopped down at her desk. Oddly she felt like Dorothy in *The Wizard of Oz* when she clicked her heels together in order to get home. She half expected to open her eyes and find herself on a farm in Kansas.

"Kansas might not be a bad idea," Charlotte said as Marty jumped from the floor to her lap.

Right after lunch, within minutes of each other, both Katani and Avery had asked Charlotte if she would be home today because they wanted to use the Tower as their campaign headquarters. She had promised both of them that they could.

"How could I not say yes?" Charlotte asked Marty as she scratched him behind his ear, setting off a rapid twitch of his back leg. "The Tower doesn't belong to me! It belongs to the BSG. It's our special place. It would be against the BSG Oath to exclude anyone. What do you think, Marty?" she asked the little dog. Marty looked up and snorted at Charlotte. "Marty, I swear you understand everything we say," Charlotte giggled as she gave Marty another little tickle on his stomach.

She hadn't asked either girl when they planned to come over. Then had realized with horror, as she walked home from school, that they might show up at the same time. Well, thought Charlotte, maybe they could divide the Tower into two rooms to separate the dueling candidates. So as soon as she had gotten home, she had found a hammer and nails, clothesline, and a large flat sheet. She had pounded in the nails and had the clothesline and sheet waiting just in case.

"I even put little loops in the ends of the clothesline, so I can hang it up quickly. Just in case," she told Marty, and he cocked his little head to one side as if to say he wasn't sure that would work.

"Well, I'm as prepared as I can be," Charlotte told him.

The doorbell rang. Charlotte left Marty in her room, shut the door, and ran down the stairs to answer it. It was Avery. Just moments after Charlotte helped carry all Avery's things up to the Tower, the doorbell rang again.

Oh, no! Charlotte thought. But she didn't say anything as she went downstairs, hoping it was UPS or FedEx, or even a traveling salesman.

But, of course, it wasn't. There on the other side of the door was Katani with her campaign file box, three-ring binder, stereo, easel, and bulletin board. Katani was in a great mood.

"You're a lifesaver, Charlotte," she said as she handed the last of her campaign supplies up the ladder. She climbed up and froze the minute she saw Avery. She turned to Charlotte. "What's she doing here?"

"What am I doing here? What are YOU doing here?"

Avery asked.

"I'm using the Tower as my campaign headquarters," Katani said.

"The Tower is my headquarters."

They both turned to Charlotte. "Who asked first?" they asked at the same time.

"You promised me, Charlotte, that I could use the Tower!" Avery exclaimed.

"What?! You promised ME! How could you promise us both?" Katani was so mad at Charlotte.

Charlotte was stuck. She did technically promise both Avery and Katani.

Charlotte tried to sidestep the issue by saying, "I don't see why you both can't use the Tower as your headquarters." Even as she said it, she had the sinking feeling that this could never work, but there was no way they were going to make her choose between the two of them.

"How's that going to work?" Katani asked.

"Maybe if we set up a schedule," Charlotte said. "We could alternate even and odd days."

"Nope. Won't work for me," Avery said, crossing her arms in front of her. "Not with basketball and indoor soccer practice to work around."

"Look," Katani said, stepping forward and coming toe-to-toe with Avery. "I NEED the Tower. I share my bedroom with Kelley and can't spread out stuff. Why can't you use your huge bedroom, or your carriage house?"

"Katani!" Charlotte gasped.

"Because I get the best ideas here!" Avery said, not backing down, even though Katani was towering over her.

"Then you'll just have to share," Charlotte said.

"Share?" they both said at the same time, in a way that

made it seem like a totally ridiculous idea. It seemed to be the only thing they could agree on.

"I'll divide the room in half." Charlotte was glad she had thought ahead and put the nails up and tied the loops in the clothesline already, or the moment would have been even longer and more awkward. If that was possible.

Charlotte mobilized into action. In an instant, she had the clothesline up and was tossing the sheet over the line. It would take two sheets to completely divide the room, but one sheet was enough of a divider between the two candidates. Charlotte pulled the sheet almost totally over where the Tower steps came up through the floor.

Katani and Avery stood in the opposite corner—Maeve and Charlotte's corner—watching in amazement as Charlotte straightened the sheet and created two distinct working spaces.

"Well, what do you think?" Charlotte asked.

"But Avery can still see my stuff when she comes up," Katani said.

"I'm not a spy! Besides … what's worth seeing except a bunch of feathers and sequins?"

"I think you should both get to work," Charlotte said before anyone could say anything else.

Reluctantly, each girl moved to her side of the sheet. Charlotte sat at the end of her window seat closest to the corner so she had a view of each girl's side of the sheet. She grabbed a pen and notebook and paged open her library book. She was reading a great book called *Lyddie* by Katherine Paterson and couldn't wait to get back to it. It was about a girl who lived in 1843 and moved from Vermont to Lowell, Massachusetts, to work in a textile mill. Charlotte couldn't believe that girls as young as sixteen worked ten to twelve hours a day, six days a week, in cold, smelly, dimly lit rooms.

Katani got out her portable stereo, popped in a CD, and cranked it up.

Avery marched to the sheet divider. "Hey! Isn't that a little loud?"

Katani kept her back to the sheet and shrugged. "Deal with it," was all she said.

Charlotte choked back a laugh when Avery leaned toward the sheet and stuck out her tongue.

Her friends were acting so childish that Charlotte felt like she was babysitting a pair of kindergarteners. On the other side of the sheet, Katani set up a portable easel and put a bulletin board on it that was neatly divided into categories with jewel-toned yarn and labeled with matching construction paper. Katani sat primly on the edge of the Lime Swivel chair, pulled her file box toward her and started sorting through papers as music blared around her.

Across the room, Avery pulled out a dry erase board, set it on the floor, and propped it up against her window seat. She pulled a folder of papers out of her duffle bag and started sorting them out. Suddenly, Avery grabbed her duffle and dumped the contents on the floor. Different sized and shaped Nerf ball equipment rolled in every direction.

Avery had hung a Nerf basketball hoop weeks ago, so Charlotte was used to seeing her bounce and toss the Nerf basketball around, but this was over the top. Charlotte couldn't hide the surprised look on her face. It was Nerf City on Avery's side of the room.

"I don't get ideas by sitting," Avery said when she saw the look on Charlotte's face. "I get ideas by moving around." She dribbled away from the basket, turned, and shot a fade-away jumper. "Avery Madden for two!" Avery shouted when it went through the hoop.

"Hey, Charlotte," Avery asked, dribbling around her side of the room. "Where's Marty?"

Charlotte held up one finger. She'd intended to bring Marty up to the Tower right away, but had been sidetracked by hanging the sheet. Charlotte tiptoed across Katani's side of the room and down the ladder. When she returned to the ladder with Marty in her arms, Katani's music poured through the opening. The base beat of the music shook the floorboards, punctuated by loud thumps and thuds. It sounded like someone was performing a hippo ballet up there.

Avery'd switched to Nerf baseball by the time Charlotte settled into her seat with Marty in her arms. Charlotte noticed there were a few things written on her dry erase board. Ironically, Avery, "the green candidate," was using an orange-colored marker to write with.

Marty usually loved greeting visitors, especially Avery, but even he seem stunned by the loud music and the frantic activity on Avery's side of the Tower. He was very content to stay on Charlotte's lap.

Charlotte couldn't blame him. It was all a little overwhelming. Charlotte had been trying to think of ways to make a special space for Isabel, but the Tower had never seemed smaller. The election had overshadowed everything in their BSG world.

Avery threw the Nerf ball up in the air and smacked it hard with the Nerf bat. She dropped the bat just before the ball hit the sheet divider, dove for the rebound, miraculously catching the ball as it bounced off of the sheet divider. She landed on the floor with a monstrous thud, but quickly jumped to her feet. She raised the Nerf ball above her head as if showing the ball to an imaginary crowd. "And the crowd goes wild!" she said.

She dropped to her knees in front of the dry erase board and scribbled out a few more ideas before she popped to her feet to repeat the whole process. This time she hit the floor extra hard. Charlotte was sure even Miss Pierce had heard the crash from her first-floor apartment.

"What are you doing over there?" Katani asked, looking back over her shoulder at the sheet divider. "It sounds like a herd of rampaging elephants."

"I am creating, if you want to know, Miss Perfection!" Avery shouted back.

Katani popped out of the Lime Swivel, tiptoed to the sheet, and peered around the edge to see what Avery was up to.

"You are being rude, Avery," said Katani in her most haughty Kgirl voice.

"Hey! Stop peeking!"

"At what? You're not doing anything!"

"Yes I am! I'm thinking, and you're disrupting the process."

Charlotte cleared her throat. Both girls took the hint and went back to their separate headquarters.

When Katani cranked up the tunes even louder, Marty began whining.

"I can't think with that noise, and you are hurting Marty's ears!" Avery shouted.

"Listen! I can't play music loudly in my room because of Kelley. That's why I came here. If you don't like it, leave!"

"What about Marty?!" Avery retorted

"Put him downstairs."

"That's not fair!"

"Candidates, in your corners, please!" Charlotte said as if she were reffing a boxing match. "I think you should just concentrate on your campaigns—and not talk to each other … you both are upsetting Marty."

Katani reluctantly turned back to her bulletin board with a big sigh.

Avery switched back to Nerf basketball. After a few perfect baskets that hit nothing but net, one shot hit the rim. Avery dove for the rebound. She caught it, but she ran into the sheet before she hit the floor. The sheet pulled off the line and wrapped around Avery as she rolled across the floor. She rolled right into the legs of Katani's easel. Katani's poster board catapulted off the easel and knocked the cord of the stereo loose as it fell. The Tower was plunged into instant temporary silence. The falling bulletin board hit Katani's equipment box, which slid off her portable file box. The corner of the equipment box hit the floor and sent the contents—multicolored paperclips, markers, push pins and rolls of tape—skidding across the wooden floor.

A large roll of masking tape rolled across the floor with such force that when it hit Avery's dry erase board, it fell over and smacked the floor.

"What was that?" Avery asked in a muffled voice. She was rolled up like a mummy in the divider sheet.

Katani rose up from the Lime Swivel and looked at her wrecked side of the room. Before she could say anything, Marty jumped from Charlotte's lap. He seemed to think this whole thing was for his benefit and started yapping and jumping on Avery, who was wrapped in the sheet. As he jumped and danced about, he scattered the markers and paperclips further across the room.

"Help! Get me out of here," Avery called.

Hearing Avery's voice, Marty jumped right on top of her. His puppy feet must have tickled because the sheet—

wrapped Avery started laughing and wiggling about like a giant silkworm.

Just as Avery wiggled enough to get her head out, they heard a car horn from the street below. Charlotte went to the window to see Mrs. Madden's car in the driveway.

"Your mom's here, Avery. I'll run down and tell her you're … wrapped up in your work, but will be along in a minute."

That did it. Katani had been wavering between laughter and outrage and Charlotte's comment pushed her over the edge. She laughed so hard she couldn't stand any more. She sank down into the Lime Swivel as Charlotte disappeared down the ladder.

Charlotte felt she could leave Marty as referee between the two and climbed down the ladder stairs and then down to the first floor. She was surprised to find Mrs. Fields climbing up the porch steps. She welcomed her inside.

"Would you tell Katani to get her things ready? I'm going to stick my head in the door and say hello to Sapphire—Miss Pierce—while I wait."

Charlotte said that she would, wondering what it was like for two best friends from middle school to suddenly rediscover each other almost fifty years later. And to think that the BSG had gotten the two together. It was a pretty cool thing, she thought.

She bounced out the front door and down the porch steps to the waiting car to tell Mrs. Madden that Avery would be along in a few minutes.

Avery had her dry erase board and papers packed up by the time Charlotte returned.

"Don't worry about the Nerf mess. I'll pick all that up for you," Charlotte said.

Avery glanced back at Katani. "Sorry," she said before she disappeared through the Tower opening.

Katani waved her off.

"Your grandmother stopped to say hello to Miss Pierce while you pack up," Charlotte told Katani. "I'll help you. I'll start with the paperclips."

"Charlotte ..."

"What?"

"Avery is so ..."

"I know ..."

And they both started to giggle.

Avery's Blog

The campaign is going pretty well. My slogan is: Vote Avery! For the Best Junior High Ever! When I become class president, I want our school to be more environmentally friendly. We have to learn "green habits" when we are young. I like to think of my generation as the one that will really save the planet.

Campaigning is a little more work than I thought it would be. And the whole poster thing ... what a royal pain in the you know what!!!!

Survey:

What is your favorite way to help the environment?

A. Pick up litter

B. Recycle cans and bottles

C. Buy environmentally friendly products

Results from the last poll:

What is your favorite way to compete with friends?

a) trivia games (11%)

b) one-on-one games (38%)

c) cards/board games (22%)

d) team sports (29%)

CHAPTER 9

෬

MISSING IN ACTION

AFTER days of going to school early, Katani felt like it was a real treat to arrive later than normal. Her mother had offered to drop Katani off later so she could put the finishing touches on her new campaign headquarters location in her own bedroom.

Katani still couldn't believe what happened in the Tower yesterday. She thought sharing a room with Kelley was bad, but after an afternoon with Avery, she'd have to rethink that. She would have been really upset if it hadn't been so funny. No, from now on, she'd keep her campaign headquarters at home. Besides, carting everything back and forth had been a real pain.

The first bell rang, and Katani walked quickly up the steps to the seventh-grade entrance and made her way to her locker.

"Did you hear?" Maeve asked as soon as she got her locker open. "There are more posters missing. Are any of yours gone?"

"I don't know, I just got here," Katani said quickly, retrieving the things she needed for her morning classes from her locker. "Will you help me look?"

Katani and Maeve made their way up and down the seventh-grade hall. They could see where a few of Betsy's, Dillon's, and one of the vice-presidential candidate's posters were missing. Katani could tell they had been quickly ripped away. Nothing remained but balled-up masking tape and sometimes a thin piece of the poster board that had peeled away when the poster was ripped off the wall.

"Are any of your posters missing?" Isabel asked when Katani and Maeve joined Isabel and Charlotte outside of Ms. Rodriguez's classroom.

Katani shook her head.

"Wow, that's surprising! Especially since you have so many. You probably have more posters than any of the candidates, and none of them are missing?" Charlotte said.

"What's going on?" Avery asked.

"Did you hear? There are more posters missing," Maeve said.

"Yeah, I heard! Henry Yurt got hit the hardest. All of his banners are missing, and he only has one poster left," Avery said.

"How 'bout you, Avery? Were any of yours taken down?" Isabel asked.

Avery shook her head. "No, and good thing. I don't have that many. But my posters are up pretty high. By the time I got them done, the only space left to hang them was above the lockers. I had to borrow a stepladder from the janitor to put them up. Whoever's taking the posters would have to have a chair to reach them. Katani? Are you missing any?"

Katani shook her head. Before she could say anything else, Anna and Joline walked up.

"Well, I see there are more posters missing today," Anna

said. "Are any of yours missing, Katani?" She made it sound like she not only knew that none of Katani's posters were missing, but that she also knew why.

Katani shook her head. "But mine are right next to classroom doors," she explained. "Maybe whoever is taking them is afraid there might be a teacher in the classroom."

Anna rolled her eyes and looked at Joline. They exchanged a look that said, "No one believes THAT!"

"How long did it take you to think up that one, Katani?" Anna asked.

"What do you mean by that?"

"I mean, it's pretty suspicious, girls. Pretty suspicious." And with that, Anna breezed past Katani and into the classroom.

Before anyone could say anything, the bell rang, and they rushed inside to their seats. As Katani took hers, she couldn't help wondering if Kelley had been alone in the seventh-grade hall this morning. *Oh, please*, she thought, don't let it be Kelley doing this!

☙

As Ms. Rodriguez took attendance, Avery stared at the back of Anna's head. If only she was one of the characters in a cartoon that had laser eyes so she could bore a hole into Anna's pea brain. Anna made it seem like Katani was taking down posters. Even though Katani was her competitor, Avery thought it was the most ridiculous thing she had ever heard in her whole life! Katani Summers would never do something like that.

Besides, if Katani was going to stoop low enough to take posters down, she wouldn't waste time with Dillon or Henry. Avery was sure that Katani would take her posters down before she'd take down Dillon's or Henry's. "I'm her main competition," Avery said under her breath. Besides, Katani was probably one of the few people in the seventh-grade class tall enough to take Avery's posters down without a chair. Obviously, it couldn't be Katani!

As soon as she'd decided that Katani was NOT the one, another thought crept into Avery's brain. Did that mean that whoever was taking posters down wasn't taking her seriously? Didn't the others consider her the leader in the campaign? The one to beat? She suddenly felt sick inside.

"Could I have your attention?" Ms. R said, interrupting Avery's thoughts. "As faculty advisors for the seventh-grade student elections, Mr. Danson and I have decided to teach you more about the democratic process by holding debates next week. To help students start formulating debate questions for particular candidates, each candidate will make a short five-minute speech at an assembly on Friday."

A low murmuring rippled around the room. Pete Wexler shouted out, "One in a Million!" Dillon raised his hand in acknowledgment. A few kids clapped.

"Let's save the campaigning for Friday, shall we?" Ms. R told Pete as she gave him the look.

Avery wished someone had shouted something out about her. She missed having her own cheering section.

"Before we begin," Ms. Rodriguez said, "I have something to say. I don't know who is taking down the posters, but I will say this to you all: it's not right or fair." There was dead silence in the classroom. Ms. Rodriguez looked around the classroom challenging everyone to think about what she had just said.

Then she continued. "Since I seem to have a handful of candidates in this class … are there any comments from the candidates?" They all looked around at each other. "If you think of something later, don't hesitate to ask me," Ms. Rodriguez said.

Avery wrote in giant red letters on the cover of her notebook: Speech. Friday. Assembly! 5 min.

Avery caught Katani looking over at her. Katani shook her head. Katani was writing the dates in her assignment book. Avery didn't understand why other people liked assignment books so much. They only worked when you had them with you and you looked at them constantly. Random was fine with Avery, because once she wrote something down she never forgot it. Random was a system that worked very well for her.

"Now ... for the rest of you, as your classmates are preparing for the speech and debate, you should also be preparing, thinking of what you want to ask the candidates," said Ms. Rodriguez.

As Ms. R went on about what sorts of questions would be appropriate for a town hall debate, Avery couldn't help visualizing how the debates would go. She could see herself being able to answer any question—batting them like perfectly hit baseballs into the crowd. She'd wow them. This was a great opportunity for Avery to show her stuff. So far, Dillon was treating the campaign like a popularity contest, Henry as a stage to tell jokes, and Katani as an art project.

Avery was sure that the debates would help her classmates see that she, Avery Madden, was the only true choice for class president. Yes, the debates and speech would finally give her the opportunity to shine.

Good thing she had been the first one to ask Charlotte for help on the speech! She didn't want to go through again what had happened yesterday when she and Katani had tried to share the Tower. That didn't make any sense! How did Charlotte think that would work? It was like two opposing teams trying to share the same locker room. From now on, she was going to use her first walk-in closet as campaign headquarters. She was sure Walter wouldn't mind.

PICTURE PERFECT

"Help!" Maeve called out to Isabel in a stage whisper as she came into the school library during study hall. "I'm so glad to find you here," Maeve said, sitting down next to Isabel at the library table.

Isabel had her sketchpad open and was working on a cartoon.

"I need help! Isabel, do you think you could spare a minute, or are you in the middle of something?"

"I'm trying to get the cartoons for the next issue of *The Sentinel*. I don't have much time … or any ideas," Isabel said.

"Why don't you do the cute little birds? I love your birds!"

"Jennifer wants something edgy. She was thinking something about the election would be a good subject. But I'm having a hard time coming up with ideas for political cartoons. I think I'm better with birds."

"What have you come up with so far?"

"A big fat zero! Well, that's not exactly true. I've come up with some bird ideas." Isabel showed Maeve her latest bird creation.

"I love it. Love it!" Maeve said.

"Thanks. What did you need help with?" Isabel asked.

"Oh, the 'My Pet Looks Perfect in Pink' Contest," Maeve said, shoving the flyer from Think Pink! in front of Isabel.

"What a cute idea!" Isabel said.

"The deadline's coming up pretty soon, and I have to have a costume. I was hoping Katani could sew something. I know she's busy, but maybe if I had the idea of what it should look like and bought the materials, it would be easier for her to put together. I have a few ideas … I just can't quite sketch them out."

"Sure, I'd be happy to help," Isabel said.

Maeve rattled off her list of ideas. As Isabel drew Maeve's ideas, Maeve pulled out her laptop and made a list of her own.

Maeve's Notes to Self

1. Go through closet and pull out
   ~~anything pink that would work for a~~
   costume.
2. Ask Charlotte, Isabel, and Katani to
   do the same.
3. Don't ask Avery—there are no teams
   with pink as a team color.
4. Talk Mom into taking me to the fabric
   store ASAP!
5. Send "chill" cards to Avery & Katani—
   JK

CHAPTER 10

CR

SPEECH, SPEECH!

AS SOON AS Ms. Rodriguez announced that the candidates' introductory speeches would be this Friday and the debate would be the following Friday, Charlotte sprung into action. She knew exactly what was going to happen, and she knew she had to be the one to make sure that what had happened yesterday in the Tower wouldn't happen again. Instead of waiting for Katani and Avery to come to her, she approached each of them before lunch.

Charlotte saw Katani first. "Wanna work on your speech right after school?" Charlotte asked. Luckily, she did.

She caught Avery just before social studies. Figuring that Avery would have basketball practice after school, she asked if she could meet her later in the evening. "Would you mind meeting in the Tower after basketball practice? You could join us for dinner?" She had hoped that two hours between meetings would be enough of a buffer.

CR

Katani and Charlotte walked home from school together. After going over the major points of Katani's campaign, they pieced together a five-minute speech. Katani practiced the beginning. Charlotte admired her poise. The way she stood tall and confident said as much about her capability as the words Charlotte had helped Katani put together.

As Katani went through the speech, Charlotte glanced at her watch. It was getting very close to the time that Avery was supposed to arrive.

"When will you girls be ready for dinner?" Mr. Ramsey called up the ladder steps.

"I don't know if I can stay for dinner," Katani said. "I'll call home and see."

Charlotte scrambled down the ladder-steps. "Not Katani, Dad. Avery," Charlotte whispered.

"Oh, sorry," Mr. Ramsey apologized.

Charlotte nodded and rolled her eyes. Sometimes dads were so clueless!

"Thanks for inviting me for dinner," Katani said as she climbed down from the Tower, "but my grandma is already on her way to pick me up."

Charlotte shot her father a look to make sure he didn't say something stupid like, "We have plenty and your grandmother can stay too." She turned back to Katani. "We better go clean up," she said, climbing back up to the Tower.

"Charlotte, what's this?" Katani pointed to a new quote on her bulletin board.

"Oh, it's for my social studies report. I picked Abigail Adams because I didn't know much about her! I didn't really have a lot of American history in school overseas. She was a pretty cool lady."

"'*We have too many high sounding words and too few actions that correspond with them,'"* Katani read out loud. "That's a really cool quote, Char."

"Isn't it? You know I got the idea for putting my favorite quotes up on a wall from your grandmother ... on the first day of school."

Just then, Mr. Ramsey called up the ladder that Mrs. Fields had arrived, and they heard a beep beep coming from the big, blue Buick in the driveway.

"Thanks for helping me out. I think I'll be able to piece together a great speech from what we talked about," Katani said.

The two scampered down the ladder stairs from the Tower, down the stairs to the first floor, and out the heavy front door. Charlotte stood on the porch and waved as Mrs. Fields backed out of the driveway. No sooner had the taillights of Mrs. Fields' car disappeared around the corner, then Mrs. Madden's white Navigator pulled to a stop in front of the house.

Avery popped out of the SUV. "Thanks, Mom. You can pick me up at nine," she shouted to her mother before slamming the door.

"You didn't have to wait for me on the porch!" Avery said to Charlotte as she jogged up the porch steps.

ʘ

As Avery climbed the stairs, the smell of food cooking got more and more intense. "Mmm! Can we eat first?" Avery asked.

Avery was glad that Charlotte said yes because she was starved!

"Dinner will be ready in about five minutes," Mr. Ramsey called from the kitchen.

Five minutes! Avery didn't know if she could wait. "Where's girl's best friend?" she shouted. At the sound of her voice, Marty ran out of Charlotte's room as fast as his little legs could carry him with Happy Lucky Thingy, his favorite toy, dangling from his mouth.

Avery and Marty played a fast-paced game of chase around the couch several times. When Avery collapsed to the floor and flipped onto her back, Marty pounced on her chest, dropped his toy, Happy Lucky Thingy, and began furiously licking her face. Lifting him into the air, the "little dude" twisted and wiggled until Avery turned him loose.

"Dinner, girls," Mr. Ramsey called.

Marty yapped excitedly.

"Sorry, pal, you'll have to wait for your dog chow."

"Mmmmm. Smells good! What's for dinner?" Avery asked.

"This is Charlotte's favorite. Croquettes."

"Croquette? Do I have to eat them with a mallet?" Avery laughed at her own joke.

Mr. Ramsey smiled. "No, this is our most favorite French dish."

The croquettes were scrumptious. It was tiny pieces of meat in a yummy sauce surrounded by a crisp breading. Delicious! By the time Avery finished her second, she was stuffed. When she leaned back in her chair, a burp bubbled to the surface.

"Oops. I mean, excuse me," Avery said, blushing.

"That's OK. In some cultures, a burp after a meal is the

greatest compliment you can give the chef. In fact, the chef is insulted if you don't burp," Mr. Ramsey said with a smile.

Charlotte gave her dad a pained look and started clearing the table.

"No, I'll take care of the dishes tonight. You two have lots to do," he smiled at his daughter.

As soon as they were up in the Tower, Avery went over all her ideas. Charlotte listened patiently as Avery listed all the things she wanted to include in her speech.

"My father said the most important thing is to start strong and end strong," Charlotte said. "People tend to forget what's in the middle."

They debated which two points were the strongest and then worked to fill in the middle of Avery's speech. Charlotte wrote down the important points. While she was thinking out loud, Avery wandered around the Tower.

"What's this?" Avery asked, picking up a knit hat from the floor.

"Oh, Katani must have left her hat here," Charlotte said.

At first, Avery figured Katani had left the hat there yesterday. Then she remembered seeing Katani wearing her bright hat today.

"Katani was here today?"

"Well, this afternoon …"

"Katani was here this afternoon?"

Avery started looking around to see if there were other things left behind.

"So you know her speech?"

"Well, not word for word. I just helped her decide on key statements and helped her organize her ideas."

"But that's what you're doing for me!"

"Well, yes …"

"Is my speech better than her speech?"

"Well …"

"It's not as good? What do I have to do to make it better?"

"It's not worse."

"But it's not better? Is that what you're saying?"

"I'm not saying anything. I don't want to compare. One is not better than the other, they're just … different."

"But the whole purpose of the speeches is for the students to compare the candidates. So, since you've already heard both speeches …"

"Please can we just talk about the speech? YOUR speech? You are getting too obsessed with all of this."

Avery sat quietly looking out the window at the spot where the lights of Brookline blended into the lights of Boston. "This is new," she said, pointing to the Abigail Adams quote.

"Yes. I'm doing my report for social studies on Abigail Adams. I found out so many interesting things. Did you know Abigail Adams tried to convince her husband that women should have the right to vote over 100 years before it became law?"

"Abigail Adams rocked," Avery said.

"It's so cool that our school was named for her," Charlotte said. "I really like this quote."

"It IS cool." Avery read the quote again, just as she heard her mom beep from the driveway below. She gathered her things together, bent down, and let Marty give her one last slurp before she trotted down the stairs and out the front door.

"Thanks, Charlotte! See you tomorrow," she called back to Charlotte, who was waving to her from the porch.

"Good luck on your speech," Charlotte called after her.

Why did she say that? Avery thought, as her mom backed

down the driveway. Avery wondered if her speech was good enough. Maybe it needed a stronger ending, something that would really wow them. Avery really liked that quote she had on the wall from Abigail Adams. The more she thought of it, the more she thought that ending with the Abigail quote would be great. Besides, it would be different, and the school was named after her.

Avery jumped in the car and gave her mother a big grin.

"Mom, I've got the best ending to my speech," she said, her enthusiasm bubbling over.

"Terrific, sweetheart," her mom answered and reached over to ruffle her daughter's hair.

"I think I'm definitely going to win this thing," Avery continued with excitement.

"Well, you know you have my vote," her mom said, flashing Avery a smile.

There was a brief pause and then Mrs. Madden asked, "How is Katani's campaign going?"

"Good, I guess. We don't really talk about it much," Avery said as she looked out the window.

"You two still pals?"

"Yeah," Avery said slowly.

"Avery …"

"It's no big deal, Mom. Katani and I are just concentrating on our own campaigns," Avery explained impatiently.

"OK, honey. But remember, Katani is one of your best friends, so don't get too heated up about all of this. School elections come and go, but good friends are hard to come by. Just be aware."

Avery leaned her head back on the head rest. There was just so much to think about. She wanted to win really badly. But how badly was the question.

Chat Room: BSG   `_ □ X`

File Edit People View Help

3 people here

lafrida
skywriter
flikchic

lafrida: How's the speech writing going?

skywriter: Better than organizing campaign headquarters

flikchic: guess what I heard

lafrida: What

skywriter: Tell us

flikchic: Anna's spreading a rumor that it's obvious that ONE of the two BSG must be stealing the other candidates' posters

skywriter: Where did you hear that?

flikchic: That's not important. What if it's true?

lafrida: No way!

skywriter: Doubtful!

flikchic: a lot of people think it might be

skywriter: Who?

flikchic: You know who!

skywriter: The queens of mean?

lafrida: but who'd believe that?

flikchic: the queens of mean can be very convincing

lafrida: think so?

flikchic: know so!!!!!!

skywriter: m's right.

lafrida: but it's not true ... right?

flikchic: if it's Ave and K they would never do that ... right

lafrida: Winning is so important to both of them

skywriter: Neither are used to coming in second

flikchic: yikes!

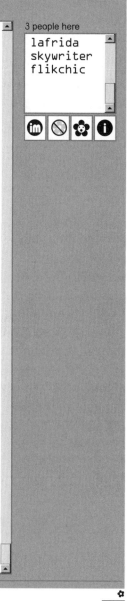

3 people here

lafrida
skywriter
flikchic

CHAPTER 11

❧

HIGH SOUNDING WORDS

KATANI looked at her watch and squirmed in her seat. Ms. Rodriguez and Mr. Danson gave the vice president, secretary, and treasurer candidates the option of speaking or not speaking. And of course, Betsy was the only one who wanted to speak, and it went on and on—well over her allotted five minutes. Actually, now that Katani thought of it, she was sure that Ms. Rodriguez had told Betsy she only had three minutes and the presidential candidates had five minutes to speak.

The candidates had gathered ahead of time to draw numbers to decide the speaking order. Katani had hoped for the last spot, but she got third. Avery had won the last spot. She acted as if she'd just stopped a corner kick to win the World Cup. She threw her arms up in the air and cheered.

At least I don't have to go first! Katani thought.

Henry was first, followed by Dillon, then Katani, and then Avery. Katani wished that the two of them weren't right after one another. It felt too close. What if one of their speeches was noticeably better than the other's? How bad would Avery feel? What if Avery got more cheers than she did? This election was really getting on her nerves.

Katani brightened when she thought about what she was wearing for today's big event. She had needed an outfit that looked good on her tall frame and also made her look a little more mature. Last night she'd spent an hour going through her closet, trying on this and that. She almost wore her yellow chiffon shirt, but she thought the ruffled cuffs might be distracting. She'd finally settled on black pants, a white shirt, and her short-waisted, red jacket. She looked like a president in that outfit, and the red, Isabel told her, projected confidence.

Henry got up when Ms. Rodriguez introduced him and walked up the three steps to the platform. Henry obviously thought bow ties were what politicians wore. Katani still thought it looked more like what a clown would wear. She wouldn't have been surprised if he wore a carnation that squirted water. "Good afternoon, Ladies and Germs ..." Henry started.

Katani rolled her eyes. That might be a great way to start a humorous speech, but Katani didn't think it was appropriate for a presidential campaign. As Henry went on, Katani tuned him out, going over her own speech in her head. She'd written the key lines on cards and had memorized the rest.

"Eye contact. Remember to use eye contact," her sister Patrice had told her as she was practicing last night. Usually, Katani thought Patrice was the bossiest sister on the planet, but she had actually been very nice last night and had helped Katani practice. Kelley did her best to help, too. Each time Katani finished her speech, Kelley clapped loudly and shouted out, "I'm Kelley Summers and I approve of this message!"

Katani and Patrice busted out laughing every time Kelley announced her approval. It was funny last night, but Katani was happy this was a seventh-grade ONLY assembly. If Kelley shouted

❀

out her approval at the end of her speech today, Katani was positive she would absolutely wither and die!

She was going over the first half of the speech in her head when she was jerked back into present time by lots of laughter and clapping. Henry was finished with his speech. He held up two fingers for victory as he walked across the stage. He motioned to the crowd at the top of the stairs, pointing first to his neon sticker and then putting his hand to his ear. The crowd responded, screaming out, "Smile! It's a Yurt Alert!" Henry applauded and thanked the group as he trotted down the stage steps.

Katani clapped politely. OK, she thought. She had to give Henry credit, he was certainly entertaining, but she was also sure no one took the Yurtmeister seriously.

Ms. Rodriguez announced the next speaker. Dillon Johnson stood and walked confidently up the steps and across the stage to the podium. Pete Wexler and a few others started chanting, "Vote for Dillon. One in a Million! Vote for Dillon. One in a Million!" At least Dillon looked like a presidential candidate in his khakis and long-sleeved blue shirt.

When Dillon started talking, Katani went over the last half of her speech in her head. She couldn't wait to see Charlotte's face. Last night when she was practicing, she had decided the end of the speech was a little flat. At the last minute, she had changed the ending. She was sure that Charlotte would love it as much as she did. Suddenly, the student body burst into applause. Pete Wexler started chanting, "Vote for Dillon! One in a million!"

Ms. Rodriguez let them go on for a minute before she hushed them.

"Katani Summers." Katani heard Ms. Rodriguez announce her name, but she was so nervous, she really didn't hear anything else. Had anyone clapped for her? She couldn't be sure. She took a deep breath, threw back her shoulders, raised her chin, and plastered a huge smile on her face even though she didn't quite feel like smiling at that moment.

She seemed to float up the stairs. She didn't remember walking across the stage, but suddenly she was at the podium, looking out on the sea of students in the auditorium. The first words of her speech flew out of her head. Then … blankness. Fortunately, she remembered Maeve always said to breathe when you are nervous. So, she took a deep breath and looked down at her cards. The first words that Charlotte had helped her write jumpstarted her brain. Once she began the first few words, the other words followed just as they had planned. All those hours of practice had paid off! She tried to remember Patrice's suggestion of scanning the room by looking right and then middle and then left.

She was into it. It was happening. Before she knew it, it was time for the big finish!

"But enough talk. As Abigail Adams said, 'We have too many high sounding words and too few actions that correspond with them.' Vote for me and you can count on action. Thank you!"

Katani couldn't help looking at Charlotte, who looked pleasantly surprised. She was sitting directly behind Avery. Avery's mouth had dropped open, and she looked like one of those fish at Wulf's Fish Market.

As Katani finished, the students clapped. She couldn't tell how the crowd's response compared to how they applauded for Dillon and Henry, but it was clear who was NOT applauding … Avery Madden. Instead she was glaring at Katani in fury as she came down the steps from the stage. Dillon and Henry were at least making a polite attempt to clap. What was with Avery? Even if she didn't like Katani's speech, couldn't she at least be polite and clap anyway? Well, Katani would show some manners. Even if Avery wouldn't clap for her she would applaud for Avery.

SCRAMBLE

Avery listened to the end of Katani's speech in total disbelief. She looked at the neatly typed speech in front of her. That was how she had planned to end her speech ... using the same quote from Abigail Adams. Charlotte and Katani ... two of her best friends ... had betrayed her.

"Avery?" Ms. Rodriguez said from the podium. The students were clapping. She'd already been introduced and here she was in a fog trying to figure out what to do next. Avery rolled up her speech and trotted up the steps.

She'd read her carefully written-out speech over and over and over again last night. It took exactly four minutes and thirty-five seconds for her to read. As Avery stared out at the crowd, she was stumped, totally stumped. How would she end? She had been so excited about going last. Not now. Now, she wished she had gone before Katani. But she couldn't think about that. She had to start her speech.

She had been nervous while she was listening to the first three presidential candidates and had rolled and unrolled her speech as she waited for her turn. She tried to smooth it out as she stood at the podium, but was having a hard time keeping the ends from rolling up. Her palms started to sweat, and they felt gooey. Focus, she told herself. Focus.

She flattened her paper and started reading her speech. By the second paragraph, she'd settled in ... focusing in on the words in front of her rather than the crowd beyond the podium. It was only when she got to the end and the words about Abigail Adams slipped out and she stopped. She looked out, and there in the second row behind her empty chair was Charlotte, looking horrified. Charlotte looked much worse than she felt. Then there was Katani, who had a scowl on her face. What was she so mad about? She was the one who had stolen Avery's idea!

Avery had already said half of the quote, so she figured she might as well finish it. She paused. She couldn't just end like that. Avery had no idea what to say next. So she just opened her mouth and said the first thing that came out.

"I mean, Katani is right," she said, and immediately cringed. What was she saying? She shouldn't mention Katani in her speech! How would that sound? Like she thought Katani should be president?

"I mean, about this ... it's one of the few things I could agree with ..." No! She didn't want to slam Katani either, at least not in front of the whole class! Avery hated trash talkers, even if they deserved it.

"What I mean is ..." Avery paused and looked around. "I mean, there are two girls running for office. Wouldn't Abigail Adams be proud ... and ... uh, she wouldn't even imagine that we could play sports, too." Avery wished she could sink right through the podium floor. What did sports have to do with anything?

She unrolled the speech, looking for the words to end her speech. Not finding any, she rolled it up again as she watched kids squirm in their seats, uncomfortable for her. *Oh, this was bad*, Avery thought. Very bad. Her mind was blank. She went with what was in her hands. She picked up the rolled speech and held it up to her eye. "I'm looking ..."

What am I doing? she thought breathlessly. "What am I doing?" she asked out loud. "I'm looking for leadership in the seventh-grade class," she said in a rush as she put down her rolled-up speech.

She paused. What was she going to say next? She had no idea. Besides, she wanted to be the leader of the seventh-grade class.

"But I can't find it out there … do you know why?"

She was scrambling now … looking for anything that would make sense and sound like a logical ending to this botched speech.

"Because the only leader for the seventh-grade class is right here standing behind this podium and looking out at you. I'm the best leader for the seventh-grade class."

Avery didn't wait for applause. She bolted for the stairs, taking them two at a time and popped back in her seat.

Sparse applause started after she hit the seat. Avery crossed her arms in front of her and wished that she could die.

"Let's give a hand to all the candidates," Ms. Rodriguez said.

She invited them all back on the stage, starting with the two candidates for class secretary, then Betsy, the lone treasurer candidate, then the vice-presidential candidates, and one by one the candidates for president, starting with Henry, then Dillon and Katani and finally Avery. Avery was almost expecting kids to boo her for the strange ending to her speech, but they cheered. It occurred to Avery that maybe it wasn't as bad as she thought. Maybe, somehow what had seemed a hodgepodge had actually worked. She wondered, was that actually possible? A tiny seed of hope started to grow.

Avery smiled and waved at the crowd as she went down the stairs. She posed at the end and scanned the crowd with her makeshift spyglass. The crowd cheered. Avery filed out of the auditorium behind all the other candidates. It was over. OVER! And she had somehow survived.

"Good job, everyone. One week down, and two weeks to go," Ms. Rodriguez said. "I'll see you all again right before the debates."

As soon as Ms. Rodriguez left the candidates, Katani turned to Avery. "I can't believe you did that!"

"Can't believe that I did what?"

"Stole the end of my speech!"

"Me! You're the one who stole the end of my speech!"

"Charlotte!" they both shouted when they saw her approaching.

"How could you do that?" Katani asked.

"Do what?"

"Give us both the same ending to our speeches," Avery said.

"Wait a minute. That's not fair. I didn't suggest that ending to either of you." Charlotte turned to Isabel. "It's a quote I put up on the wall of the Tower. I didn't know either one of you would see it or use it."

"Great minds think alike," Isabel said.

Katani scowled. "I'm nothing like this immature goofball," she said angrily, moving away from Avery.

Not one to back down, Avery took two steps toward Katani. "And I'm nothing like this superior snob."

The two stormed off in opposite directions, leaving Isabel, Charlotte, and Maeve wondering if the BSG would survive the seventh-grade class election.

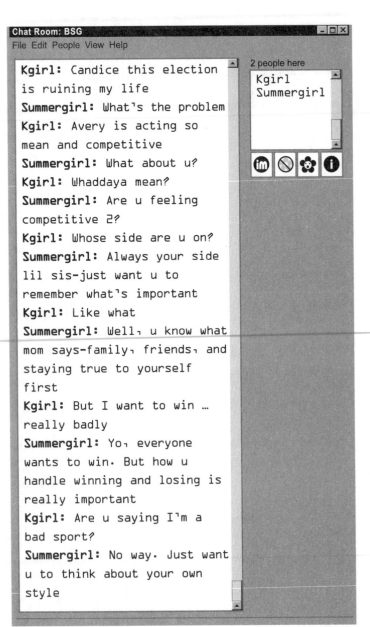

Chat Room: BSG

File Edit People View Help

2 people here

Kgirl
Summergirl

Kgirl: Candice this election is ruining my life

Summergirl: What's the problem

Kgirl: Avery is acting so mean and competitive

Summergirl: What about u?

Kgirl: Whaddaya mean?

Summergirl: Are u feeling competitive 2?

Kgirl: Whose side are u on?

Summergirl: Always your side lil sis-just want u to remember what's important

Kgirl: Like what

Summergirl: Well, u know what mom says-family, friends, and staying true to yourself first

Kgirl: But I want to win ... really badly

Summergirl: Yo, everyone wants to win. But how u handle winning and losing is really important

Kgirl: Are u saying I'm a bad sport?

Summergirl: No way. Just want u to think about your own style

PART TWO

MILES TO GO

CHAPTER 12

❧

THE ENDLESS WEEKEND

"CHARLOTTE, I'm sorry that I can't take you to the football game Friday. My students would camp outside my office en masse if I didn't get them their papers by Monday," Mr. Ramsey explained.

As a result, it had been a long, lonely weekend for Charlotte. Her father, who taught English and creative writing at Boston University, had been buried beneath a stack of papers he was grading for mid-terms.

So Charlotte had spent the night writing in her journal, playing with Marty and Happy Lucky Thingy, and catching up on assignments. She hadn't been able to reach any of the other BSG, but hadn't really felt like going out anyway.

Charlotte's Journal

I wonder if real politicians get as angry at each other as Katani and Avery. It seems like they have both lost sight of their friendship and only care about winning. I mean, we all like to win, but I don't think I would want to lose a good friend over something like this. It's all so confusing. How do you compete over something and still stay friends? I certainly don't have the answer!

All day Sunday, Charlotte had traipsed up and down the stairs of the stately Victorian house on Corey Hill, in hopes of finding the sliding panel door to Miss Pierce's apartment ajar. She was hoping that the two of them could have a cup of tea and chat about Miss Pierce's research on comets for NASA's Deep Impact mission. But it was tightly closed, and Charlotte couldn't drum up the nerve to knock.

Charlotte hadn't heard a sound from Miss Pierce's apartment all day. It was almost as if she had gone out, but Charlotte didn't think that could be true. Miss Pierce hardly ever went out. She was what her dad called a recluse.

Charlotte loved the way the word "recluse" sounded. She'd added it to her Word Nerd list. It meant "somebody who lives alone and deliberately keeps away from other people." It made her think of a lighthouse on a lonely cliff— far, far from any human. It was a lovely image, but to imagine someone being a recluse in the middle of the city was kind of sad.

Miss Pierce and Mrs. Fields, Katani's grandmother, had been the original Beacon Street Girls—Sapphire and Ruby. Charlotte thought it was so great that the two friends had used the Tower for a clubhouse, and created the original BSG OATH of LOYALTY.

It was just too bad that Miss Pierce had withdrawn from the world. Being a little shy herself, Charlotte knew how hard it was for shy people to reach out. But she never wanted to hide away like Miss Pierce. There were too many adventures to be had, she reasoned.

Although, after what had happened at the speeches on Friday, Charlotte felt like she might want to be a recluse, too. The idea of closing herself away in her room with her two constant best friends—books and stars—sounded heavenly. It was certainly less complicated than having two friends running for class president.

But after one weekend of being a recluse, Charlotte had had enough. She was ready to be with people again. Especially the BSG. Charlotte felt just horrible about the whole speech fiasco. She'd been thrilled when Katani ended her speech with the Abigail Adams quote. But when Avery followed with the same quote, Charlotte was mortified!

And she was so hurt when they both blamed her! She hadn't known that they were both using the quote. She'd only been trying to help!

Without anyone else to turn to, Charlotte sat down at her computer to send an email to her friend Sophie in Paris. If only she could shrink down and electronically follow her email across the Atlantic Ocean to France.

```
To: Sophie
From: Charlotte
Subject: Class Election


Bonjour sophie—


I miss you. Comment ça va? how is
paris? Have u been to deux garçons?
I want so much to have a café au lait
and walk along the Seine. Lots going
on here. We are having class elections.
Katani and Avery are both running for
```

president. It is hard to support either of them without making the other angry. Quel problem! I will only be able to vote for one. How can I choose between friends? To make it worse, I helped both of them write their speeches. Somehow, they ended up with the same ending. It was affreux! I was as embarrassed as they were. It was almost as bad that time I walked into the boys' bathroom! Even though I didn't give either of them the ending, they both blamed me. Wish I could run away to Paris! Miss you so much. Au revoir, BFFAE love, charlotte.

A STITCH IN TIME ...

Katani carefully pinned the empire bodice to the sleek A-line skirt. If she finished stitching the major pieces together tonight, that meant she would have a week to do all the handwork—hemming, tacking, sewing on the hook and eye, and voilà ... she'd be finished!

She had set up her sewing corner as soon as she had come home from school on Friday. She kept her sewing materials tucked out of sight behind a folding screen. She loved the piles of neatly folded fabric and the containers of thread and sewing notions stacked and organized on the shelves above her sewing table. She'd spent most of the weekend designing, snipping fabric, and piecing together a dress for the upcoming dance. It was so much fun! She couldn't wait until she was a grownup fashion designer.

Unable to find the perfect pattern, Katani bought two—one with the neckline that she wanted, and another with the A-line skirt that she wanted. She'd had a few frustrating moments when she tried to meld the two patterns together. Thankfully Grandma Ruby had been there. Between the two of them they had figured out how to make it work. Katani glanced at the sketch she had made of the completed outfit. The dress was stylish enough for the dance, and yet when she added the burgundy jacket she'd made last month, it would be dignified enough for making her acceptance speech.

. Katani pulled the light a little closer to the seam she'd just stitched and began removing the pins. She loved her swivel halogen light because it was the perfect combination of style and function.

Katani took a big breath. She couldn't wait til the campaign was over and she was president of the seventh-grade class. It would start with her acceptance speech. Katani tried to push that thought aside. She needed to concentrate on the outfit she was making.

For the rest of the afternoon, Katani's grandmother kept Kelley busy in the kitchen making pumpkin bread. Katani could smell the rich cinnamon aroma when Kelley opened the door to their bedroom.

"I made pumpkin bread, Katani," Kelley said. "Want some? Maybe you will turn into a pumpkin when you eat it." Kelley laughed hilariously at her own joke. Then she shoved her half-eaten piece of pumpkin bread in Katani's direction.

"Kelley, be careful," Katani said through a mouthful of pins. She put her hand out to keep Kelley from coming any closer. "Don't get any of your crumbs on my dress."

"What are you making?" Kelley asked.

"A dress," Katani said, not turning from the work in front

of her.

"For a dance?"

"Yes, for the post-election dance," Katani said, taking a pin from her mouth.

"Why are you worried?" Kelley asked.

"What are you talking about?" Katani asked, taking the last pin from her mouth.

"You are sad," Kelley said.

"I'm NOT worried and I am NOT sad," Katani answered, clearly annoyed with her sister. She had said this louder than she should have.

Kelley took a step back and put her hands over her ears.

"Sorry," Katani apologized to her sister. She was angry with herself for snapping at her sister. Still, Kelley was a little oversensitive to noise. She hadn't been THAT loud.

"Katani's worried; Katani's sad," Kelley repeated stubbornly in a singsong voice and still standing with her hands on her ears.

Katani shook her head. She didn't want this to erupt into a major meltdown for Kelley.

"Uh huh," Kelley said. "Are too!"

Katani glanced up at her sister, who was gazing at her with her head tilted slightly to the right.

"Katani's worried," Kelley said again. It was as if by looking at her sideways, Kelley could see things that other people couldn't see.

In the silence that stretched between them, Katani felt an uneasiness ripple through her body. When she decided to run for class president, she was certain all the BSG would be on her side. Maybe she should have dropped out of the race and avoided all this trouble. No, she thought angrily. Avery should have dropped out. She was the one who said she

◆

wan't going to run in the first place.

Katani stuck the last pin into the pincushion on her sewing table. She wasn't even sure if she had those three votes.

No matter how she tried to project confidence, Kelley and her X-ray eyes could see even what Katani couldn't admit ... she was worried.

"It's OK," Kelley said and hugged Katani.

Kelley wasn't much of a hugger, but when she did hug it was more of a full body slam. Katani held the dress at one arm's length to avoid getting stuck with a pin.

She seemed to sit there forever with Kelley's arms wrapped around her. Slowly, Katani felt her annoyance melt away. The hug felt good. She could always count on Kelley for unwavering support. But could she count on the BSG? Whose side were they on?

Suddenly, Katani needed to know.

NEW GAME PLAN

"Woo-hoo!" Avery and her brother jumped up from the couch, high-fiving in celebration. A last-second field goal had just put the Patriots up 24–21 over the Jets.

"Whoa, they had me worried for a second there," said Scott.

"I wasn't worried," said Avery. "Adam Vinatieri always comes through in the clutch."

"So true," said Scott as he walked out of the room. "Later, Ave. Homework calls!"

"Later!" Avery shouted after him. Avery was psyched that the Patriots had won again, but she didn't feel like listening to the postgame babble.

As she trudged up the winding staircase to her room, Avery wondered about the Abigail Adams football game on

Friday night. She hadn't heard who had won. She really hoped the Wildcats had pulled through. They were five and one in their division and had a good chance of having the best record.

Avery had a lot of catching up to do and not just about the football game. Her schedule for next week was jammed. She had two nights of soccer practice, tons of homework, and she still had to prepare for the upcoming debate.

Avery groaned when she pushed the door open to her room. She had sort of pushed her soccer stuff into the closet over a week ago, but had never put it away. It seemed pointless to keep putting equipment in her closet and taking it out over and over, so she left it in a heap in front of the open closet door. In her other closet, Walter's cage now had a snakeskin in it. Avery had missed the big shedding day.

Carla, the Madden's housekeeper, had complained that she couldn't vacuum Avery's room until she picked up, but the cleaning would have to wait. Avery had more important things on her mind.

The second week of the campaign was over, and the most important part was ahead of her ... the debate. She pushed a pile of clothes off her desk chair and sat down to brainstorm issues, reminding herself that she was good at debates, Avery drummed on the desktop with her pen. Nothing popped to mind.

She grabbed the note cards and plopped on the floor, clearing away a stack of books so she could lean up against the bed. "How do people think in chairs?" Avery muttered out loud. She flopped on her stomach and continued to think about her campaign for class president. Nothing. She was getting desperate. She decided to IM her brother Tim. He'd have a good idea. College was supposed to make you smart.

✿

Before she could start typing, she noticed her dad was
IM-ing her from Colorado.

```
┌────────────────────────────────────────────────────────┐
│ Chat Room: BSG                                  _ □ ✕   │
│ File  Edit  People  View  Help                           │
│ ┌──────────────────────────────┐ ▲  2 people here        │
│ │ Skimad: WU with my favorite  │   ┌──────────────────┐  │
│ │ daughter—haven't heard from  │   │ Skimad        ▲  │  │
│ │ you lately                   │   │ 4kicks           │  │
│ │ 4kicks: Sorry, Dad. I'm like │   │                  │  │
│ │ super busy                   │   │                  │  │
│ │ Skimad: How's the election   │   │               ▼  │  │
│ │ going?                       │   └──────────────────┘  │
│ │ 4kicks: Mom told you I was   │   🅘  🚫  ✿  ⓘ          │
│ │ running?                     │                          │
│ │ Skimad: She did              │                          │
│ │ 4kicks: Well, I have to      │                          │
│ │ prepare a debate and I can't │                          │
│ │ get started                  │                          │
│ │ Skimad: Think about your     │                          │
│ │ opponents as the opposing    │                          │
│ │ team—yk—analyze their        │                          │
│ │ strengths and weaknesses and │                          │
│ │ plot your strategy           │                          │
│ │ 4kicks: Awesome idea Dad.    │                          │
│ │ I gotta go plot ... now      │                          │
│ │ Skimad: TTYL                 │                          │
│ │                              │                          │
│ │                              ▼                          │
│ └──────────────────────────────┘                          │
└────────────────────────────────────────────────────────┘
```

Finally, Avery decided to approach her campaign like she would a game. The first step was to be prepared by knowing her opponents and their weaknesses. She mentally went over each candidate in her head. First there was Dillon. He was Mr. Smiley and quick to say, "Sure! Whatever you want!" Katani said she was worried about him, but Avery figured that everyone could see through that slick exterior. Maeve's feathers got ruffled when Avery said Dillon was slick … but he was.

Next, there was Henry Yurt. Avery was sure no one would take the Yurtmeister seriously. He was such a goof.

It wasn't a huge leap to realize that Katani was her toughest competitor. Avery figured her classmates would take Katani seriously. Everyone knew that she was a good student. And since the Talent Show, everyone also knew that she was responsible and could get the job done. Because Katani had gone first with her speech on Friday, Avery was sure that some of her classmates thought that Avery had copied Katani instead of the other way around.

The debate would show the entire class what the candidates were really all about. Since none of them knew what the debate questions were going to be, Katani wouldn't have a chance to copy her. It would be her time to shine!

Avery was certain that when the students compared the candidates at the debate, she would win. She didn't have the most posters, she didn't have the best speech—but the first part wasn't that bad. It had only been the ending that she had fumbled. And now that she thought of it, the kids sorta liked the spyglass bit. Maybe she would use it in the debate.

She could end her victory speech by adapting her favorite John F. Kennedy quote to fit a school setting. Something like, "Ask not what your school can do for you, but ask what you can do for your school." That couldn't miss. She should have used that in her speech last Friday.

But how would she start her acceptance speech? Usually, candidates started by thanking those who had helped them get elected. With sinking reality, Avery realized she didn't really have anyone to thank. Sure Charlotte had helped her write her speech, but she had helped Katani, too. And sure, Isabel had offered her a few suggestions on how to make her posters better, but she had only been there because she was helping Katani.

Maeve hadn't done much to help Katani, but now that Avery thought of it, she realized that Maeve hadn't done much to help her either. After trying to talk her into running that night at the sleepover, had the BSG decided to support Katani? Avery felt totally abandoned by her best friends in the world.

Avery looked over at Walter. She couldn't very well thank her snake. How would that sound? Avery wished that Marty lived with her instead of Charlotte. She felt like she needed someone to cuddle with right now.

Avery leaned back on her bed. Two books on the edge slid off and hit the floor. Boom. BOOM! Avery couldn't believe it. She was a team player. She looked around her room, which was crowded with team pictures and trophies. She was used to being part of a team, where everyone was focused on one goal. Somehow she had to find out who was on her team and who wasn't.

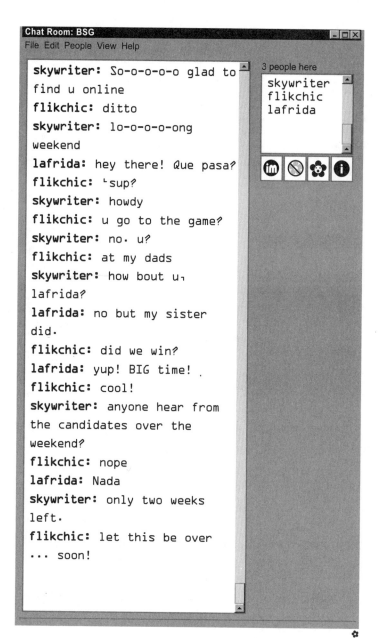

Chat Room: BSG

File Edit People View Help

skywriter: So-o-o-o-o glad to find u online
flikchic: ditto
skywriter: lo-o-o-o-ong weekend
lafrida: hey there! Que pasa?
flikchic: 'sup?
skywriter: howdy
flikchic: u go to the game?
skywriter: no. u?
flikchic: at my dads
skywriter: how bout u, lafrida?
lafrida: no but my sister did.
flikchic: did we win?
lafrida: yup! BIG time!
flikchic: cool!
skywriter: anyone hear from the candidates over the weekend?
flikchic: nope
lafrida: Nada
skywriter: only two weeks left.
flikchic: let this be over ... soon!

3 people here

skywriter
flikchic
lafrida

CHAPTER 13

❦

STUCK IN THE MIDDLE

"YEOW! I feel good!" Maeve sang to herself as she walked down Harvard Street on her way to school Monday morning. "The way that I should now," she sang as she crossed the street. When she stopped for the light at Beacon Street, she swayed to the music in her head. She felt like dancing. She couldn't help it. Her mother had an oldies station on this morning when she came down to breakfast. James Brown was blasting away singing a song she'd once heard in a commercial—"I Feel Good." Now the song was stuck in her head. She couldn't shake it, so she just gave into it.

As she bebopped down the hallway to her locker, Maeve couldn't help notice that everyone around her seemed to be in a good mood, too—especially considering that it was a Monday morning. There was a buzz of excitement in the hall. Everyone was talking about the big football game last Friday night. The Wildcats' victory had put them in first place.

"Charlotte! Wow! This football stuff is huge!" Maeve said as she opened her locker. "I just wish I understood football better."

"You're way ahead of me, Maeve," Charlotte said. "American football is pretty foreign to me. I never know who has the ball. It looks like they all run into each other and fall down."

Maeve giggled at the thought.

"Though I do like the passing. It always looks like he's throwing it to no one. Then, out of nowhere, someone ends up under the ball and catches it."

"... Or not."

"But at least I understand why they pass. Then there's punting. Why do they punt the ball to the other team? Wouldn't they keep the ball until the other team takes it away?" Charlotte asked.

"It has something to do with 'downs,'" Maeve shrugged. "Whatever they are. All I know is that you have to punt on fourth down."

Charlotte looked blankly at Maeve.

"Dillon explained it to me. I thought about going to the game with Dillon, but then I was afraid that Avery or Katani might see me with Dillon and flip out. Then I thought of going with Avery. She'd explain it to me without making me feel stupid. But then ... what if Katani showed up and saw me with Avery?"

Charlotte nodded knowingly.

"I decided it was easier just to stay home."

"Wise choice."

Just as Maeve closed her locker, she caught sight of a Wildcat football jersey. "Charlotte! Charlotte! Look! There's Daren Winsor. He's the ninth-grade quarterback," she leaned in and whispered to Charlotte.

"What's he doing in our hall?"

"Look who he's with," Maeve said, nodding in that

direction.

Anna and Joline came bouncing along after him. One on either side.

"OK—seventh graders," Anna said as if she weren't a seventh grader. "This is Daren Winsor, quarterback of the Abigail Adams Wildcats. Let's show him what we thought of the game."

Loud whoops and piercing whistles ricocheted through the hall.

Anna waved her arms and everyone went silent. Maeve whispered out loud to Charlotte.

"Do you think Anna and Joline have magical powers? It's just amazing how they always get everyone to pay attention to them."

"Well, they do have everyone enthralled," Charlotte admitted.

"Enthralled ... I love that word. It sounds so ... what does it mean?" Maeve asked.

"Spellbound," Charlotte answered, her eyes riveted to the Anna and Joline Show.

Anna counted off, "One. Two. Three. Hit it!"

"Two! Four! Six! Eight! Who do we appreciate?" Anna and Joline chanted in unison.

The seventh graders called out, "Daren! Daren! Daren!" as Anna and Joline pumped their arms in the air. "Go Wildcats!"

The hall was packed. Everyone was sticking around for Anna's and Joline's performance instead of going to class.

Charlotte and Maeve wormed their way through the crowded hall toward Room 124. They got through the door just as the bell rang; the other students poured in after them.

Ms. R allowed a little lateness in lieu of the circumstances.

Maeve saw Katani squeeze in the door right before Avery

came in. The two didn't look at each other, which wasn't a great sign. But Maeve noticed that they weren't giving each other dirty looks either, which was an improvement.

"I feeeeeeeel good!" The James Brown lyrics continued to roll through Maeve's brain as Ms. Rodriguez took attendance. Even the impromptu pep rally hadn't been able to shake that song from her head.

◌

Somehow, Maeve made it to the cafeteria before anyone else. It was deserted. She put her lunch bag on the table and closed her eyes. Slowly, she let the song in her head take over her body, swaying this way and that. She closed her eyes and broke into a spontaneous dance, singing the lyrics, starting off softly and gradually getting louder. When it came to the bridge, she sang out "Ba! Ba! Ba!" to the melody of the trumpets that were playing in her head. Now for the finale.

"So good! Ba! Ba! So good! Ba! Ba! Cause I got you!" she sang, spinning around with flourish for the big finish. She pointed out to her imagined audience and opened her eyes. Surprise! Sometime during her little song and dance, the lunchroom had filled.

"Go, Maeve," shouted Billy Trentini and a group of boys. There were a few whistles. Maeve was momentarily embarrassed, but then the performer in her kicked in, and she took a bow. Maeve turned around and sat down.

Charlotte and Isabel had suddenly appeared at the other side of the table carrying their lunch trays in front of them.

"Way to go, Maeve!' Charlotte cried out as she sat down.

"Sorry! I can't get that song out of my head. Do you ever get songs stuck in your head?" she asked.

Isabel nodded as she closed her sketchbook. "I know

what you mean!"

"Sorry. Am I interrupting something?" Maeve asked.

"No. Not at all," Isabel said. "Charlotte and I were talking about *The Sentinel*. I need her professional opinion. We can talk later."

"Great! Because I wanted to discuss Marty."

"Marty?" Charlotte asked.

"The pink thing?" Isabel guessed.

"Yeah! Did you tell Charlotte about it?"

Isabel shook her head again.

"About what?" Charlotte asked.

"Think Pink! is sponsoring a contest called 'My Pet Looks Perfect in Pink!' Isn't that so cute? Anyway, it's really great because all the proceeds from the entry fees go to the local pet shelter. I want us to enter Mr. Marté. I brought the sketches," Maeve said in a singsongy voice. "I wanted everyone to look at them and vote on which one they like the best before I go on."

"Maybe you shouldn't use the word ... vote," Isabel said wryly.

Maeve tipped back her head and laughed. "How about if I ask everyone to pick the one they like best?"

Charlotte cringed.

"Give me their input?" Maeve tried again.

"Score!" Charlotte said.

"Where are our two candidates?" Maeve asked.

The three looked around the cafeteria, scanning each line. "Hmm," Maeve said. "It's not like Avery to be late for anything—especially lunch!"

"Where do you think they could be?" Isabel asked.

"Hopefully, not taking down posters," Maeve said.

Charlotte and Isabel exchanged looks.

"I'm joking. Great! Here comes Katani!" Maeve stood up and waved Katani over.

"Katani, just in time ... I have sketches of pink costumes for Marty," Maeve said, pointing to the sketches in front of Charlotte.

"What?" Katani asked.

"The 'My Pet Looks Perfect in Pink' contest at Think Pink!"

"Not now, Maeve ... maybe I'll look at them later. I have to ask you something before Avery gets here." She looked around and checked both doors to the cafeteria before she went on. "Which way are you leaning?"

"I'm not leaning at all! I'm sitting straight," Maeve said.

"Ha. Ha. Very funny, Maeve," Katani said. "I'm serious! Which way are you leaning?"

"I wasn't trying to be funny," Maeve said.

"You know what I mean," Katani said, looking tense.

"No, I don't," Maeve said.

"Maeve—I'm asking ..." Katani took a big breath and launched into her even-toned political poller's voice. "If the election were today ... who would you vote for?"

Katani looked expectantly at Maeve, who looked to Charlotte and Isabel.

"Look ... Katani, I thought we decided that the lunch table was one place we weren't going to talk about the election," Maeve said.

"Sure, when we're both here ... but we're not. So before Avery gets here ..."

"Forget it."

"Forget it!? I have a right to know who's working with me and who's working against me."

"Working against you?" Maeve asked in total disbelief.

This was getting way out of hand, she thought.

"Why would you think," Charlotte asked, looking up at Katani, "that any of us are working against you?"

"Well, I'm not sure. That's why I have to ask," Katani said, looking concerned.

"Katani, we're not against you," Isabel said.

"You're not against me, but you're not FOR me? Is that what you mean?"

"Enough!" Maeve said. "Isabel spent hours helping you with your posters, and Charlotte helped you with slogans and your speech. It's not fair to question their loyalty!"

"I need to know if I can depend on my friends."

"This is why we shouldn't talk about this during lunchtime," Isabel said.

"Since when are you making the rules?" Katani asked, staring directly at Isabel.

"Since when can you change the rules whenever you want?" Maeve asked.

Katani opened her mouth to say something, but Maeve held up her hand before she could say anything. "Stop. Just stop! This whole election thing is pulling us all apart because you're letting it go to your head. It's bad enough with you and Avery going at it whenever you're in the same room, but don't start yelling at us!" Maeve said.

Katani opened her mouth again. She knew Maeve was right. But instead of saying anything, she closed it, and turned and walked away from her friends.

Well, that did it. For the first time since she left the house, Maeve didn't have the urge to sing "I feel good."

"Are you OK, Maeve?" Charlotte asked as she watched Katani storm off. No sooner had Katani disappeared through the west doors, than Avery appeared through the east doors. She paused for a second at the door, scanned the room, then made a beeline for the Beacon Street Girls' table.

"Hey! Avery supporters ... I have special stickers for all my campaign workers."

No one said anything as Avery rummaged through her bag.

"Look! We just went through this with Katani," Maeve said.

"So ..."

"I refuse to go through this again," Maeve said to Charlotte and Isabel. "I'm outta here. I'm late anyway." With that, Maeve stood up and flounced out of the room.

Avery opened her lunch bag and pulled out orange stickers—neon orange and about two inches in diameter. She'd written "Avery for President" on them.

"Here," Avery said, pushing two Avery for President stickers toward Isabel and Charlotte.

"Thanks," Isabel said, taking the sticker and holding it in her hand.

Charlotte took one, too. Charlotte couldn't say anything. And she definitely couldn't put this on. What would Katani say if she saw her with it?

"Aren't you going to put them on?" Avery asked.

"Maybe later," Charlotte said.

"You two are voting for me, right?"

Charlotte gulped. "I'm undecided," she said, using the phrase from Katani's poll.

Isabel only shrugged.

"Undecided? How can you be undecided? You guys were the ones who talked me into running in the first place! Now you're undecided?"

"Avery ..." Isabel started, but it was clear she didn't know where to go from there.

"I guess I should be spending time with people who are planning on voting for me, or at least will tell me to my face whether they are or not."

Avery snatched her lunch bag with one hand, and pushed back from the table with her other hand. In an instant, she plopped down at the table where Nick, Adam, and Robert were sitting. She never looked back.

Isabel looked bewildered. "This is a total mess," she said, dispirited.

Charlotte clung to the edge of the nearly empty and silent BSG table like it was a life raft in the noisy school cafeteria. She glanced at Isabel. Charlotte was glad she wasn't alone.

Charlotte and Isabel ate in silence for a while.

"Can I look at your cartoons?" Charlotte asked quietly.

"I can't deal with my cartoons right now, OK?" Isabel said abruptly. When she saw Charlotte's hurt expression, she added, "I'm not mad at you; I'm just ... stressed."

Charlotte nodded and the two finished their lunch in silence.

Both were thinking the same thing ... what would the Beacon Street Girls be like after this election was over?

GUILTY BY ASSOCIATION

Katani went straight from the lunchroom to the teacher's lounge to ask Ms. Rodriguez for a pass to work in the library. She felt woozy and not because she hadn't had any lunch. She wasn't sure which direction to take.

Well, she wasn't going to waste any more time on the BSG. If they weren't going to vote for her, then she didn't want their help. She would get elected on her own. There were plenty of other class votes to concentrate on. She passed out her campaign flyers to everyone who passed her by. She got a few thumbs up, which lifted her confidence enormously.

As she walked down the hall to the library, she saw space after space where posters once hung. Somehow, between homeroom and lunch, someone had ripped down more posters. Only the rolled masking tape and sometimes a part of the poster remained on the wall. She noticed that most of the posters that were missing had been located between Kelley's locker and the classroom where Kelley had speech each morning.

All of a sudden, Kelley's favorite commercial tagline came to mind … "And I approve of this message."

What if Kelley was taking down her opponents' posters because she didn't approve of their messages? What if Kelley really did it and everyone found out? The notion hit Katani like a brick. Would anyone believe that Katani hadn't put Kelley up to it? Worse, would anyone vote for her if it was Kelley taking the posters down?

CHAPTER 14

❧

ON EDGE

TUESDAY MORNING started off gray and dismal. Isabel felt grayer than gray as she walked down Harvard Street on her way to school. She felt exactly like a character in a cartoon with a little cloud over her head.

As she walked, an idea popped into her head. Isabel saw it clearly in her mind ... a little bird with a cloud over its head in an otherwise clear sky. She couldn't wait to sketch it, so she stopped at the trolley stop, took out her sketchbook, and began drawing. She penned the tagline underneath. When she was finished she held the sketchbook at arm's length to scrutinize her work.

Isabel was pleased.

How come bird ideas came to her so easily? Where were all the ideas for edgy political cartoons? Not one idea for a political cartoon had popped into her head, yet. Maybe her brain just wasn't political. Maybe she was a birdbrain. She chuckled at her own joke.

However, like any artist, Isabel knew that sometimes you couldn't wait for inspiration. Last night, she had put pen to paper, adapting two political cartoons—one found in *The Boston Globe* and the other in *Newsweek*—to fit the election at Abigail Adams Junior High. At least she had something on paper.

The problem was Isabel didn't like either of them. They just didn't seem right. She liked the bird cartoon she had just drawn much better. Perhaps today would be the day that the political edgy part of her brain opened up and a super election cartoon would present itself.

With that thought in mind, Isabel slipped her sketchbook under her arm, slung her backpack over her shoulder, and trudged down Harvard Street. One block from school, she heard her name and turned to see Jennifer Robinson jogging toward her.

"Isabel, I'm glad I caught you. I wanted to touch base with you to see how the cartoons for *The Sentinel* are coming," Jennifer asked.

"I've had a couple of ideas," Isabel said.

"You know the deadline is a week away. A week from tomorrow."

"Yes, I know."

"Do you have any finished?"

"Well, just two … they're really still in the planning stage."

"Ooohhh! I'd love to see them!"

"I don't know," said Isabel, holding her sketchbook close to her chest. "I mean, they're not finished yet."

"Come on … let me take a peek."

Reluctantly, Isabel opened her sketchbook and quickly flipped past the cartoon she had just drawn to the first attempts at political cartoons she had worked on last night.

Jennifer looked at the first one. She read the line below. The ends of her mouth curved up into a small smile. She nodded and then flipped to the next one. Jennifer read the tagline and chuckled a bit.

"Isabel! These are great! I love them."

"Really? I thought maybe they were a little much."

"Perfect! They're perfect! Bring them by the office today and we'll photocopy them."

"Oh, no," Isabel said, reaching toward her sketchbook. "There are some smudges, and well ... these are rough. I need to redraw them, and the lettering is off ... see. I need to redo them. Make sure they're centered."

Jennifer reluctantly handed the sketchbook back. "Well, OK. Oh, and sign them. I noticed you didn't sign these. Don't forget ... the cartoons are due next Tuesday, or Wednesday morning at the latest. We go to press right after school on Wednesday so the paper will be out on Thursday before the election. Two more just like these."

Jennifer turned and headed toward school, leaving Isabel to put her sketchpad back into her backpack.

Isabel looked at the cartoons again. She wasn't as excited about them as Jennifer was. In fact, she was just thinking she would be embarrassed to sign her name to them when someone tapped her on her shoulder. Her first instinct was to hide the cartoons and she crushed them against her chest.

"Guess who!" Maeve said. "What's that?"

"Oh, just cartoons I'm working on for *The Sentinel*."

"Let me see!"

"No, they're not ready for general viewing yet."

"Oh ... but I'm not 'general.'"

"Not yet ..."

"Anyway, I'm glad I ran into you," Maeve said as they started off toward school. "I'm looking for pink … anything you might have in your craft stuff … feathers, sequins, yarn, faux leather … oh, leather! Can't you just see Marty in a tiny pink biker outfit with a pink do-rag on his cute, little head?"

"Oh, this is for Marty?"

"Yes, remember, for the 'My Pet Looks Perfect in Pink' contest."

Maeve stopped at Isabel's locker and talked nonstop about all of her pink ideas as Isabel hung up her jacket and got her books organized.

"Walk me to my locker," Maeve urged when Isabel shut her locker door.

"Have you decided which costume?"

"No," Maeve said as they arrived at her locker. "I've decided to see what pink things I can collect and then fashion a costume from what I have, instead of picking a costume and then not being able to find the stuff to make it."

"Hmm, makes sense," Isabel said.

"Hey, Charlotte! What little pink things have you found?"

"Nothing yet, Maeve. Sorry, I didn't have time to look last night."

The three continued to discuss outfits for Marty as they walked to homeroom together.

"Oh, can't you just imagine him in a little pink clown outfit?" laughed Isabel. Charlotte and Maeve giggled at the absurd image of Marty as they headed into homeroom.

"Hey," they heard someone call to them. Avery was rushing in their direction.

"They're gone! I can't believe it! Gone! Gone! Nothing left but a little tape with poster board stuck to it," Avery said.

"Chill, Avery. What are you talking about?" Maeve asked.

"My POSTERS. Every single one of my posters is gone ...
all six of them!"

They didn't have a chance to let that news sink in yet
before Katani rushed up behind them. "I don't believe this,"
she said.

"What?" Maeve asked.

"My boards!"

"Are yours missing, too?" Charlotte asked.

"Well ... at least there are few left." Katani pointed to
the one still hanging between the row of lockers and Ms.
Rodriguez's door. "Did you see, Isabel? They're gone. Hours
and hours of work down the tube."

"What's going on?" Avery asked.

Katani turned to Avery. "I haven't had a chance to count,
but some of my posters are missing. A LOT of them are
missing."

"Big deal, Katani! All of mine are gone. ALL of them!"

"It's not the same thing, Avery," Katani said. "You didn't
have that many to start with. And ..."

"And what?" Avery asked.

"Well, it's not like you had much time invested in them,"
Katani said with a shrug.

"So, how is that important?" Avery demanded.

"My posters—well, they weren't really even posters, they
were boards. They represented a lot more thought, planning
and effort! We worked on them for hours. HOURS!" Katani
said, looking directly at Isabel, her eyes brimming.

Avery scrunched her face into a scowl. "Well, I'm running
for class president, not some artsy award. Besides, you had
help! I had to do mine all by myself. Everyone was too busy
to help me."

Katani rolled her eyes to the ceiling. "A good leader

would be able to get people to help."

"At least I'm not a backstabber, Katani."

"Backstabber! Who are you calling a backstabber?" Katani asked, putting a hand on her hip.

"You! That's who! 'Oh, Avery, you really should run for president!' is what you said to my face, when all along you were planning on running yourself."

"I was NOT!"

Isabel felt helpless watching the argument escalate between her friends. Katani and Avery were such a mismatch in height, but they were standing toe-to-toe—Katani leaning down and Avery stretched up practically on her toes, her arms straight out behind her. Isabel couldn't focus on the words anymore. They were both yelling, the angry tones swirling around them. Other students stopped milling around the hall and gawked at the spectacle Avery and Katani were creating.

Isabel felt frozen to the spot next to Charlotte. Both were wide-eyed staring at the scene in front of them. Neither had moved since the yelling started.

Maeve waved her arm to get their attention. "Stop it! Both of you! Stop it!" She moved forward to break them up. Before she could get between them, Ms. Rodriguez stepped into the hall.

"Katani! Avery! My class! Right now."

Everyone in the hall stood still for what seemed a whole minute before they started talking again and shuffling about the hall.

"This is getting way out of hand," Maeve said. "I hope Ms. R can straighten them out."

Charlotte nibbled the ends of her nails. She did not like arguing—not one bit. Maybe it had to do with being an only child, she thought nervously.

The three quietly moved into the classroom and took their seats, unable to speak or comment on the scene they'd just witnessed.

Dillon walked into the room and tossed his books on his desk. He looked directly at Isabel, then Charlotte and Maeve. "I told you this was gonna happen! It was just a matter of time," he said before he sat down. "They should have listened to me."

Isabel's heart was beating in her throat. She felt slightly sick to her stomach. Oh, how she wished she knew a way to make everything right! A way that this election would end so that Katani and Avery would both be happy and they would be a group again. She missed her friends.

SHORT DIVISION

Avery marched into Ms. Rodriguez's office and sat in one of the two chairs in front of her desk.

"This is all your fault," Katani said under her breath as she sat down in the chair next to Avery.

"How is this my fault?" Avery asked.

"Quiet. Not another word!" Ms. Rodriguez said. She stood there for a moment watching the two girls before she walked around to the other side of the desk. "I want you both to take a deep breath ... now."

Avery took a deep breath and for some reason hearing Katani, who was sitting right next to her, taking a deep breath at exactly the same time made her angry. She clutched the arms of her chair, picked a spot on the floor to stare at, and tried to zone out. She tried not to even think about Katani sitting in the chair next to her.

Ms. Rodriguez sat across from them and looked at them for what seemed like forever. Outside in the hall, lockers banged and kids shouted back and forth to each other. Inside the office, the room was heavy with silence. The fluorescent light flickered, giving off angry little jerks of light. The clock on the bookshelf behind Ms. Rodriguez's desk ticked way too loudly. To Avery it seemed to be shouting, "Hurry up! Hurry up! Let's get this over with so we can get out of here."

The warning bell rang, and Avery flinched and scooted to the edge of her seat so she could bolt when Ms. Rodriguez gave her the OK.

"Hang on. I'm not finished," Ms. Rodriguez said.

What is she talking about? She hasn't even said anything yet, Avery thought.

"Before we go across the hall to homeroom, I want you two to think about something. The qualities of a leader—trust, respect, and commitment—are more important than the position itself. There's not much point in being elected if you have to give up your values in order to win. Do you understand what I'm saying?"

Avery nodded and she could see Katani nodding to her left.

"On top of that, you two are good friends. You should remember that you are friends first and candidates second. Do you want this election to ruin your friendship?" Ms. Rodriguez asked.

The final bell rang.

Neither of the girls moved.

Avery continued to stare a hole in the yellowed vinyl floor.

Ms. R sighed.

The clock ticked.

"Let's get to class."

Avery shot up from the chair and beat Katani to the door. She didn't want to see Katani or look at her face.

"Wait," Ms. Rodriguez said.

Avery stopped and let Ms. Rodriguez walk across the now empty hall in front of her. Their homeroom was buzzing with conversation, but as soon as Ms. Rodriguez opened the heavy wooden door, the conversations withered to a murmur. Most students tried to ignore Avery and Katani as they took their seats, but a few stared openly.

"Got a staring problem?" Avery asked Anna as she took her seat.

"Let's get started, shall we?" Ms. Rodriguez asked the class and calmly went about the business of homeroom.

Avery was still steaming. Here she was all upset that her posters—every single one of her posters—were missing, and Katani was being all snooty, acting like because her posters didn't have globs of feathers and sequins, they didn't matter. She dug her pen into her notebook.

Ms. Rodriguez passed out a form they needed to fill out for school pictures.

Avery fished a pencil out of her backpack, just in case she had to erase. Ms. R was wrong. This wasn't about friendship. A friend wouldn't encourage you to run for president when she was planning on running against you all along. In fact, Katani had probably only said all that stuff that night in the Tower because she wanted the others to jump in and say, "No, Katani, that sounds like you!"

Avery's cheeks reddened, and she clutched her pencil so tightly her knuckles were white. When she started to write, she pressed so hard on the pencil that the lead broke, shooting across the aisle and hitting Robert in the ankle. It left a charcoal smudge on the paper and bits and pieces of graphite scattered about the form. Avery dug another pencil out of her backpack and started writing again.

She'd push all those words that Katani had said behind her. This wasn't a team effort, that was for sure. She would have to approach this the way she did soccer or tennis. Focus. Visualize. Execute. She would start by making more posters. She wouldn't even waste time asking for help. It was all up to her now. The BSG had let her down.

After the emotional rush of the morning, the rest of the day felt flat. Avery walked from class to class like a robot, doing only the bare minimum of what she needed to do to get by. Who knew this election was going to be such a big drain? she thought. She hadn't even had time to take Marty to the park. Well, she'd need all of her energy, all of her emotion to get through the next week and a half of the campaign. When she won, she would extend a hand of friendship to Katani—if she took it, fine. If she didn't—well, that was her choice. But for now, no matter what Ms. R said, she and Katani couldn't be friendly.

When Avery arrived in the lunchroom that day, she didn't even look at the BSG table. Instead, she went straight to the guys' table with Nick, Adam, Billy, Josh, Dillon, and Robert. She handed each of them a lollipop with an Avery for President sticker.

Avery hadn't joked around with the guys in a long time. It didn't take long before they had her laughing so hard that little snurps came out of her mouth. At one point, she thought milk would come out of her nose.

As all the guys at the table prepared to play milk carton football, Avery glanced over to the BSG table. It was almost empty. Charlotte and Isabel sat close together, hunched over Isabel's sketchbook. Katani was nowhere to be found. And where was Maeve? She'd been leaving lunch early for the last week.

EQUAL SPACE

There was no one there when Charlotte set her tray of grilled cheese and green Jell-O on the table. She looked around the cafeteria but didn't see any of the Beacon Street Girls. Where were they? It was the first time since she had been at Abigail Adams Junior High that she'd had to sit at a lunch table alone. It reminded her of all those horrible first days in other schools when she had to eat by herself, and she felt a sob catch in her throat, as Anna and Joline walked by, shooting their "you are so lame" look her way.

"Tell me it's over," Charlotte whispered to herself. She shut her eyes, and reviewed the scene from this morning in front of Ms. Rodriguez's class. She couldn't remember the angry words, but she could see the angry eyes and expressions as Katani and Avery squabbled.

"Where is everyone?" Isabel asked when she sat down. She had a salad. Somehow, Charlotte had missed seeing Isabel in the salad bar line. She was so grateful to see Isabel she could have jumped up and hugged her.

"I don't know," Charlotte said.

"I knew Maeve wasn't going to be here. She told me in gym that she had some project to work on and that she got a pass," Isabel told her.

"There's Avery," Charlotte said, nodding toward a table of boys.

"Maybe Katani is working in the library again," Isabel offered.

"I guess since Maeve said that the election is off limits they decided they couldn't handle sitting here," Charlotte speculated. "They're both pretty driven. The election is all they can think about. Talk about."

Charlotte slowly nibbled at her grilled cheese sandwich

while Isabel ate her salad.

"Well, since we're alone, there's something I'd like to talk to you about," Charlotte said.

"Me, too! You go first," Isabel said.

"Wouldn't it be funny if we both said we decided to run for class president?" Charlotte said laughing.

"No!"

"Vice president?"

Isabel smiled a crooked smile.

"It's about the Tower," Charlotte said. "When we discovered it and became the BSG, we divided it in four parts. You're part of us, and I've been trying—well, Maeve and I have been trying—to figure out how to divide the Tower five ways. We just haven't yet. We want you to know that you mean so much to us. We want you to have equal space. We're just not sure how to do it."

A small smile crept to Isabel's face. She gave Charlotte's hand a quick squeeze.

"Thank you ... but just being there with all of you is enough for me. I don't want to take away space from anyone else. I don't want to cause any more problems," Isabel said.

"But there has to be a solution."

Just then, Charlotte heard Avery laughing at the next table. Isabel and Charlotte both turned in that direction.

"Maybe we won't have to worry about the space—the way things are going, we may have two open spots. We might have to worry about dividing it three ways instead of five," Charlotte said.

"We can't think that way. We have to believe that this will all work out. Blow over."

They looked at each other.

"Actually, you know how much I love interior decorating.

I'll think about it," Isabel said.

"Great! What did you want to tell me?" Charlotte asked.

Isabel bit her bottom lip and tucked her long, dark hair behind her ears. She pushed her half empty salad bowl aside and pulled the sketchpad from her backpack. "I need your creative input. Remember I told you that Jennifer wanted edgy? Well, I adapted a few political cartoons that I saw in the *The Boston Globe*. Jennifer saw them this morning. She loved them, but I'm a little uncomfortable with being this edgy, and I wanted your opinion."

She opened the sketchbook.

Charlotte winced as she read the comics. "Ouch!"

"That's what I thought … they're really mean," Isabel said. "Especially with what happened this morning, I just don't think I should turn these in. The deadline's coming soon. I know this is the election edition, and I just don't have any 'election' ideas."

"Hmm. Well, I've been working in *The Sentinel* office all week. I know that Jennifer is writing a cameo of each presidential candidate—maybe you could do a drawing of each candidate."

"Like a caricature?"

"Yeah, have you ever done that before?"

"Not exactly, but I guess it's worth a try. Anything is better than what I have so far," she answered. "Thanks for the suggestion!"

CHAPTER 15

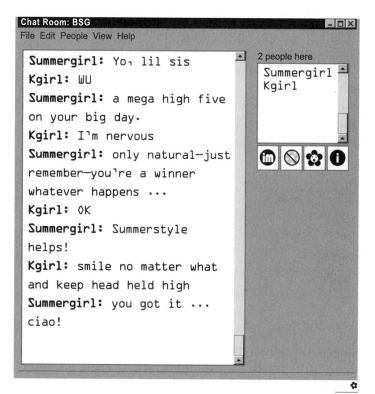

IN THE MIDDLE

Summergirl: Yo, lil sis
Kgirl: WU
Summergirl: a mega high five
on your big day.
Kgirl: I'm nervous
Summergirl: only natural—just
remember—you're a winner
whatever happens ...
Kgirl: OK
Summergirl: Summerstyle
helps!
Kgirl: smile no matter what
and keep head held high
Summergirl: you got it ...
ciao!

Chat Room: BSG
File Edit People View Help

2 people here
Summergirl
Kgirl

✿

KATANI, Avery, and the rest of the candidates arrived early for the debates.

As Mr. Danson explained the procedures for the debate, Katani watched Mr. Clauson, the janitor, slowly and methodically pull out the bleachers on the east side of the gym. He had already set up two long tables right across center court. It was a little intimidating to be right in the center of the whole gym, Katani felt, but then she remembered Candice's pep talk and she raised her chin.

"Katani, you'll be sitting here," Mr. Danson said, pointing to a chair that was in the middle of the center court circle.

Two of Katani's sisters had been centers for the Abigail Adams girls' basketball team when they were in middle school. How ironic that Katani would be sitting right here in this very spot! How many times had she watched her sisters jump in this very circle at the beginning tip-off of a game? But, today Katani was starting her own tradition. From this spot in the gym, she would "jumpstart" her illustrious student government career.

Things had been so chilly between Avery and her since their meltdown earlier in the week. Katani had talked to her mother about it and they both decided it would be best if Katani avoided Avery until the election was over ... give things a chance to cool down between the two of them. Today, Avery was chatting it up with Dillon, so it was pretty easy to avoid any contact. Her mom had also reminded Katani to try and think about the election from Avery's point of view as well. But, that was easier said than done.

Ms. Rodriguez had been right about the importance of focusing on good character, and she, Katani Summers, was going to rise above trash talk from any of her opponents. But she wasn't going to sit by and allow Avery to call her a backstabber either! Ms. R was wrong. A friend wouldn't call her something like that ever! But, feeling noble after her conversation with her mother, Katani decided that after she won, she would give Avery a chance to apologize. But if she didn't, well ... Katani was sure she would be too busy to really miss her at all!

"You each have a microphone and a bottle of water," Mr. Danson said, pointing to the table. "A podium has been set up on either side of the candidates' table for the questions from the seventh-grade student body."

By the time Mr. Danson asked if there were any questions, the seventh-grade class was filing into the gym. Once everyone was seated, Katani and the rest of the candidates watched from the hall as Mr. Danson addressed the class and explained how the town hall forum format worked. Then he motioned to the candidates. He called their names, and each candidate stepped into the gym and walked across the court to their seat.

Dillon raised his arms in the air as he walked to his seat. Katani thought he was such a showoff. Avery also waved to the crowd, pumping her arms in the air. Henry Yurt gave his bow tie a tap and it spun around like a pinwheel. Kids went crazy with laughter.

Katani sighed, Henry Yurt was so immature. This was not comedy hour. When Mr. Danson called her name, Katani nodded to the crowd, smiled, and then walked to her seat with as much dignity as she could gather.

She turned all her focus on the first question ... a challenging one by one of the smartest girls in the class, Samantha Simmons. "I would like to ask each of the candidates to tell us why their platform is better than everyone else's." Soon Q&As accompanied by cheers and whoops were flying through the air.

Debates sure were fun, thought Avery.

No Smiles Award

It was difficult for Charlotte to tell who was winning the debate. She thought all of the candidates were doing an amazing job—even the Yurtmeister, who had his classmates in stitches most of the time. Charlotte knew that she would have frozen if she'd had to debate in front of everyone.

Katani and Avery each had notecards, but it seemed they never looked at them. When they were asked a question, they didn't hem or haw, they just started right in with the answer as if they knew what question they'd be asked. They were totally prepared. How did they do that?

Charlotte thought Katani sounded great when she talked about how the class could do car washes at the football games to raise money. It made sense. It would make cents. Charlotte smiled at her pun. She loved wordplay.

When asked what projects she would push, Avery did a great job of explaining her ideas. Charlotte was really proud of her for not going overboard and listing all the things that she wanted to do for the rest of junior high, high school, etc. Charlotte wished she could catch Avery's eye and give her a thumbs up. But Avery had avoided all of them since the big incident in the hall. Instead, she ate lunch every day with the boys. Not once had Charlotte caught Avery looking in their direction.

Charlotte wondered if Avery really believed that none of them liked or supported her, or if avoiding everyone was easier than trying to get along.

Charlotte couldn't resist sneaking a quick look at Isabel, who was sitting next to her sketching the candidates as they spoke. She was drawing fast and furious. Isabel tilted the pad toward herself when she noticed Charlotte peeking over, but she gave her a smile and wink to let her know she was OK— that she liked this much more than the "edgy" cartoons she had shown her earlier in the week. Charlotte understood how Isabel felt. She didn't like to show early drafts of her writing to anyone—not until she had a chance to go over it and over it.

Charlotte turned to see another girl, Chelsea Briggs, squatting down in front of the bleachers holding a camera. She was kind of a chubby girl who kept to herself a lot. Charlotte felt a little bad for Chelsea because she didn't appear to have many friends.

Nick Montoya was now approaching the podium. As he climbed up the stairs, he looked over to Charlotte and smiled. Maeve poked her in the ribs and Charlotte felt her cheeks flush. Nick really was so cute and she knew that he really liked her. He always asked her about assignments and once he even tried to kiss her. Maeve kept telling her that she should ask him out. But Charlotte just couldn't do that ... yet.

Nick cleared his throat, tapped the microphone, and asked what was the most important thing to each of the candidates. Charlotte thought he looked very together in his blue shirt and khaki pants, and his voice was strong and clear.

Mr. Danson, who was acting as moderator, motioned to Dillon to start first.

"That's a good question," Dillon said. Charlotte noticed that was how Dillon started each of his answers. "I can sum up it in three words ... 'whatever you want!' My goal as president is to do what YOU want."

Charlotte thought Katani did a good job of not making too much of a face. Charlotte knew how Katani felt about Dillon's promises to do whatever anyone wanted. Katani had her hands folded together in front of her. She drew herself up straight and tall and cleared her throat. "Nick," she said when it was her turn to speak. Katani had started each answer by addressing the person who had asked the question. Charlotte thought it made her seem very personable and professional.

"Now that we are seventh graders, we finally have a say in how class funds are spent. We are finally at that age when we can decide what we want to do and set up plans to reach our own goals …" spoke Katani.

But before she could finish, Avery cut her off. "That's where you're wrong, Katani. We have reached a time in our life when …"

"I wasn't finished!" Katani snapped, shooting Avery a nasty look.

"So-o-o-orry!" Avery said as she rolled her eyes. A few kids laughed.

Katani finished by saying, "We are at an age where we can not only decide what we want, but also HOW we're going to achieve those goals. I feel the best way to do that is proper management of our budget. As class president, I'll make sure we'll be able to do more by properly managing what we have."

Avery put her hand over the microphone, but Charlotte could hear her from her front row seat. "Are you finished NOW?" Avery asked Katani.

Katani didn't say anything. She just narrowed her eyes and glared at Avery.

Charlotte couldn't believe Avery was being so insensitive.

Avery turned back to her microphone. "What my …"

Charlotte hoped Avery was going to say friend, but instead she stressed the word, opponent.

"What my OPPONENT said is wrong. We should stop thinking about ourselves all the time and always wondering 'what's in it for me?' We are at a point in our lives when we should start thinking, planning, and DOING what we can to make the world a better place. You know … save the planet." Everyone cheered at that one.

While Avery was right, making Katani look bad in front of everyone left a bitter taste in Charlotte's mouth. Avery was so oblivious sometimes … just saying things to make a point and forgetting that sometimes that could hurt people's feelings.

Charlotte was so busy looking from Avery to Katani that she missed the beginning of Henry Yurt's answer. Whatever it was, it made everyone laugh, and he smiled at the crowd before he went on.

"Who says school has to be dull and boring?" Henry asked. "I want to make school a fun place. We can make that happen! Ask yourself right now, 'Who have I made smile today?' I think there should be an award for the person that brings smiles to the people around them. I'd call it … uh … the SMILE award. Yeah, that's it! The Smile Award!"

Henry's comment got Charlotte thinking. Who had she made smile today?

"That's all the time we have," Mr. Danson said. "Thank you all for your participation."

There was a round of applause before students started filing out of the gym.

The candidates were gathering their cards. But, Katani was staring at Avery.

As soon as Mr. Danson left to supervise the north entrance of the gym, Katani's glare intensified.

"What?" Avery asked.

"You know what! You cut me off!"

"I said I was sorry!"

Katani rolled her eyes.

"Careful, Katani, or you won't win Yurt's Smile Award," Avery said when Henry was out of earshot.

"That's the dumbest thing I've heard. Vote for me! Let's all smile about it!"

Avery giggled.

"Too bad for you he's not giving out a Laughs-At-Anything-Award. You'd win that for sure," Katani huffed.

"Well, at least it's an award," Avery quipped.

Katani struggled to keep the corners of her mouth from turning up, as she walked toward Isabel and Charlotte.

At that moment, Charlotte thought Henry's idea about making someone else smile was brilliant.

OUT OF ORDER

When the bleachers finally cleared out enough, Maeve bounced down from her top row seat to where the other BSG were standing. Maeve wasn't sure how she ended up on the top. She wished she had been in the front row with Isabel and Charlotte.

Maeve hoped that the fact they were all together meant that Katani and Avery were finally getting along.

"Great job, everyone. Let's go to Montoya's for hot chocolate to celebrate!" Maeve called out.

It took a little persuasion. But the two candidates agreed that getting away from school sounded like fun, like it used to be! They went to their lockers, gathered their books, and met on the front steps.

The fresh air felt good as they walked to Montoya's Bakery, with Maeve leading the way. Behind her, Charlotte walked with Avery. Bringing up the rear were Isabel and Katani.

They each ordered hot chocolate and a cookie and carefully carried them to their table.

Maeve was keenly aware that this was her chance to reunite the five of them on something they all loved, Marty. She chattered on about the Think Pink! contest.

"Hold up, Maeve," Katani said. Katani's expression was divided perfectly between confused and annoyed. "What are you talking about?" she asked.

"The 'My Pet Looks Perfect in Pink' contest at Think Pink!" Maeve said.

"Tell me you aren't seriously thinking about putting Marty into a pink outfit," Avery said.

"That's the whole point of the contest, Avery," Maeve snapped.

Avery's jaw dropped. "Pink! Marty can't wear pink—he's a boy! This is crazy! You can't do this!"

"Too late. We are! You two have been so wrapped up in the election. You haven't been paying attention to anything else," Maeve said.

"Sorry. But count me out," Katani said.

"What?!" Maeve shrieked. "But we need you Katani! We were counting on you to sew Marty's costume."

"Tell the little guy I'm sorry, but priorities are priorities," Katani said.

"Nothing's a priority with either of you except winning the class election," Maeve said.

"And what else is there right now?" Katani asked with a haughty tone.

"Fun, and helping the local pet shelter. Why do you two have to be so serious about everything?"

"Caution! Caution! Yurt Alert!" Avery sounded the alarm.

Katani laughed. "Are you sure it's not a 'My Pet Looks Perfect in Green' contest?"

"Hey!" Avery said, sitting up straight and staring at

Katani. "There's nothing wrong with being green!"

Katani laughed. "I meant the color, not the cause, Avery."

Isabel raised her hand slowly from the table and held it out like she was a crossing guard directing kids at a dangerous intersection. "I think we shouldn't talk about the election while we're all together."

"I agree," Charlotte said, looking worried.

"I'll totally and completely second that!" Maeve said. The group had dangerously come close to talking about the election again. It seemed no matter what subject Maeve threw out there, it always came back to that one topic.

Avery flopped back in the chair and folded her arms across her chest.

Katani sat up straight, crossed her arms in front of her and leaned on the table. As Maeve talked on about the new arrivals at Think Pink!, Katani tilted her chin to study the ceiling fan in the center of the room.

Avery finished her muffin and started chewing on her fingernails instead.

Katani caught sight of her and made a disgusted "tsk" sound and looked away.

"What? What!" Avery asked.

"Nothing!" Katani said. "Nothing that you would understand."

"Stop it!" Maeve shouted. "You are both acting so obnoxious! You're ruining this for all of us!"

Katani snapped her mouth closed and glared at Maeve.

Avery flopped back in her chair and crossed her arms in front of her in a classic pout.

Their silence was almost worse than the arguing.

Maeve took a deep breath. Clearly, this had been a huge mistake. She thought if she got them all together things would be better, but it looked as if until the election was over, nothing was going to work. The question was ... once the election was over, would they ever go back to normal again?

Chat Room: BSG   `_ □ ✕`

File Edit People View Help

Skimad: Hey #1 daughter
4kicks: Hi Dad
Skimad: How'd the debate go?
4kicks: OK I got a big cheer for saying we had to save the planet
Skimad: that's great but I don't sense your usual enthusiasm WU?
4kicks: I don't know
Skimad: Having a tough time of it?
4kicks: Katani's mad at me and I'm mad at her. It's no fun.
Skimad: Too much competition, huh.
4kicks: I guess
Skimad: Winning isn't everything, Avery.
4kicks: You always say that, Dad
Skimad: Sorry—old man—repeat myself. Can't help it

2 people here

Skimad
4kicks

❖

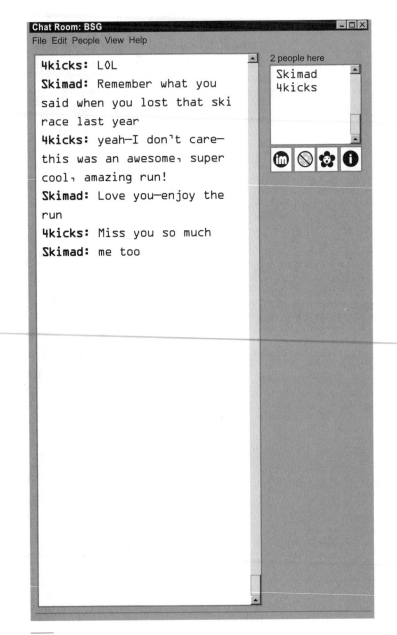

CHAPTER 16

౧

STAR SEARCH

CHARLOTTE leaned up against the window. A fine mist had been falling all day. It was too wet to sit on her balcony tonight. Since she had moved to Brookline, the balcony had been her special spot. A place just for her.

Charlotte scanned the evening sky. She was looking for the Seven Sisters—a constellation of the seven stars that travel the skies together. She remembered the night that her father had first shown her that constellation. It had made her think of the Beacon Street Girls and how they were traveling through life, or at least junior high, together. Secretly, she had added Sophie to that group. She exchanged letters at Christmas time with Shadya from Africa and Anabel from Australia, but Sophie had been her most faithful correspondent. Charlotte went online, hoping to find a response to the email she had sent Sophie earlier in the week. She scanned down the list of names and her heart jumped when she saw the familiar name in the message box.

```
To: Charlotte
From: Sophie
Subject: re: Class Election
```

ma cherie,
I cry for you. you sound so sad. It is
hard to make friends and harder still to
be in fight with friends. They will come
around, no? They will understand when the
surprise is gone. But if they don't you
are free to runaway to Paris. I would
take you in toute de suite. Speak of
runaways, I saw glance of a small chat
near the docks. Your lost Orangina? Alas,
I am not sure. I cannot say. I don't want
to get your hopes up. There are so many
stray chats in Paris. I will keep my eyes
open for her.
Bisous
Sophie

Charlotte wished Sophie were here right now to help her understand all that was going on. Sophie might have seen Orangina? What better reason for Charlotte to run away to Paris for a while! She missed that little orange furball.

There was a soft knock at her door.

Charlotte closed the email from Sophie. "Come in," she said.

"Hey, pumpkin, sorry I've been so busy with work lately. What's up in Charlotte's world?" Mr. Ramsey said, sitting on the bed next to her desk chair.

"Nothing much. This week's going to be crazy. Class

elections are on Friday. I can't wait until it's over," Charlotte said, sinking down on the bed next to her father.

"Rough campaign?"

For the first time in a long time, Charlotte started to cry. "It's been horrible," she said, the words catching in her throat. And before she knew it, she poured out her heart about the events of the past two weeks.

"What about the other candidates?"

"Dillon is just Mr. Popular ... saying just what everyone wants to hear. Everyone laughs at Henry, but he made some good points," Charlotte said. "I just wish Avery and Katani could get along. It's been so ... hard. I'm afraid none of us will be the same again."

Her dad patted her knee and then put his arm around her. "Well, it's hard to compete against friends. On the sports field and court you have referees to help make sure things don't get out of hand, but an election ... well, as you can see from some of the political ads on TV, even adults have a hard time not letting things spin out of control."

"I'm just afraid," Charlotte sighed as she sunk close to her father's side. "We promised we would be friends forever. Now I'm not sure if we'll all make it."

"Don't give up on them yet. Things will calm down after the election is over. And those two girls are good kids. Just hang in there!"

"Woof, Woof," barked Marty as he jumped up in Charlotte's lap.

"See, Marty knows. Don't you, little guy?" said Mr. Ramsey, scratching the little dog behind his ear.

And then Mr. Ramsey told her that he was working on an article about Paris. "Who knows, Char, we might be drinking café au lait on the Seine again ... you never know."

Charlotte's heart skipped a beat. It was amazing how one little word, in this case, *Paris*, could change your whole outlook.

THE RED PEN STRIKES AGAIN!

When Katani walked down the hall the next morning, the first thing she noticed was that everyone was looking up. The second thing Katani noticed was that everyone's mouth was open. Only Anna and Joline were laughing. Anna pointed at one of Katani's few remaining poster boards and there right in the center was a Post-it note: "Don't Vote for this Beanpole," was written in red ink.

Katani was outraged. Steaming, she ripped the note from her board and examined it closely. In the bottom right hand corner it was signed, "The Red Pen will strike again!" In the bottom right-hand corner, there was a little smiley face sticking its tongue out. Who would do this? Katani's first thought was that it was Avery, but she immediately shook that thought away. No way Avery would be this heartless. Besides, there were Post-its on Avery's poster that were downright cruel!

Katani dropped her books in front of her locker and continued down the hall, angrily ripping the Post-its from the posters, lockers, and walls. She tried not to read them as she stacked them in her hand, but she couldn't help it. Who would say such awful, hurtful things?

Even though she was mad, truth be told, Katani was also relieved. For the first time since the posters started disappearing, Katani knew that Kelley wasn't responsible. It couldn't be Kelley. It wasn't her handwriting. Besides, Kelley didn't know how to be cruel.

Mr. Danson was on one side of the hall ripping down the notes and Ms. Rodriguez was on the other side of the hall doing the same. Quietly, Avery joined them.

"Girls, I would like those as evidence," Mr. Danson said when they had finished.

Katani walked over and handed her pile to Mr. Danson.

"Do either of you have any idea who may be behind this?" Mr. Danson asked, a stern look in his eyes. "This is *very* serious," he added.

Avery looked to Katani and they both shook their heads that they didn't.

"Well, don't let them get you down," Mr. Danson said.

"We won't," they said at the same time. It was the first time in weeks they had agreed on anything. It felt good to be on the same side for a change.

BACK TO THE DRAWING BOARD

Charlotte was happy when she arrived at lunch at the exact time Isabel did. That meant they went through the hot lunch line together and arrived at the empty table at the same time. Charlotte hated sitting at the table by herself.

"I finished the caricatures," Isabel said, pulling her sketchbook from her backpack. "I want you to look at them and tell me what you think."

"How do you feel about them?" Charlotte asked.

"I like them better than I did the EDGY stuff. Still— they're not my usual thing. The more I try to focus on political cartoons, the more 'birdy' ideas I have. I've also been working on something else all weekend."

"What?"

"An idea for the Tower."

"Really?"

"Yes, I think I figured out a solution that will make everyone happy."

"Ooooo! Let me see."

"First things first," Isabel said, putting the sketchpad on the table. She thumbed it open to the first character sketch.

Charlotte peered down at the first caricature and saw Henry Yurt smiling up at her. Isabel had done a great job of portraying the Yurtmeister's zest for living. "This is great," Charlotte said before she flipped to the next caricature.

Isabel smiled as she sipped from her milk cartoon.

"They're so good!" Charlotte said. She flipped back through the caricatures again and ended up on the picture of Avery. It was so full of energy, it practically buzzed. "But, personally I like your bird ones better, too."

"Yeah, I know," sighed Isabel. "Birds are me, but Jennifer wants something about the election."

Without warning, the table jolted. Applesauce sloshed from Charlotte's divided tray into her macaroni and cheese. Avery had arrived.

"Hey guys, what's up?" she asked as she twisted the top off a yogurt smoothie and downed it in one long gulp. "Hey! That's me," she said, pointing at the caricature of herself. "This is awesome. Can I use it for my campaign posters?"

"I don't think so. These are for *The Sentinel*," Isabel told her.

"There're more? Let me see the others!" Avery lurched, grabbing for the sketchpad.

"Dillon looks so funny. These are awesome, Isabel!" When Avery flipped to Henry's caricature, she slapped the table and busted out laughing. When she paged to Katani's, she fell forward in silent convulsive laughter like she was having a seizure.

"Avery, breathe!" Charlotte said. Avery looked as if she might pass out. Her uncontrollable giggles were contagious.

❀

In an instant, Charlotte and Isabel were laughing as hard as Avery. They were laughing so hard, they didn't hear Katani walk up to the table.

"What's so funny?" Katani asked as she glanced down at the caricature of herself. Katani's eyes widened, and she backed up a step. "So you're all laughing at me?"

"No!" Charlotte said. She'd tried to stop laughing so fast that the "no" came out with a huge snurp, which sent the three of them back to uncontrollable giggles.

"Isabel, out of all the BSG, I thought you were the only one who truly supported me. How could you?" Katani asked as she turned on her heels and headed toward the door.

"Wait! Wait!" Isabel shouted after her and caught her right outside the door.

"I drew caricatures of everyone. It's for *The Sentinel*," Isabel told Katani.

"You're going to put THAT in the school paper? I thought you were my friend! But you want everyone to laugh at me?"

"It's a caricature ..."

"You think that's the way I look?"

"I didn't think you looked bad in it at all."

"My head is huge. My body is so small."

"Katani ... caricatures of everyone look like that. Please come back to the table and I'll show you."

"I'm not like EVERYONE. I have never wanted to be 'just like everyone.' Look, I can't handle this right now. I gotta get out of here." Katani pushed through the double doors, leaving Isabel standing speechless.

"She didn't like it?" Charlotte asked when Isabel returned to the table.

"She hated it," Isabel said. "I don't know what to do ... Jennifer wants something by tomorrow."

"Maybe you could draw a new one of Katani," Charlotte suggested.

"I don't think she'll like anything I draw," Isabel said. "I just can't take that chance. I don't want to hurt Katani's feelings."

"If she can't take a joke, that's her problem," Avery said, matter of factly, and in between crunching on her sunflower kernels.

"It wasn't supposed to be a joke."

"Are you kidding? Caricatures are supposed to be funny. Look at mine! I'm funny! Go ahead. Turn it in," Avery said. "Later," she said and headed back to the boys' table.

"I can't turn this in. And what if Katani finds whatever I

draw insulting?"

"Maybe it's just as well, I didn't want to say anything, but I found out yesterday that Chelsea Briggs is taking photographs of all the candidates," Charlotte admitted.

"Who?"

"Chelsea Briggs. You know, she was the one who did the ventriloquist act with the Cabbage Patch doll for the Talent Show."

"Oh yeah, Chelsea. I remember now. Too bad she had a sore throat that night. She was so good in the rehearsals."

"I think she must have practiced too long. Anyway, I just found out she took some candid pictures of the candidates, and Jennifer is going to use them in *The Sentinel*."

"Photographs?" Isabel asked.

"Yeah. Actually, Chelsea's pretty good. When I said something to her about her pictures, she told me she liked being the photographer because that way she's always behind the camera and never in front of it."

"Why would she say that?"

"I don't know. Maybe she's a little embarrassed about you know ... how she looks," Charlotte said uncomfortably.

"What's the matter with the way she looks?" asked Avery.

"Well, you know ... she is kind of chunky," Isabel said as a picture of Chelsea appeared in her mind.

"Oh, that," Avery said, clearly disinterested in the topic.

"What are you going to do now?" Charlotte asked. "The deadline is tomorrow."

Isabel shrugged. "Since the caricatures aren't going to work, I guess it's back to the drawing board. Look, I'm going to get a pass to go to the library ... maybe I'll find something to inspire me there."

Isabel left Charlotte sitting at the lunch table alone. She

wondered briefly where Maeve was again today, then she couldn't help thinking about Chelsea's comment that she'd rather be behind the camera than in front of it

Charlotte was thinking the same thing. "Cabbage Patch Chelsea." She said that to remind herself that her name started with a "C," just like Cabbage Patch. But Charlotte couldn't help thinking that Chelsea kind of looked like a cabbage patch doll: the full round face, the dimpled elbows and the curly blonde hair. Of course, she would never say that to anyone else. Not even to the BSG. It was almost too mean to think! Charlotte chased the thought from her mind.

Luckily, the bell rang, and she was off to her afternoon classes.

Avery's Blog
Campaign Update

The mudslinging has begun! Except no one knows who's slinging mud or why! Whoever it is seems to hate all the candidates. What's up with that? This election will go down in the history of Abigail Adams Junior High as one of the most contentious (cool word, huh?) ever.

Quote:
You can't make yourself look good by making someone else look bad.
—My Mom

Survey:
What's your favorite Fall Activity?
a. Hayride
b. Jumping into a pile of leaves

c. Wiener roast
d. Football games.

Results from the last Survey:
What is your favorite way to help the environment?
A. Pick up litter 28%
B. Recycle cans and bottles 68%
C. Buy environmentally friendly products 4%

SWEDISH FISH FIX

"Mrs. Weiss!" Maeve called as she burst through the door of Irving's. "Help! I need Swedish Fish ... immediately, if not sooner!" Maeve pretended to faint, and then collapsed into giggles. It felt good to be silly. Things were so tense with the BSG these days, and it was stressful just to be around Avery and Katani.

Mrs. Weiss chuckled as Maeve sprung up and took a bow. "My, you certainly are energetic this afternoon. Did you have a good day at school?" she asked as she made change for Maeve's dollar bill and handed her the package of Swedish Fish.

Maeve opened the bag and popped two fish into her mouth. "Well, school was OK. But my friends are still fighting about the school election, and I'm totally fed up. I wish they would realize how ridiculous they sound. And how bad it's making the rest of us feel."

Maeve had been keeping Mrs. Weiss posted about the drama surrounding the election. It was nice to talk to someone on the outside—someone who wasn't wrapped up in all the emotional friendship stuff.

"I'm sorry, Maeve. It sounds like this campaign has

gotten out of hand," Mrs. Weiss said sympathetically. "Sometimes people want to win so badly that they forget about everything and everyone else. But I know you girls have a special bond. And I think it will hold you together through this."

"Thanks, Mrs. Weiss. I hope you're right. But things aren't looking too good right now," Maeve said and then filled Mrs. Weiss in on her failed attempt to reunite the BSG after the debates.

"Well, it sounds like Avery and Katani aren't making things easy for the rest of you girls. I'll send extra good thoughts in your direction until the election is over ... even more good wishes than usual," Mrs. Weiss said with a smile. "And how is your special project going?" Maeve perked up again and grinned. Mrs. Weiss was the only person who knew her secret. "It's going GREAT." She gave a thumbs-up to Mrs. Weiss, stuck the Swedish Fish into her school bag, and bounced out the door.

CHAPTER 17

ॐ

GIANT ZINGERS

AVERY couldn't believe her eyes when she arrived at school early the next morning. The seventh-grade hall looked like a gigantic "zinger" graffiti wall. There were zingers everywhere—on every poster—giant-sized yellow Post-its in bright red markers. Somebody got totally carried away.

None of the comments were nice. Usually, Avery considered herself immune to attack. When she was playing sports, she was in the zone and didn't hear trash talk. Her teammates sometimes filled her in afterwards on some of the things she was called. Sure, the comments made her angry, but she chose to focus on the game.

But, walking down the hall and staring up at all the Post-it notes made her grit her teeth.

Outraged, Avery ripped a zinger note off her poster that said "Don't vote for this Munchkin." Avery was sure of one thing—even though Katani sometimes called her Munchkin, there was NO WAY Katani was behind this. She would never ever stoop this low. She took a few zingers off Henry Yurt's poster. Henry wouldn't do this either.

Dillon? She wasn't sure. No, Avery shook her head. The more she thought about it, the more she was certain that nasty notes like these weren't Mr. Popular's style.

Avery saw Ms. Rodriguez come out of her office. "Avery! Stop right there!" she called out. Avery froze as Ms. R came toward her, her high heels ringing loudly in the empty hall. "Avery! What are you doing?"

"Taking down these ... zingers," Avery said, continuing down the hall, ripping down the ones that were within reach. "Ms. R, I can't reach this one ... could you?"

"Of course," she said, reaching up and pulling a zinger from one of Avery's posters. "For a minute, I thought ..."

"You thought I put them up?"

"Well ... yes. It's just that when I went down this hall twenty minutes ago, none of these were here. Whoever did it, just did it. What are you doing here so early?"

"I came to put more posters up," Avery said, pointing to the stack of posters lying on the floor in front of her locker. "But it seemed more important to get these down before anyone saw them." Avery showed a particularly nasty zinger to Ms. Rodriguez: "Dillon is a fake loser."

"This is inexcusable," Ms. Rodriguez said. "We need to get to the bottom of this ... Now."

During first hour, Avery got a hall pass to go to the office. When she got there, the other candidates were there as well as Ms. Rodriguez and Mr. Danson. Mrs. Fields was not happy. None of the candidates looked very pleased either. Dillon didn't have his million-dollar smile on and even Henry himself couldn't find anything to joke about.

"If anyone in this room has any idea who is doing this you better tell me now!" Mrs. Fields said firmly.

Katani had never seen her grandmother so mad.

They all shook their heads.

"No matter what, I can't imagine anyone in this room saying—writing—those things!" Avery said.

"Avery's right," Katani said.

They all nodded grimly.

Mrs. Fields looked out at the group of candidates and teachers and said, "Nothing like this has ever happened while I have been principal at Abigail Adams Junior High. This election has created a very negative atmosphere in our school, and I don't care for it one bit."

Everyone was stunned. No one had ever heard Mrs. Fields speak that way before; even her own granddaughter was worried. *Did Grandma Ruby think that she was a negative influence?* thought Katani as she chewed on her nail.

Mrs. Fields sent everyone on their way with a stern warning to behave in an honorable fashion.

Katani and Avery walked out of Mrs. Fields' office and stood for a moment together.

"Gotta get back to art. What class are you going to?" Katani asked.

"Math," Avery said.

"If I ever find out who's doing this ..." Katani said.

"Don't worry. I know it's not you," Avery responded.

"What's that supposed to mean?" Katani asked, whirling around to glare at Avery.

"That even you aren't that ruthless," Avery said. She didn't understand what Katani was getting all upset about. "You gotta hearing problem? I said I knew it WASN'T you!"

"Because even *I* wouldn't be that cruel?!" Katani looked like steam was about to shoot out of her ears.

"Right!"

Katani had both hands on her hips.

"What?" Avery asked.

"You are …" Katani huffed.

"Whatever," Avery said and took off down the hall in front of her.

Avery didn't understand Katani at all … she was soooo sensitive. But, it didn't matter. Avery was out in front. She was on her way to victory. Katani would get over it. Katani wasn't one to hold a grudge.

Katani stood there shaking. How could she behave like that after her grandmother had warned everyone? Grandma Ruby was right. "Negative" was the word. What had happened to everyone? What had happened to her … to Avery? Avery was her friend, one of her best friends. Now they were always snapping at with each other, saying mean things, and storming off like they were in first grade.

PHOTO SHOOT

"Can you believe this weather?" Charlotte asked Isabel and Maeve as they climbed the hill to her house. Even though it wasn't sunny, Charlotte couldn't believe how warm it was today. Much too warm for the jacket she'd worn this morning. On cloudy days, the leaves seemed to glisten, as if they were releasing the last stored up sunshine of summer.

"I haven't been able to figure out Boston weather yet," Charlotte said.

"Me either," Isabel said. "No matter what I pick to wear, I'm always too hot or too cold."

"Don't feel bad! I've lived here all my life and I still can't figure it out," Maeve said.

Maeve had suggested that all five of the girls go to Charlotte's house after school to help with Marty's "photo shoot." Charlotte had been a little disappointed at first that

Avery and Katani had said they were busy, but now that it was just the three of them, she had to admit she was a little relieved. Things were just too tense when Avery and Katani were around.

"Did you hear about the notes on the campaign posters this morning?" Isabel asked.

"Yeah, Avery calls them the Nasty Zinger Notes," Charlotte said.

"They were all signed, 'The Red Pen will strike again.' Just like the first set, but even nastier," Maeve said.

"Who do you think the 'Red Pen' is?" Isabel asked.

"Whoever it is … how do you think they got them up so fast? Avery said that Ms. Rodriguez had just left her room and went to the teachers' lounge only ten minutes before," Charlotte said.

"Maybe they had help," Maeve said, arching her eyebrows in surprise.

"That makes sense," Charlotte agreed.

"I know two nasties who would love to trash both Avery and Katani," Maeve said.

Charlotte knew that she was talking about the Queens of Mean—Anna and Joline.

"We don't know that," Isabel said.

"How can you defend them after what they did to you during the Talent Show?" Maeve asked.

"I only know that I can't accuse them unless I have better evidence," Isabel said.

"You should be a lawyer, Isabel." Suddenly, Maeve stopped short. Charlotte and Isabel walked on for a few steps before they noticed. "Look! That's a pretty important-looking car in front of your house," Maeve said, pointing at a big, shiny black car.

"Wow, Dad's not home right now and Miss Pierce NEVER has visitors," Charlotte said.

Just as she said that, two serious-looking men came out of the house. They were wearing dark suits and black trench coats—even on this warm day. They slipped dark sunglasses on as they trotted down the front porch steps—even though it was cloudy out—and headed toward the black car.

"Who do you think they are?" Isabel asked. "Did you catch the license plate?"

"Weird. It wasn't a Massachusetts license plate," Maeve exclaimed, craning her neck to see. "I think it was a U.S. Government plate."

The three exchanged a surprised look.

"Str-r-r-ange," Charlotte said.

"Maybe they're with the FBI," Isabel guessed.

"No, they looked too spooky for that … CIA, I bet," Maeve said.

"Wait a minute! Miss Pierce was an astronomer. IS an astronomer! What if she's found extraterrestrial life?" Charlotte whispered excitedly.

"Those guys could have been MEN IN BLACK," Maeve added.

"That's only a movie," said Isabel.

"Hey … you'd be surprised how many things in movies are really, actually true," Maeve continued, giving Charlotte and Isabel a knowing look.

Once inside, with Marty dancing around their heels, the girls quickly forgot about the mysterious men in the car and concentrated on the task at hand.

First, they took Marty for a walk in the park. The "little dude" was beyond ecstatic. His whole posse—Fly, Louie, everyone was there. The girls laughed as Marty greeted each and every dog with his woof-and-somersault routine.

"Our dog is going to be famous someday," predicted Maeve.

When they ran back to Charlotte's house and up the steps to the Tower, even Marty was out of breath.

"So who did you get to sew the costume?" Isabel asked.

"I didn't. I had to improvise and make a costume out of what I had on hand. AND what I could hot-glue together. No sewing involved," Maeve said, pulling her big pink slipper from her backpack.

"Your slipper?" Isabel asked.

"No! Can't you tell? This is a fur coat. With matching scarf and ear muffs," Maeve said.

In minutes, the three cut leg holes out of the bottom of Maeve's slipper. Maeve had already drawn on buttons down the front. She had cut apart her other slipper to make a scarf and earmuffs using a pink pipe cleaner. They duct-taped the slipper on. And voilà! Marty was transformed into a puff of pink—ready for winter.

"And for the final touch …" Maeve pulled what seemed to be large pink tongue depressor out of her bag. "A pink snow board."

"That should make Avery happy," Isabel said.

"We need a backdrop," Maeve said.

"Do you think we could borrow this piece of fabric from inside Katani's window seat?" Isabel asked. "It's perfect— the blue will off set the pink."

"Better not let Katani catch us," Charlotte warned as she looked out the window up and down the street to make sure Katani wasn't on her way to her house.

"We're going to put it back," Maeve said.

"I don't know, Maeve," Charlotte sounded worried.

"Things are bad enough."

"It'll be fine."

"Well, you have to put it back EXACTLY the way it was!" Charlotte insisted.

Maeve stamped her foot in jest, put her hands on her hip and said to Charlotte, "I will."

Charlotte crossed her eyes and made a funny face at Maeve.

Isabel began draping the fabric over the window seat and let it fall in a puddle on the floor. Charlotte put Marty in the middle and tried to get him to raise his head and look up as Maeve clicked away with the Ramseys' digital camera.

Marty was so cute that the three couldn't stop cooing at him.

"Pretty doggie."

"Good little dude."

"Smart doggie."

It was so unusual for Marty to sit still for that long. But he seemed to enjoy the attention and the posing. It's almost as if he knew how to be a doggie actor.

After a few minutes, Marty was ready for a game of chase around the room. He broke away from Charlotte and shook his scarf and earmuffs off, sending them flying. Then he flung himself to the floor, flipped on his back and the duct tape gave way with a loud rip. He shook off the pink fur coat, which looked like Maeve's slipper again once it was on the floor. Then, Marty pounced and attacked it with such ferocity that the girls went crazy.

When the three recovered from the laugh attack that Marty's little striptease had started, they flopped down on the floor to review the pictures on the digital camera and came up with their favorites.

"Charlotte, could you print these off, and then we can vote on them?" Maeve said.

Silence reverberated in the Tower.

"Don't worry," Maeve said. "After the election, everything is going to go back to normal and then we can find a space for Isabel in the Tower." Maeve clapped her hand over her mouth. "Ooops sorry, Charlotte. I know you didn't want me to say anything."

"That's OK, Maeve. I talked to Isabel about it already," Charlotte said.

"I'm so sorry, Isabel. It's so unfair! We're going to make it right!" Maeve said.

"That's OK, Maeve," Isabel said. "I told Charlotte I'm not one to worry about being exact or things being equally, evenly fair. Things always have a way of evening out in the end."

Maeve put her hands on her hips. "Oh, no! You're not going to be all goodie-goodie about this and say you don't need equal space."

Isabel shook her head. "No way … But I've accepted it as my challenge to find a space for me in the Tower without taking away from anyone else."

"Really? How's that going to work?" Maeve asked.

"Well, as I said, it's a challenge … but I have some ideas. Speaking of which, I need some measurements." Isabel pulled a tape measure from her backpack and got to work. "Actually, I'll need some help. Charlotte, will you hold this end of the tape measure? Maeve, can you write the measurements down?"

Maeve and Charlotte complied as she measured the floor diagonally from the corner-to-corner, then from the floor to the tip of the ceiling.

"Thanks," she said, taking the list of measurements from

Maeve and putting the tape measure back into her bag.

"What are you going to do? Take the top part of the room?" Maeve asked.

A hint of smile danced across Isabel's face as she looked up from the pad she was working on. "You'll see," she said mysteriously.

Maeve and Charlotte both looked at her, both hoping for more details, but Isabel was silent.

"I almost hate to ask, but ... how are the cartoons for *The Sentinel* coming?" Charlotte asked.

Isabel's smile turned to a frown.

"I turned in my article this morning," Charlotte said. "I always feel so relieved when it's done ... it's always rush, rush, rush to finish it. But once I get it done, I feel much better. What did you decide to turn in?"

"I haven't turned anything in yet," Isabel said.

"But today was your deadline!"

"For articles ... I have until tomorrow morning for cartoons."

"What ones are you going to turn in?" Charlotte asked.

Isabel sighed heavily. "I'm not sure," she said.

DRESS REHEARSAL

Katani pulled a list from her notebook, and then made a neat check next to everything she'd finished.

Kgirl *Kgirl List:*

1. *Find pair of shoes for new dress* ✓
2. *Finish hemming dress* ✓
3. *Go over vocabulary for English test* ✓
4. *Write acceptance speech*

Katani had finished hemming her dress that afternoon. The dress had an empire waist, made with fabric that was very soft and silky. She loved the way the fabric swirled around her knees. The color was perfect—burgundy, rust, and a sage green on a warm autumn gold background that accentuated Katani's skin tone. The dress was perfect for the dance, but when it was time for the election results, Katani would put on the burgundy jacket she had made last month. The jacket was made of rich velvet with a scalloped, asymmetrical front with two frog closures and a three-button mandarin collar. It was the perfect complement to the dress and in an instant transformed it from a carefree party look to the elegant style of a distinguished class president.

Katani couldn't resist trying on the full ensemble, shoes and all. She'd found mod Mary Janes in just the right shade shopping with her mother at Filene's Basement.

Now that the bulk of the campaign was behind her, Katani flipped back through her list and marveled at all she'd done. There was only one thing left to do—write her acceptance speech.

She imagined herself in her dress and velvet jacket walking up to the podium. Poise. She had to remember to stand tall and project confidence. Her acceptance speech should be about uniting the class. She would have to find a way to dispel all the negativity that had surfaced during the election, even with Avery.

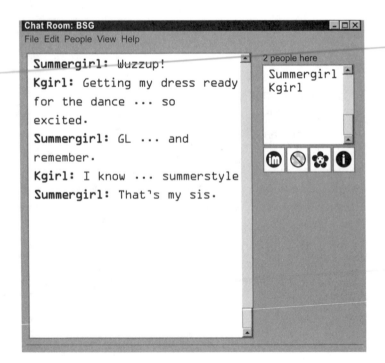

CHAPTER **18**

∞

HEART TONES

ISABEL hit the snooze button on her alarm for the second time, but didn't go right back to sleep. She rolled on her back and gazed up at the ceiling at the papier-mâché birds hanging above her bed. She smiled. Perhaps seeing the birds first thing this morning was a good omen.

She shut her eyes and dozed for a moment before her alarm started beeping again.

"You're not up yet?" her sister, Elena Maria, called from the door. "Better get moving."

"I wish I could just stay in bed today and stare at the ceiling," Isabel said to her sister.

"Well, you can't, so you better get up now or you will be late," Elena Maria answered quite unsympathetically.

"Sisters," Isabel grumbled. Sometimes they make you wish you were an only child, she thought.

Isabel groaned, rolled to the edge of her bed, and slowly sat up. She usually didn't have a hard time getting up in the morning, but she also usually didn't stay up so late. She'd been up all night drawing, putting the final touches on the cartoons.

✿

Her drop-dead deadline was in less than an hour. It wasn't like she didn't have anything to turn in. She didn't just have four cartoons, she had eight—a folder with edgy, political stuff and a folder with two bird cartoons. Even as she got dressed, had a piece of toast for breakfast, and pushed out the door, she still didn't know which folder she was going to turn in to Jennifer. She had to make a choice: go with what would make Jennifer happy or go with what she felt was right in her heart.

From the door, Isabel's mother watched her daughter nibble on her toast and stare into space. She knew she was worried about something so she walked over and lightly caressed Isabel's hair.

"What is on my beautiful hija's mind this morning? Are you worried about a big test?"

Isabel turned. She hadn't realized her mother had been watching her.

"No Mama, it's just some drawings. I don't know if I like them," Isabel answered, not wanting to concern her mother, who hadn't been feeling well last night. Her mother's illness, multiple sclerosis, was worrisome for Isabel and she didn't want to bother her mother with stuff about school when other issues were just so much more important.

"Would you like me to look at them?" offered Mama.

Isabel jumped up from the table before her mother could sit down.

"Maybe later," she said. "I'm going to be late if I don't get going."

She gave her mom a hug and raced out the door, stopping to grab her backpack in the hall.

Luckily, Isabel's route to school that morning took her past Yuri's fruit stand. Her stomach was already growling.

The one little piece of toast she had wasn't going to hold her until lunch. A nice Granny Smith apple would hit the spot. Her mouth puckered as she imagined the first, tart taste of her favorite apple. She ducked in the door and dug through her coat pocket for change.

"Ah—look what the cat dragged in," Yuri growled when he saw her come through the door.

"Hola, Yuri," Isabel said.

"Looks like not so good morning to me," Yuri said. "You have extra baggage with you today, no?" Yuri pointed to Isabel's eyes.

Isabel smiled. Her eyes felt puffy, so she couldn't imagine what they must look like.

"Big date last night?" Yuri asked.

Isabel smiled and shook her head. "No, I was drawing cartoons for the school newspaper—for the election issue."

"Ah—American election. Most important and sacred right! Always remember to vote. I have not missed an election in all the years since I have become citizen," Yuri said proudly.

Isabel nodded. She felt a twinge of guilt. She'd thought about skipping the election. "This election is hard," she admitted to Yuri. "Two of my best friends are both running for president. Voting for one of them makes me feel like I'm voting against the other one."

"To NOT vote is grave sin. You must vote! If head cannot decide—let heart decide," he said, pressing his hand to his chest. "Your heart is never wrong. Listen to your heart."

Isabel paid for her apple, thanked Yuri for his advice and headed off to school. A cool north wind tugged at the edges of her poncho. Thoughts about which folder to turn in swirled around in her mind like the wind. And Yuri's words reverberated in her head.

"Listen to your heart." That was easy for Yuri to say, Isabel thought. Her heart said vote for both of her friends but that was impossible not to mention illegal!

RUNNING MATES

Katani almost expected to see more zingers plastered on the walls when she arrived at school that morning. She breathed a sigh of relief when she noticed everyone moving about the halls as if it was a perfectly normal morning, as if nothing extraordinary was happening. Before homeroom, she knocked on Ms. Rodriguez's office door to ask for a pass so she could work in the library during lunch.

"Working in the library again?" Ms. R asked as she pulled the pass pad from her desk drawer. "How are things going between you and Avery?"

Katani faltered a little. "OK, I guess." What did working in the library have to do with her relationship with Avery? Ms. R always seemed to be able to read Katani's thoughts. It was spooky! And Katani was sure Ms. R knew what she was thinking right now.

"Remember Katani, this is just a class election."

"Things are fine between us. We've just agreed to run our own campaigns and stay out of each other's way."

"Is that why you've been hanging out in the library?"

"No—I have work to do. The campaign has taken ..." Katani took a breath and realized the campaign had taken a lot more than time from her life. "... a lot of time. Maybe things will go back to normal once it's over," she added wistfully.

Ms. Rodriguez handed Katani the library pass for lunch. "Good luck," was all she said, but her pretty brown eyes seemed to look right through Katani.

Katani put the pass in the outside zipper compartment of her backpack. The truth was, Katani wasn't 100 percent sure if things would go back to normal. And not only between her and Avery. Things had been strained between her and the rest of the BSG. She hoped they would be able to bounce back after the election. Would things ever be the same again? What if she won the election but lost the BSG? With a twang Katani realized that finding new friends as great as the BSG would be much, much harder than getting elected class president.

When lunchtime rolled around, Katani went to her locker to get her campaign folder. She heard a noise at the far end of the hall. Across from the science lab, Avery was jumping up and down, swatting at something above the lockers. Katani squinted to see if she could get a better picture of what she was doing.

Avery stopped jumping and looked at Katani. They both stared at each other for a second. Not exactly a hello, but recognition that they saw each other. Katani turned back to her locker and began to work the combination.

Suddenly, Avery was at her side and tugging her elbow. Even though Katani'd seen Avery at the end of the hall, her sudden presence at her elbow startled her and she jumped. "What?!" she asked. Katani couldn't hide the annoyance in her voice.

Avery pointed up. There on the wall high above Katani's locker was another nasty zinger left by the Red Pen.

"How? When?" Katani sputtered. She couldn't believe she didn't see this earlier. She must have been looking at the floor the entire time.

"There was one above my locker too," Avery said.

"Is that why you were jumping?" Katani asked.

Avery smiled and nodded. "I must have looked pretty stupid, huh?"

Avery's smile faded as she looked down at the note in her hand. Avery showed it to Katani. Among other nasty things, the zinger included the word "Shrimpster," something that Katani had often called Avery. "You don't think ...?" Katani asked.

Avery tilted her head and glared at Katani like she could stare a confession out of her. Things must be really bad between them if Avery thought she would ever do something like that.

"Avery you gotta believe that I would NEVER ever write anything like that!" she exclaimed.

Katani reached up and grabbed the zinger that was above her locker. "Look at this!" Katani pointed to the word "Beanpole."

"Sound familiar?" Katani asked. "But I know YOU didn't do it."

Avery nodded. "You're right."

The two stood motionless next to each other in the hall.

"Who's doing this? It's just so ... dastardly!" Avery exclaimed.

Katani smiled. "That's a Maeve word."

"I know; I stole it from her." Avery grinned.

Suddenly, Katani nudged Avery and pointed down the hall. "Maybe it's not just one person. Maybe it's two! Look! Anna and Joline are hanging all over Dillon at the end of the hallway. I bet they are behind this."

"I know they hate us ... but what else is new?"

"They probably figure if they frame us, we'll drop out of the election and Dillon will win!"

Avery's nostrils flared. Katani wouldn't have been

surprised if steam came out of them. She expected Avery to start pawing the ground any second. Avery wasn't one to stand still for long. In an instant, she was stomping down the hall! How could anyone so little make so much noise? She sounded like a Clydesdale. Katani craned her neck to see what would happen next.

Avery walked up to the group at Dillon's locker and tapped Anna on the back. "Excuse me!" Avery said, as she shoved the note in Anna's face.

Anna read the note and laughed.

"Think that's funny?" Avery demanded.

"Yeah, I do!" Anna replied.

"I want to know why you're doing this!"

"Me? Why would you think it was me?" Anna asked.

"Puh-leeze, this has the Anna-and-Joline stamp of approval written all over it," Avery said impatiently.

"Why don't you ask the ice queen over there," Anna said, nodding down the hall to Katani.

"Hey! Don't insult my friend!"

"Friend? After the little show before homeroom last week, I don't think anyone would think you two are friends," Anna sneered, with an air of self-importance.

"Oh, yeah? What do you know about friends?"

"I know more than you think, and I'm not so brainless that I think you or the ice queen will win this election. Dillon has it all over you two. You don't know anything about what it takes to be popular."

"This ISN'T a popularity contest!" Avery retorted.

"We'll see," Anna replied, giving knowing looks to Joline and Dillon before they sauntered off down the hall.

Avery stood in the hallway and stared after them. Katani walked over and stood by Avery. She couldn't be sure, but it looked like Avery was trembling all over from head to toe.

Avery whipped around. "Did you hear that?"

"Most of it."

Katani stood silently next to Avery. Both of them were breathing hard and trying to get a handle on their emotions.

"That girl makes me so angry!" Katani couldn't help stomping her right foot when she said it. She wished that Anna's big toe was beneath the heel of her boot.

"I know it's her—them. Anna and Joline don't do much separately," Avery said

"But this—" Katani said, looking down at the note in her hand. "This is pretty low and nasty even for them."

"Who would be so nasty? I mean it's just a school election! School! Not the most important thing in the world. It isn't something you should ..."

"I know. I mean ..."

Katani and Avery caught each other's eyes, embarrassed and ashamed.

"I guess we kinda let things get out of hand," Katani finally said.

Avery nodded, but she didn't say anything.

Katani took a deep breath. "Avery, I'm really sorry about all of this. I just wanted to win so badly I ..." Katani paused not quite knowing what to say next. She wanted to gather her things and go to lunch, but she couldn't. She couldn't leave Avery standing alone in the hall. Katani realized she wanted things to be the way they were before the campaign started. But she didn't know how to undo the things that had been done ... unsay the things that had been said.

"I guess you were right," Avery said.

"About what?"

"About it not being a good idea that we both run for

president. I didn't realize … I didn't think about …"

Katani nodded, "What the heck, Avery. We are only seventh graders. How would we ever know that things would get so crazy?"

"I've felt so alone the last couple of weeks," Avery said.

Katani had an urge to hug her. But she didn't. Avery wasn't big on hugging her friends. She said it was too sappy.

"I meant what I said that day in the cafeteria when we both found out we were running," Avery said. "I can't think of anyone who would be a better, more worthy opponent. I kind of wish we had just tossed a coin. Or maybe one of us should have run for president and the other for vice president," she wishfully added.

"We would have made an awesome team." Katani smiled.

"Can we still be friends? Even if we're running against each other?" Avery asked. "Even after the election … no matter what happens?"

"We will be loyal to our friends," Katani promised.

"New Tower Rule #3," added Avery proudly.

And the two linked arms and headed toward the lunchroom.

CHAPTER 19

❦

ALMOST ALL TOGETHER AGAIN

CHARLOTTE carried her lunch tray to the BSG table. Although lately it was just the Charlotte and Isabel table. As soon as Isabel joined her with her salad, Charlotte asked her if she had turned in the cartoons that morning. Isabel hadn't gotten past a "yes" when Avery made a crash landing at the table.

"Hey," Avery said, sliding out a chair and sitting down.

"You're eating with us?!" Isabel asked.

"Yup ... power food," Avery said, dumping the contents of her brown paper bag onto the table. "Veggie wrap with sunflower seed kernels and a strawberry yogurt smoothie. I sound like a TV commercial," she added.

Surprised at Avery's good mood, Charlotte and Isabel watched silently as Avery chugged her entire smoothie. No sooner had she slammed the empty bottle on the table than Katani showed up, pulled out a chair and began unwrapping her deli sandwich.

"Mmmm. That looks good," Katani said, pointing over at Avery's veggie wrap. I've never had one of those spinach tortillas, are they good?"

"Yup! Want to try a bite?"

"Ooooo. Could I?"

Now Charlotte and Isabel were really shocked. They watched, mouths open, too stunned to eat or talk. Charlotte couldn't believe her eyes or her ears. Katani and Avery were behaving as if they were best friends, not battling head-to-head for class president.

"Mmmm. That's great! Thanks," Katani said.

"No prob!"

"What's up with you two? You're really quiet," Avery said, through a mouthful of veggie wrap.

"Well, come on! Someone say something," Katani said.

Charlotte looked to Isabel. She opened her mouth, but nothing came out.

"It's OK ..." Avery said, nodding to everyone.

"Win or lose, we're still friends," Katani added.

"Well, it sure isn't like competing in a basketball game," Avery said, before she took another bite of her wrap. She chewed quickly and swallowed. "I guess this is what my mom means when she says, 'Live and learn.'"

Before Charlotte had a chance to gather her jumbled thoughts into words, Dillon jumped up on his chair and asked for everyone's attention. "Ladies and Gentlemen ... you too, Montoya ... I'd like to be your class president. Hit it!" he called down to Pete Wexler who turned on Maeve's karaoke machine.

The opening strands of the song "If I Had a Million Dollars" came blaring out the speakers. Dillon started singing, "If I had a million votes ..." Kids around them began dancing and clapping wildly.

Charlotte, caught up in the fun and excitement, started clapping. Avery and Katani looked at each other and and joined in. The cafeteria was rocking. Avery whistled when Dillon finished.

Pete Wexler started passing out Dillon's million dollar bills.

"I don't suppose this table wants any of Dillon's Millions," he said as he passed by.

"Let's see what you got!" Avery said.

Pete tossed a few in the center of the table.

The front side had Dillon's picture in the center of a million dollar bill. The back side read, "Vote for Dillon—One in a Million" with a list of all the things he was pushing in his campaign.

Katani rolled her eyes. "Can you believe this?"

"He didn't lie. Dillon IS one in a million," Avery said. "Hey … isn't that Maeve's karaoke machine? Where's Maeve?"

"So you two are OK with each other," Isabel said, looking over to Katani and Avery. It was more of a question than a statement.

"Yup! Win or lose, we're still friends," Katani repeated.

"If there was only a way both of you could win," Charlotte said. Even as she said it she knew it sounded stupid. How could the seventh-grade class have two class presidents? But it was what she hoped.

Katani shook her head. "Real life isn't like that, Charlotte. It may not seem fair, but only one of us is going to win." Katani looked at Avery. "But if Avery wins maybe she'll let me give her an idea or two on how to expand the budget."

Avery laughed. "If Katani wins, maybe she'll let me be her environmental advisor."

"You got it." Avery reached up to high-five Katani, who responded enthusiastically.

Charlotte wished that Maeve was there. It would be so nice to have the five of them together again!

As if she had read her mind, Katani asked, "Where's Maeve?"

"I don't know. She's been skipping out halfway through lunch for a couple of weeks now," Isabel said.

"Huh," Avery said. "Anyone know what that's all about?"

The group shared a collective shrug.

"I hope she's not in trouble with her schoolwork again," Avery said.

"I hope ..." Charlotte started, but the bell rang and they gathered up their lunch gear and pushed toward the exit. There was a bottleneck at the door, so it took forever for them to push their way through. On the other side of the door there was a big group around Henry Yurt.

"Vote for smiles," he shouted as the crowd pressed toward him. "This should put a smile on your face. Here you go. Do something nice for someone today!" he said, placing a candy bar in every hand extended his way.

"Hey Katani ... what are you going to do to buy our vote?" Nick asked as he crunched into a KitKat bar.

"I'll be a great class president," Katani shouted back.

Nick rolled his eyes, took another bite of his KitKat bar and walked on.

"These guys just don't get it, do they, Katani?" Avery asked.

"I'm glad my worthy opponent isn't into buying people's votes," Katani said, slipping her free arm around Avery's shoulder.

Charlotte felt a warm glow spark inside her. She couldn't resist putting an arm around Isabel's shoulder. "There might be hope after all," she whispered into her ear and the two shared a smile.

MOMENT OF TRUTH

"Isabel! Wait up! Isabel!"

Isabel heard someone call her name and stopped in the middle of the crowded hallway.

Suddenly, Jennifer popped out of a wall of people. She had Isabel's folder in her hand. "What's this?" she asked.

Isabel stared down at the folder like she had never seen it before.

"Isabel, what happened to the edgy cartoons we talked about? The ones you showed me?"

People streamed past them on either side. Isabel was aware that Charlotte was nervously shifting from foot to foot, but was still standing by her side.

Isabel looked at her shoes.

"Isabel?"

"I didn't feel comfortable with those. They seemed too mean," Isabel finally said.

"Political stuff *is* mean."

"It doesn't have to be," Isabel said flatly.

"Well, I guess I'll have to use what you turned in. It's the only thing I have that will fit the space available."

Isabel was quiet.

"Don't get the wrong idea," Jennifer said. "It fits size-wise ... but not content-wise. It isn't about the election."

"Read it again," Isabel said softly. "I think it kind of is, considering what's gone on."

Jennifer leafed through the cartoons, looking briefly at each one and then shrugged.

"I'll guess they'll have to do," she said before she rushed away.

Isabel and Charlotte watched her disappear into the crowd of students.

"I feel like I let her down," Isabel said.

"But you didn't let yourself down," Charlotte reminded her.

Isabel didn't move. It felt as if the school was rushing around her and she was rooted to that spot.

"Hard to do what you think is right, but at the end of the day you have to be able to live with yourself," Charlotte said.

"I think you may have a theme for another cartoon," Isabel said with a tiny smile.

The two linked arms again and headed for Charlotte's locker.

"Maeve," Charlotte called out as they approached. "We were looking for you."

"We missed you at lunch," Isabel said.

"Great news!" Charlotte said. "Avery and Katani ate with us today."

"You're kidding!" Maeve replied.

"Yes … they sort of made up," Charlotte said.

"Temporarily at least," Isabel added.

"That's great. But … what if one wins and the other doesn't?" Maeve wondered out loud.

The three looked at each other and didn't say anything.

"Whatever happens, I think we should have a sleepover at the Tower on Saturday, is that OK, Char?" Maeve asked. "I think it's important that we're all together."

"I'll ask my dad, but I'm sure he'll say yes," Charlotte said.

"Great!" Maeve said happily as she scooted off to class.

Isabel thought of her new design for the Tower as she hurried on to class. Saturday would be a great day to make it happen. "Charlotte, would it be OK if I came over early on Saturday? I was hoping that I could do some … redecorating," Isabel asked as soon as they sat in their seats.

Charlotte looked a little uneasy. "Do you think we should vote on it first?"

"Don't worry. I think this one is a no-brainer. So can I come over early?"

"Hmm. Actually, I have a little project that I'm working on. It'd be great if you could help me with it," Charlotte said.

Isabel gave her a thumbs-up as she took a last sip of milk.

If a promise sounds too good to be true,
it might be too good to be true ...

CHAPTER 20

ᘓ

ELECTION DAY

"TODAY'S THE DAY," Avery called out as she pushed back the comforter and climbed out of bed. Draped over her desk chair was the outfit she picked out last night before she went to bed. Avery rarely put much thought into what she was going to wear, and she almost NEVER laid out clothes for the next day. Usually, she wore whatever she grabbed first out of the closet in the morning that was clean and comfortable.

But election day was a big day and Avery wanted to look just right. It hadn't taken her long to decide. She slipped on a pair of jeans and a red-white-and-blue hockey jersey—a replica from the 1980 USA Olympic Hockey Team.

She loved the story about the "Miracle On Ice." LOVED IT! Many of the players had been from New England ... they were local boys who did the impossible. They beat the Russian hockey team against all odds and then went on to win the Olympic Gold match against Finland. It was totally inspirational.

Avery checked her appearance in the mirror. Yup! She looked like a winner. Next she checked on Walter. He was in

❁

his sleep box. She could only see the shiny black scales from the middle of his coil. She changed his water as she did every morning and headed off for breakfast. She was starved!

"Hey, shorty. So today's the day, right?" her brother, Scott yawned.

"Yup!" Avery replied. "And I'm ready!"

"How 'bout a special election smoothie to power you through the day?" he asked.

Smoothies were Scott's specialty. No way could Avery turn down one of those. "Thanks," she said.

"I see you're wearing your USA hockey jersey," Scott said as he dumped ingredients into the blender.

"Yup! A win against all odds," she said as Scott hit the switch on the blender.

Not that she felt her campaign was against all odds. It just made her feel good to wear this jersey. It made her feel like a winner.

It was sad to think that in order for her to win, Katani had to lose. Avery didn't feel sorry for her opponents when she was playing sports. This campaign had been totally different from any sporting competition she'd ever been in. She thought running for class president would be like sports—prepare, practice, execute. But without specific rules and a referee or umpire to enforce them, the election had been brutal. She'd almost lost a good friend over politics.

At least she and Katani had made their peace before the election. She hoped that Katani wouldn't be too disappointed when she lost. She wished now that she had suggested that Katani should run for vice president. It would have been nice to have Katani for VP—they would've been a great team. Avery was voting for Robert Worley because she thought he would be easy to work with.

Avery downed the smoothie and wiped the frothy smoothie mustache from her upper lip. "Now can I have one of your cheesy omelets?" she asked.

"You got it!" Scott said.

POLLS ARE OPEN

Katani's mom grabbed her briefcase and dropped a kiss on top of Kelley's head first and then on the top of Katani's.

"I have an early court date this morning. Good luck with your election, Katani. I'll be thinking about you today," Mrs. Summers called as she moved toward the door.

"Mom, as you know, luck doesn't have much to do with it," Katani said, checking over her to-do list. "I've done all I can do. Now all that's left is for me to practice my acceptance speech."

Mrs. Summers blew her daughter another kiss. "Win or lose, I'm proud of you," she said. Her eyes caught Katani's eyes, and she held them for a moment before she went out the door.

"Katani for class president. And I approve of this message," Kelley said as she crunched into her second piece of toast. "I approve of this message."

Katani glanced over at Kelley and smiled. She couldn't believe she had actually thought it was Kelley taking down the posters!

When Katani arrived at school a half hour later, every person she met reminded her that today was the day. "Good luck with the election," she heard over and over again.

Ms. R dedicated the whole homeroom period to describing how the election would be run. "The ballots are being passed out in homeroom," she explained. "You have between now and the end of lunch to vote. Ballot boxes are in the cafeteria. You may vote between classes, or if any of you have study period between now and lunch, you can vote during study period."

Katani glanced over at Avery and smiled as Ms. Rodriguez went on.

"Mr. Danson and I will collect the ballot box after lunch and will count the votes after school. The results will be announced tonight at the dance."

Katani hoped Avery wouldn't be too disappointed when she lost the election. Avery had lots of good ideas so Katani would try her best to make her feel welcome at the class meetings. She made a mental note to create an environmental committee and appoint Avery as chair.

Katani was not surprised to find Avery wearing a hockey jersey. But she was surprised to see how big the jersey was. Avery was swimming in it! Didn't she realize that wearing such a huge shirt made her look small and kid-like? "That jersey is super-sized!" Katani said to her at lunch.

"No, it's not," Avery said, twisting around to grab the tag at the base of her neck. "See. It's a small. I had to special order it. They usually don't carry small hockey jerseys in the stores."

"What team is Eruzione?" Katani asked.

"USA? You might have heard of it?" Avery said. "Mike from Winthrop Massachusetts Eruzione was the captain of the 1980 U.S. Olympic Hockey Team?"

"That was like over a decade before I was born!" Katani said.

"It's world famous!" Avery told her. "Katani … they made a movie about it. *Miracle*, remember?"

Katani shrugged. "I'm not into hockey at all."

"How can you live in Boston and NOT be into hockey!" Avery's voice rose.

"Good thing that wasn't an election issue," Katani said to Charlotte.

Charlotte smiled, but her cheeks reddened a bit. She was grateful Avery was babbling on about hockey and the Bruins and hadn't heard what Katani said.

Katani tuned Avery out and turned her attention to Charlotte and Isabel. She had seen them put their ballots in the ballot box before they got in the hot-lunch line. She was dying to ask who they voted for, but didn't.

"Where's Maeve?" she asked when there was a break in Avery's diatribe about hockey.

"I don't know. We asked her yesterday where she's been disappearing to and she got all mysterious on us," Isabel answered.

"Is everything alright at home?" Katani asked.

"Maybe it's just been too tense for her at lunch," Isabel said.

"Things have been tense at lunch?" Avery asked innocently.

Katani rolled her eyes.

"What?" Avery wanted to know.

"Think about it Avery," Katani said.

The light bulb finally popped on in Avery's head. "Oh, you mean about the election and all," she said.

"Yeah, about the election and all," Charlotte echoed.

Katani hung her head. She wanted to be class president more than anything else. But at what price? What if she became class president, but because of the strain of the election, the BSG fell apart?

"Well, we've all neglected Maeve these past few days. I've been preoccupied with the cartoons for *The Sentinel*. I mean, she was really serious about the Picture your Pet in

Pink thing," Isabel said.

Katani suddenly felt bad that she told Maeve she couldn't help with Marty's costume. "How did that turn out?" Katani asked.

"Still think that was a crazy idea," Avery said.

"Well, we narrowed it to three. I don't remember if we ever picked just one," Isabel said, ignoring Avery's comment.

"Did we?" Charlotte asked.

"I don't think so. But all three were good," Isabel said.

"You guys took pictures of Marty in a pink outfit and sent it out for other people to see?" Avery asked.

"Avery!" Isabel said. "He was adorable."

"Marty in pink is not my idea of adorable," grumbled Avery.

CHAPTER 21

CR

THE RESULTS ARE IN

"OK, EVERYONE! On three," Maeve said. "One! Two! Three!"

"Go Wildcats!" Charlotte, Maeve, Isabel, Avery, and Katani screamed in unison before collapsing together in a wave of giggles. The quarterback handed off to #28, who dashed to the right, found a hole in the Bulldogs' defense, and rushed ten yards before he was tackled and dragged to the ground.

Maeve jumped to her feet and screamed, "Wooohooo!"

The rest of the crowd groaned.

Avery pulled on Maeve's coat. "Maeve, he didn't make first down. We're going to have to punt," she told her.

"What? But he ran a long way that time! The last two times he was hit as soon as he got the ball!"

"But it was third and fifteen and he only made ten yards," Avery explained.

"I don't get it," Maeve said.

"Me either," Charlotte said with a sigh.

"Obviously," Avery said, "I'll have to have you guys over for Football 101 some Sunday afternoon."

✿

The kicking team ran out onto the field to set up for a point. The Wildcat center hiked the ball back to the kicker and he kicked it to the waiting Bulldog player. It was a beautiful play.

It was one of those rare, warm October afternoons, and the first time since hot chocolate at Montoya's that the five of them had all been together. The election was over. Whatever was going to happen had already been decided. Maeve thought that would have made everyone feel a bit more relaxed, but her friends still seemed a little tense—everyone but Avery, who was totally into the game.

Maeve had wanted to invite everyone to her house tonight to get ready for the dance, but she was staying at her father's place tonight. And, there wasn't room for all of them to get dressed in that tiny room she shared with her brother Sam.

Suddenly, the crowd roared and Maeve jumped to her feet because everyone else did.

"What? What!" she asked Avery.

"The Bulldogs just got a penalty flag for holding, so that last play doesn't count," Avery said.

"What's holding?" Maeve asked.

"When a player literally grabs on and holds another player back," Avery explained.

"You mean you can knock someone down, but you can't hold them?" Maeve asked.

"Yup," Avery said.

"I'll never understand this game!" Maeve said.

"Me either," Charlotte agreed.

"Stick with me," Avery said. "I'll keep explaining it until you get it."

Maeve had to admit that by the end of the game, she understood football a little better. She loved the fact that her team had won! Everyone in the stands went wild. No one wanted to leave. Winning was such a rush!

Of course winning only made Maeve think of losing. Only one of her friends could win the election. That meant one of them would lose. Losing wasn't as fun as winning. Not by a long shot.

AND THE WINNER IS ...

After the win on the football field, each of the BSG had returned home to get dressed for the dance. For the first junior high dance of the year, they had all gathered at Maeve's house to get ready together. It had been so much fun! Katani was Chief Personal Problem Solver, in charge of making the lives and looks of her BSG sisters more beautiful. Everyone wanted Katani's fashion advice. Well, everyone except Avery perhaps.

Fashion was a non-issue for Avery. Katani knew that if she could, Avery would have worn that ridiculous too-big-for-her hockey jersey. Instead, Avery wore the same outfit that she had worn for the first seventh-grade dance last month. Not the most trendy outfit, but Katani realized that Avery's fiery nature compensated for her lack of fashion sense. Kids were drawn to her because of her personality and endless energy. Avery was her own fashion statement.

Katani took off her velvet jacket the moment she walked into the gym. Her dress was perfect for the fall theme. Katani was wowed by the decorations. The decorations committee had done a nice job of decorating the gym with fall colors.

Riley Lee and his band were on a riser at the front of the gym. Riley was in Katani's homeroom, but he was so quiet that she rarely noticed that he was there. So it seemed odd to see him in front of the whole seventh grade, playing a guitar and singing into a microphone. He looked like a completely different person.

Katani got a cup of punch and joined Avery at the edge of the dance floor. For the first time in weeks, Katani and Avery were on the sidelines and not the center of attention. Neither Avery or Katani were into dancing right at the moment. Besides, Maeve and Isabel were the real dancers of the group, and they were out on the floor dancing with a big group of girls. Nick had asked Charlotte to dance and considering the klutz factor, Katani thought Char was very brave to accept.

One song blended into another and then another. Maeve, Isabel, and Charlotte continued to dance. Avery and Katani nervously watched the clock. Time ticked by so slowly ... too slowly. They chatted about soccer for a little while, and then about Abigail Adams and how cool it was that she was able to tell her husband, President John Adams, that women needed the vote.

Betsy Fitzgerald eventually wandered by. She didn't look nervous at all, but that was because Betsy was running unopposed, so she KNEW she would be class treasurer by the end of the evening.

Betsy leaned in close so Avery and Katani could hear her over the band. "I want to wish you luck. The seventh grade is lucky to have two such qualified candidates to choose from. You would both make good presidents. I'm looking forward to working with either of you," she said.

Avery, for once, was speechless. Betsy had had the best election manners of anyone, Avery suddenly realized. Katani smiled politely. "Thanks for your support," Katani told her.

The song ended then and everyone around them clapped and cheered. A few people on the dance floor whistled.

When Betsy walked away, a very handsome eighth-grade boy headed toward Katani.

"Wanna dance?" he mouthed and pointed toward the dance floor.

Katani looked behind her. He couldn't be speaking to her! But there wasn't anyone behind her. She looked back at the eighth-grade hottie. What was his name again? He looked amused. Katani, her confidence a little rattled, wondered if he was serious or if he was making fun of her.

He nodded toward the dance floor again. His smile was warm, not taunting. Her heart jumped in her throat and she swallowed hard to force it back down. She wasn't sure what to do. Before she could do anything, the song ended.

"Maybe another time?" he asked.

Katani smiled and the mysterious boy disappeared back into the crowd.

Katani and Avery shared a surprised look as Maeve wove through the crowd, climbed the steps on the riser, and joined Riley on stage.

"This is a song I wrote myself. It's called, 'You Got Me,'" Riley said and handed Maeve the microphone.

It was a great song—bouncy with an infectious beat—that even had Avery and Katani swaying to the music. The lyrics were fun and catchy and by the end everyone was singing the refrain, "You Got Me!"

Katani couldn't take her eyes off Maeve, whose stage

presence was wonderful. She not only had a great voice, but she had the moves, the smile, and the facial expression to make the song come alive.

Maybe it was time for an *American Idol* Maeve, thought Katani. When the band finished, Maeve took a bow as the room erupted in cheers. Then she bounced off the stage and straight into the group of BSG that had gathered to greet her.

"That was great," Katani said.

"Awesome," Avery shouted.

"How could you just get up there and sing … impromptu without rehearsing or anything?" Isabel asked.

Maeve blushed. "Well … We've … I've been rehearsing now and then with Riley's band."

"Let me guess. During lunch?" Charlotte asked.

Maeve nodded.

"Why didn't you tell us? I would have borrowed my mom's digital video recorder!" Avery said.

"Well, you guys have had other things on your mind …"

Maeve glanced back at the stage. Riley lifted his chin in recognition. Just then, Katani caught the look between Maeve and Riley.

"Is there something going on between you two?" Katani whispered in Maeve's ear.

"Well … I'm not sure if Riley's my destiny or not, but I'm willing to explore the possibility," Maeve whispered back, blushing at the same time. "We really like the same things."

"Katani! Katani! Get ready. It's time," Avery said, tugging at Katani's arm.

Katani turned to see her grandmother already at the microphone. The long wait was over. It was time for the election results to be announced.

"I'd like to thank Riley and his band, *Mustard Monkey*,"

Mrs. Fields said.

The seventh-grade class cheered. Avery whistled loudly, "Way to go, Maeve," she shouted out.

"He named his band *Mustard Monkey*?" Isabel asked, making a face.

"What's wrong with monkeys?" Avery wanted to know.

"Nothing … but when I think of monkeys, I think bananas … and bananas with mustard are just gross!" Isabel shuddered.

"And now, to announce the results of today's seventh-grade class elections, I'll turn you over to the seventh-grade class advisors, Ms. Rodriguez and Mr. Danson," Mrs. Fields said, nodding to the teachers as they approached the stage.

To Katani, it seemed the entire room went dead silent as Ms. Rodriguez and Mr. Danson climbed the stairs to the riser. "Poise," she whispered to herself. She instantly lifted her chin, threw her shoulders back, and felt three inches taller.

"First we'd like to thank all the candidates who ran for office," Mr. Danson said when he reached the podium. "A round of applause, please."

"Get on with it," Avery said under her breath, but all the BSG heard her.

Maeve grabbed Avery's hand and squeezed it.

"We'd like to start with the position of treasurer," Mr. Danson announced.

Betsy didn't even wait for the announcement, but started moving toward the riser … she was halfway up the stairs when Ms. Rodriguez read out, "Betsy Fitzgerald."

"Next for Secretary we have …"

Ms. Rodriguez stepped over to the podium, "Yuko Osawa."

Everyone clapped as Yuko let out a little screech and ran

for the stage steps. She was so excited she tripped and almost fell flat on her face.

"The new seventh-grade vice president is ..." Mr. Danson paused and stepped back so Ms. Rodriguez could step up to the microphone.

Katani took that opportunity to go through the opening of her acceptance speech in her head. "I'd like to thank ..."

"Jessica Bentley," Ms. Rodriguez announced in a loud clear voice.

A cheer went up from around where Jessica was standing. Katani couldn't see Jessica, but the whole group seemed to surge toward the stage steps.

"Remember. Poise. I am calm and confident," Katani silently repeated to herself.

"And now, the results for seventh-grade class president," Mr. Danson said. Everyone quieted down right away.

Ms. Rodriguez stepped to the podium and scanned the crowd. "The new president of the seventh-grade class is ..."

Katani took one step forward.

"Henry Yurt."

Katani felt a shock wave run through her from the top of her head all the way through the soles of her feet. Her ears were ringing. A loud sound filled her ears. Slowly, she realized the sound she was hearing was her classmates around her screaming and clapping.

She was stunned. Unsure. What just happened? Isabel was patting her back. Had she misheard? Had Ms. Rodriguez really said Katani Summers, and she had only thought she had heard her say Henry Yurt? Was Isabel patting her on the back or urging her toward the stage? Katani was confused. Dizzy. She looked to the left, where she saw kids cheering with their arms raised, punching the air with one fist and shouting, "Yurt! Yurt! Yurt! Yurt!"

Only when she saw Henry Yurt trot up the steps to the riser and watched Ms. Rodriguez and Mr. Danson shake his hand did she realize that she hadn't misheard. Henry Yurt had won. The Yurt Alert had triumphed.

When she looked to the left and saw Avery's face, her mouth hanging open and tears dancing in her eyes, Katani realized she must look as shocked and stunned as Avery did. She couldn't let anyone see her like this! She turned and ran to the nearest exit and out into the night. She remembered Candice's cheer "Summerstyle," but she just couldn't smile … not now. And how could she hold her head up? She had just lost big time to, of all people, Henry Yurt! She was crushed.

The cool air stung her face. Hot tears oozed from the corners of her eyes. She didn't really know where she was going, but she had to keep moving. She ran around the back wall of the gym to get out of sight.

How could this be? Had she been so worried about Dillon and Avery that she hadn't taken Henry seriously? How could anyone take the suspender-snapping, bow-tie-wearing Yurtmeister seriously?! Was it the Smile Award thing? Was it the candy bars? Whatever it was, they had chosen him—the goofster—over her, Katani Summers. The thought caused her to run, as if by running she could put all those thoughts behind her. Tears were flooding her eyes and she was running blinded when … oof! She ran into something. Someone.

She looked down to see that it was Avery. The two collapsed into one another's arms. They stood there with their arms around each other for a while before Avery pushed away. They sat down on the steps leading up to the gym entrance.

"Sorry," Avery said, sniffing loudly. "I hate crying."

✿

235

"Me, too," Katani said, sinking down on the cold concrete next to her.

"I hate letting anyone see me snivel," Avery said.

"Me, too," Katani sniffed.

"I never cried when I got smacked in the eye with a field hockey stick."

"I didn't cry when Kelley ruined a dress I'd been working on for three weeks," Katani said.

"Oh, yeah? I have no idea what that would have felt like, but I know what you're going through now!" Avery said.

Katani choked back a laugh that oddly sounded like a sob.

"I'm not used to losing," Avery said. "I mean when I lose I can always say there'll be another game … next week. Next season."

"I wouldn't know about that. I'm not much for organized sports. I mean that's my sisters' thing. Maybe it's because they're so good at sports and school, and everyone has always compared me to them all my life, that I'm really careful about what I take on. I mean I won't try anything that I don't think I can …" The word stuck in her throat. *"Win."*

Neither of them said anything for a moment, and suddenly Katani felt very cold.

"Now what?" Katani asked.

"I'm not sure what will happen after this," Avery said.

"Well, at least it's over," Katani said looking down at her mod Mary Janes.

"Over," Avery echoed.

"No more campaign posters," Katani said.

"Or debates."

"Or polls."

"Back to being friends."

"Yeah," Katani said gently. The wind whipped up the

edges of her dress and she smoothed it back down with her hands.

"I suppose we should get back in there," Avery said, rubbing at her tearstained eyes as she stood up. "Coach G says that win or lose after a game, it's good sportsmanship to shake hands and congratulate the winner."

"I guess ..." Katani said, rising to her feet and then half laughing. "Is my mascara running?"

Avery studied Katani's cheeks. "Nope. Looks fine. Ya know, I thought running for office would be like any other sports competition. Somebody wins, somebody loses. But this feels different than losing a soccer game. It feels ... I don't know ... *personal*."

"I know what you mean," Katani sighed as she peeled off her velvet burgundy jacket. She was going back into the gym as just another seventh grader going to a dance. The jacket seemed out of place now. "It feels ... like being rejected."

"Besides, I'm used to having a team. A cheering section at least," Avery added.

"Well, you have me," Katani said, giving her short friend a quick hug.

"Running against you was hard. But losing together ... well, it's better than losing alone ... Beanpole," grinned Avery.

"You're right. Let's go ... Shrimpster."

The two went back to the dance arm-in-arm.

CHAPTER 22

❦

SEVEN SISTERS

MAEVE couldn't believe her eyes!

"He won! Marty won!" she shouted, not caring that the people passing by on the sidewalk were looking at her like she had lost her mind.

There in the middle of Think Pink!'s front window was a huge blow-up of Marty. Suspended by wires and hanging in the center of the window, Marty's photograph was the largest picture of the dozen or so pictures displayed in the window. Each picture was matted in pink with the title of the picture in bold hot pink letters below the photograph. Maeve was happy with the title they had come up with … Klondike Pink. It fit.

The tiny bell above the door jingled as Maeve pushed through the shop door.

"Good morning! How can we put you in the pink this morning?" The woman behind the counter this morning was Razzberry Pink, herself.

"Good morning, Ms. Pink," Maeve said.

"Please, call me Razzberry," she said.

"Razzberry," Maeve said, sure her cheeks were now the

most perfect shade of pink. "I'm already in the pink. That's my photo in the center of the window."

"Oh, yes ... Klondike Pink! What a delightful entry! I have something for you ..." she said, opening the drawer, pulling out a pink envelope and handing it to Maeve.

"Is this first prize?"

"Well, they're all first prizes," Razzberry Pink said.

"But I thought ..." Maeve paused. "I mean it was in the middle and it was bigger than all the others ... so I just figured it was the winner."

"They are all winners!"

"You mean it wasn't a contest?"

"Ma cherie ... our society puts way too much emphasis on winning. As Dr. Robert Anthony once said, 'You were placed on this earth to create, not compete.' That is why all who entered My Pet Looks Perfect in Pink will be rewarded! Of course, all the entry fees will be donated to the Brookline Pet Shelter. Those little darlings need our help, you know!"

Maeve nodded. They were all winners? Maeve couldn't help feeling that the picture of Marty was better than all the others and should be recognized as the best. But she smiled politely and thanked Ms. Pink. "I can't wait for my friends to see the window," she said.

Maeve didn't open the envelope until she was outside the shop. It was a $20 gift certificate. Immediately, Maeve started calculating. The twenty dollars plus this week's allowance would put her over the top. She now had enough money for the boa. Her first instinct was to run home for the rest of the money, but she stopped. This, after all, had been a group effort. The gift certificate belonged to the BSG, not to her. They could decide together what to get with it. They could buy pink treats for an upcoming sleepover, or maybe

Rose   Pink

Think Pink

Klondike Pink

The store for people who love pink

Pink   Rosa

new décor for the Tower. Maeve's mind started spinning with all the possibilities.

They could decide tonight. Maeve was happy that together with Isabel and Charlotte, she had planned the sleepover—even before they knew the election results. Not that she enjoyed seeing Katani, Avery or even Dillon lose, but Maeve was almost happy that none of them had won. She wasn't sure what the long-term effects of having any of those three win might have had on the BSG.

But, Avery and Katani had looked so sad at the dance last night. Hopefully, the news of Marty's picture in Think Pink!'s window and the gift certificate would put them in the pink, too.

Avery's Blog
Election Update

Sadly, I lost the election for class president. But as my dad told me when I called to tell him—"the important thing is that we learn from our losses."

Did you know that Abraham Lincoln was one of the biggest losers? Before he became president he had lost two elections and had two failed businesses. But, despite his losses ... and his successes ... Lincoln knew what was important.

Quote:
The better part of one's life consists of his friendships.
—Abraham Lincoln

❀

UNVEILING

Charlotte asked her dad to have a fire in the fireplace ready and waiting when the girls arrived. Avery had called to say that she was bringing dinner—Fenway franks to roast over the fire.

This was Charlotte's first hot dog roast—definitely a new experience. Avery brought it all—hot dogs, buns, roasting forks, and all the fixings, including sauerkraut and relish.

"A hot dog roast was only the second top vote getter in my recent blog, but it got me thinking about hot dogs and I couldn't stop! I've been hungry for hot dogs ever since. It's been a while since I've had a really good dog. Fenway franks are the best! Really—the best!" Avery explained as she unpacked the feast in Charlotte's kitchen. Maeve thought Nathan's were the best, but since Avery was a Red Sox fanatic, she decided to keep quiet.

After their roast, they had s'mores, which had become a BSG tradition after their first slumber party back in September. It was only after she'd polished off her second s'more that Maeve announced she had news.

"I brought pink ginger ale to celebrate," she said and carefully poured it into five plastic glasses.

"I'd like to make a toast," Maeve announced with a flair that only she could get away with. "To Marty—otherwise known as Klondike Pink."

The five clinked their plastic cups together. "To Klondike Pink," they said in unison.

Avery giggled because the ginger ale tickled her nose.

"Klondike Pink?" she asked when she recovered from her giggle fit.

"Marty's Think Pink! costume," Charlotte explained.

"You didn't make him look ridiculous—you know, like a girl, did you?"

"There' s nothing wrong with looking like a girl," Katani told Avery.

"There is if you're a guy!" Avery replied.

"That's right! You two never saw the photo. Hang on!" Charlotte said. She ran to her room and returned with a photo.

"Aww!" Katani crooned. "Marty, you're such a cute little boy."

"Let me see," Avery said, tugging at the picture.

"Awesome!" she said when she spied the snowboard. "Where'd you get the mini-snowboard?"

"It's poster board," Maeve said.

"Really? From this angle, it really looks like a puppy-sized snowboard. So, did he win?"

"Well, yes and no."

"Huh?" Katani said.

"Well, I thought it was a contest, but it turns out it was just 'an invitation' for Think Pink! customers to be creative."

"What's up with that?" Avery asked. "What exactly does that mean?"

"All that work for nothing?" Isabel asked.

"Well, not exactly nothing," Maeve said. "Everyone who submitted a photo got this!" Maeve showed them the gift certificate. "And Marty's picture is blown up and in the center of the Think Pink! window. And he helped raise $10 for the Pet Shelter."

"Cool," Avery said, clapping.

Charlotte added, "We should walk down and see it tomorrow."

"The money goes to the BSG ... unless you want to buy something pink for Marty with it."

"NO!" Avery said.

"Snacks? Décor for the Tower?" Maeve suggested.

"I think the money should go to Maeve to replace the slippers she sacrificed," Isabel said.

"Here, here," Avery called out taking the certificate from Maeve and holding it in the air for all to see. "The motion on the floor is to let Maeve have the $20 to reimburse her for the loss of her pink slippers. All in favor say 'aye.'"

"Aye!" the entire group said loud and strong.

"Motion carries," Avery said.

"Thanks," Maeve said. "But if you don't mind, I had my eye on a boa."

"Constrictor?" Avery asked.

"Eewww," Isabel said with a full-body shudder.

"No, Avery—a feather boa," Maeve said. "A pink one."

This time, it was Avery who shuddered. "I'd rather have

a boa constrictor," she said.

"Now that THAT's out of the way …" Katani said. "I have news, too. Avery, this is for you." Katani handed Avery a business envelope.

"What's this?"

"Open it and find out," Katani said.

Avery ripped open the envelope, quickly scanned the letter inside and jumped to the bottom of the sheet to see who it was from. "Haley Yurt! Haley Yurt was the Red Pen?! What? How!" Avery sputtered.

"HALEY Yurt!" the other BSG exclaimed.

"I can't believe it," Maeve gasped.

"Poor Henry," said Charlotte.

"Poor Haley," Isabel said quietly.

Isabel, Charlotte, and Maeve chorused, "Poor Haley."

"Well … she must be pretty mad inside to do something like that. What if no one ever talks to her again?" Isabel asked.

The girls were silent.

Then Katani took a breath and started in with the story. "My grandmother somehow found out—she wouldn't tell me how—that Haley Yurt was behind all the election nastiness. Haley'd made a big stink about the eighth-grade elections, saying they were stupid and just a big popularity contest. So when her little brother Henry decided to run … I don't know, I guess she just snapped or something," Katani said.

"I really thought it was those two Queens of Mean— Anna and Joline!" Avery said.

"Me, too," Maeve said.

Charlotte nodded. She had been so convinced that Anna and Joline had something to do with the zingers in the hall that she actually felt a little guilty knowing it was Haley.

"Anyway, my grandmother made Haley write a letter of

apology to every candidate," Katani said.

"Is that all?" Avery asked indignantly.

"No," Katani said in hushed tones. "She was suspended for two weeks."

The BSG gasped. They had never known anyone who was suspended before.

Charlotte was relieved that it wasn't anyone she knew very well. She was even glad that it wasn't Anna and Joline. It was hard enough to be around girls like that every day without adding one more reason to distrust them. Everywhere she had lived there had been girls like Anna and Joline. Girls who thought they were better than everyone else and weren't happy until they made everyone else feel small and unworthy. Charlotte was glad she didn't have to face girls like that alone. She was glad she had the BSG.

"I have a surprise," Charlotte announced. "I had tea with Miss Pierce the other day and she told me an old Chinese proverb: 'At home one relies on parents; away from home one relies on friends.' I'm so glad I have all of you to rely on. And so you never forget, I made bracelets to remind you who you can depend on."

Charlotte took the five bracelets out of a bag and passed them out. The beads were on a coil of wire that circled the wrist four times. She made a different color for each girl: yellow for Katani, pink for Maeve, green for Isabel, blue for Avery, and purple for herself. Interspersed between the beads and spaced so they could easily be read in the correct order were BSG Forever written on shrink plastic.

Delighted, her friends murmured their thanks. Maeve gave Charlotte a huge hug.

"And now … for the big news of the evening," Charlotte said. "Remember how I said that Isabel needed her own equal space, but I couldn't figure out how to do it? Well, Isabel did! Wait til you see this!"

The group rushed up the ladder steps to the Tower.

"Wait for me at the top of the ladder. No turning on the lights until we're all up there!" Charlotte told them.

Charlotte was the last up. There was a quiet energy in the Tower. Charlotte fumbled along the wall feeling for the light switch. When she threw it, there was a collective gasp from the group.

Over the center of the room hung a hoop about the size of a hula-hoop. Hanging from the hoop was fabric, the most beautiful shade of blue—dark and deep, but still true blue. "Corners, everyone," Charlotte said. Everyone went to her different corner of the tower, while Isabel disappeared inside the ring of fabric.

"Pull the cords now," Charlotte said. Each girl pulled the cord that was hanging in her corner, and the ends of the fabric that were really triangular pieces opened like five petals on a flower when they were pulled up to the corner of the room.

"Wow!"

"Awesome! It's like a BSG flower," marveled Katani.

Maeve threw her arms in the air dramatically and sang out, "It's BSG Flower Power."

"Look at this!" Avery called rushing to the center where Isabel stood. Avery pushed aside a beanbag chair to look at the brightly painted compass rose on the floor. Each direction had one of the girls' names written on it.

"You painted on the floor? Miss Pierce is going to flip out!" Avery said.

"No," Isabel said reaching down and raising an edge. "Look, everyone … it's painted on canvas and cut out and shellacked. It's really just a floor cover, even though it does look like it's painted on the floor. I can move this wherever we want and that will be my space."

"Isabel," said Katani in a burst of awed enthusiasm, "you are just so … so … artistic."

Isabel bowed and with a flourish directed each girl to her petal.

Each girl sat down where her name was painted and looked up. Above them, inside the hoop, Charlotte had used a rope of lights to write Isabel's name, just like she had written their names on their windows.

From the hoop hung three of Isabel's papier-mâché birds.

"Inspirations for your cartoons?" Maeve asked.

Isabel nodded.

Their eyes were all drawn to the petals or wings of fabric that stretched from the center hoop to the corners of the Tower. On the inside of the fabric, Charlotte and Isabel had painted stars with metallic silver paint.

"Wow! Our own stars show no matter what the weather!" Avery said.

"It's Persius," Isabel said. "The constellation known as the Seven Sisters—the brightest constellation in the sky. Charlotte helped me paint it on this afternoon."

"The Seven Sisters?" Katani asked.

"Yes. Seven stars that travel the sky together," Charlotte said.

"Just like the five of us!" Maeve said.

"… and two more stars—Ruby and Sapphire—the original Beacon Street Girls," Charlotte said.

"… Moving through the universe together …" Katani said.

"… Forever and always …" Isabel promised.

"Woof," Marty barked, as if adding the exclamation point.

Charlotte's Journal

We made a friendship promise tonight. Isabel said that the BSG would be friends "forever and always." I hope that that is a promise we can keep, no matter where we go or what other friends we meet. But one thing is for certain—some promises are really, really hard to keep. So, I guess you better make sure that when you promise something, you keep to your word. Otherwise, the word promise won't mean much. And I don't think I want my life to be full of empty promises. The other day, I read this anonymous quote in a magazine ... "Say what you mean—mean what you say." I'm going to add it to my quote wall because I think it's a really great motto. And no one knows who wrote it ... I think that makes it even more special. It's a reminder to all of us—no matter if we're famous, or just a regular person—to keep the promises we make.

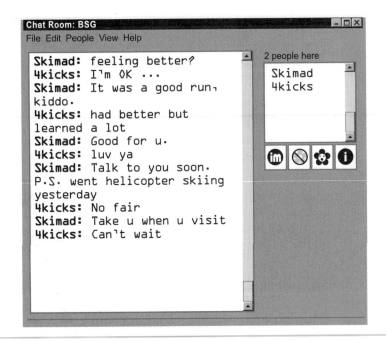

Chat Room: BSG

File Edit People View Help

Skimad: feeling better?
4kicks: I'm OK ...
Skimad: It was a good run, kiddo.
4kicks: had better but learned a lot
Skimad: Good for u.
4kicks: luv ya
Skimad: Talk to you soon. P.S. went helicopter skiing yesterday
4kicks: No fair
Skimad: Take u when u visit
4kicks: Can't wait

2 people here

Skimad
4kicks

CR

To be continued ...

sneak preview!

BOOK 6: lake rescue COMING SOON!

ALSO AVAILABLE AT:

www.beaconstreetgirls.com and **www.amazon.com!**

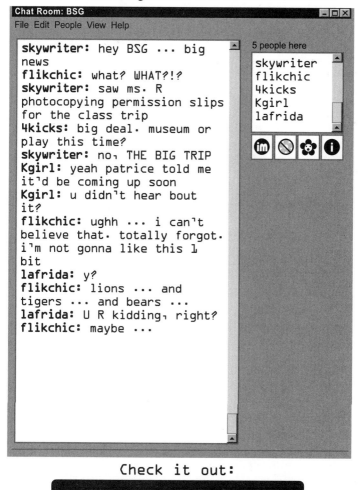

```
Chat Room: BSG                                    _ □ ✕
File Edit People View Help

  skywriter: hey BSG ... big        ▲   5 people here
  news
  flikchic: what? WHAT?!?               skywriter  ▲
  skywriter: saw ms. R                  flikchic
  photocopying permission slips         4kicks
  for the class trip                    Kgirl
  4kicks: big deal. museum or           lafrida
  play this time?
  skywriter: no, THE BIG TRIP       ▼
  Kgirl: yeah patrice told me
  it'd be coming up soon
  Kgirl: u didn't hear bout
  it?
  flikchic: ughh ... i can't
  believe that. totally forgot.
  i'm not gonna like this 1
  bit
  lafrida: y?
  flikchic: lions ... and
  tigers ... and bears ...
  lafrida: U R kidding, right?
  flikchic: maybe ...
```

Check it out:

www.beaconstreetgirls.com

THE NEW TOWER RULES
CREATED BY THE NEWEST ORDER
OF THE RUBY AND THE SAPPHIRE

Be it resolved that *all* girls are created equal!

1. We will speak our minds, but we won't be like obnoxious or anything.
2. We won't put ourselves down, even if we aren't super-smart, super-coordinated, or a supermodel.
3. We'll be loyal to our friends and won't lie to them even if they make a mistake or do something totally embarrassing.
4. We will go for it—how will we know what we can do if we don't try?
5. We will try to eat healthy and stay active. How can you chase your dream if you can't keep up?
6. We won't just take from people and the planet. We'll try to give back good things too.

❧ . . . . ❦

AMENDMENTS:

1. We can add as many amendments as we like.
2. We will dare to be fashion individualistas—like we're all different so why should we dress the same?
3. Sometimes we'll veg out—just because we feel like it!
4. We should have as much fun as we can.
5. We should try to save money so if we ever want to we can start a business or something someday.
6. We will try to keep an open mind about new people.
7. When in doubt ... phone home!
8. We won't let people take advantage of us ... we deserve respect!

Note from Avery
Proposed new amendment:

9. We won't let competition ruin the BSG—friendship is way more important than winning.

What's the vote?

Katani—I second the motion.
Maeve—That's music to my ears.
Isabel—Friends forever.
Charlotte—BSG forever!

10 Questions For You and Your Friends to Chat About

1. Do you think that Avery and Katani made the right decision to run against each other for class president?

2. What were some of things that caused the competition between the BSG to get out of hand?

3. If you were running for class president ... what important school issues would be part of your campaign?

4. Why was Isabel so worried about her cartoons for *The Sentinel*?

5. What are the qualities of a good leader?

6. Who, out of all the candidates, would you have voted for?

7. What important message does Maeve learn—and pass on to her friends—from the "My Pet Looks Perfect in Pink" contest?

8. Have you ever been in the middle of an argument between your friends? What did you do?

9. What important lessons did the BSG learn about competition?

10. If you were dressing up Marty, what kind of costume would you create?

✿

Charlotte's Word Nerd Dictionary
BSG Words

Fantabulous: (p. 8) adjective — *so fantastic ... so fabulous.*
Chillaxing: (p. 29) verb — *chilling out and relaxing — a cool combo.*
Kludgy: (p. 41) adjective — *awkward.*
Zinger: (p. 193) noun — *a sticky note that has a nasty message written on it.*

French Words & Phrases

Croquettes: (p. 118) noun — *ground up pieces of meat breaded and fried into yummy cakes ... like French chicken fingers.*
Comment ça va?: (p. 136) — *How's it going?*
Garçons: (p. 136) noun — *waiters, boys.*
Café au lait: (p. 136) noun — *coffee with hot milk.*
Quel problem!: (p. 137) — *What a problem!*
Affreux: (p. 137) adjective — *awful.*
Voilà: (p. 137) exclamation — *like Ta-dah!*
Bisous: (p. 182) noun — *kisses.*
Chérie: (p. 182) noun — *my dear.*
Papier-mâché: (p. 205) noun — *glued together pieces of paper that can be molded and dried into cool shapes.*

Other Cool Words ...

Ferocity: (p. 3) noun — *a fierce, strong, and rough way of handling something.*
Paparazzi: (p. 4) noun — *photographers from magazines and newspapers who follow famous people around relentlessly.*
Mayhem: (p. 5) noun — *total craziness and confusion!*

Optimistic: (p. 8) adjective—*always seeing the good side of a situation.*

Obsessive: (p. 9) adjective—*being really concerned that things should be a certain way.*

Mandatory: (p. 63) adjective—*someone makes a rule so that something has to happen—no matter what.*

Gimmicky: (p. 65) adjective—*getting other people to believe you by having a slick phrase or plan.*

Tagline: (p. 78) noun—*a short phrase that companies or organizations use so that people will remember their message.*

Hodgepodge: (p. 130) noun—*mixed up and jumbled together.*

Recluse: (p. 135) noun—*someone who lives alone and keeps away from other people.*

Bodice: (p. 137) noun—*the top part of a dress.*

Enthralled: (p. 148) verb—*being full of enchantment about something or someone.*

Q&A: (p. 171) nouns—*question and answer.*

Contentious: (p. 190) adjective—*characterized by arguments and disagreements.*

Dastardly: (p. 210) adjective—*really mean; planned by someone who is too scared to confront other people.*

Diatribe: (p. 225) noun—*a long explanation or speech.*

Impromptu: (p. 232) adjective—*something happening without being planned.*

✿

1. What part of Maeve's wardrobe becomes Marty's Perfect Pink Costume?
   A. Her favorite pink T-shirt
   B. Her pink fuzzy slippers
   C. Her pink nightshirt
   D. Her pink polka dot socks

2. What class office does Betsy Fitzgerald run for?
   A. President
   B. Secretary
   C. Vice President
   D. Treasurer

3. Avery LOVES which kind of pizza?
   A. Mushroom
   B. Hawaiian
   C. Spinach
   D. Extra Cheese

4. What is Henry's catchy campaign slogan?
   A. Yurtmeister for President
   B. Yurt Alert
   C. Yurt for Prez
   D. Vote Yurt

5. Whom does Katani suspect is responsible for the missing campaign posters?
   A. Avery
   B. Henry
   C. Ms. Rodriguez
   D. Kelley

6. What is the name of the salesgirl at Think Pink!?
   A. Ms. Rose
   B. Ms. Magenta
   C. Ms. Fuchsia
   D. Ms. Pink

7. What is Isabel's favorite cartoon inspiration?
   A. Elephants
   B. Tigers
   C. Birds
   D. Monkeys

8. What is Avery's word for the mean notes that are put on the posters?
   A. Wingers
   B. Thingers
   C. Clingers
   D. Zingers

9. What's the name of Riley Lee's band?
   A. Mustard Monkey
   B. Kickin' Kangaroo
   C. Crazy Chicken
   D. Purple Panda

10. What's Marty's pink nickname?
   A. Pretty in Pink
   B. Pink Marty
   C. Klondike Pink
   D. Pink Perfection

(Answers right below!)

SCORING

8—10 Points: Congrats ... You're a Beacon Street Girl at heart! We can never have too many BFFs!

5—7 Points: Nice work ... How 'bout we hang out at Montoya's after school?

0—4 Points: No problem ... let's go get some Swedish Fish!

ANSWERS: 1. B. Her pink fuzzy slippers **2. D.** Treasurer **3. C.** Spinach **4. B.** Yurt Alert **5. D.** Kelley **6. B.** Ms. Magenta **7. C.** Birds **8. D.** Zingers **9. A.** Mustard Monkey **10. C.** Klondike Pink

BOOK 1

*Worst Enemies/
Best Friends*

BOOK 2

*Bad News/
Good News*

BOOK 3

*Letters From
The Heart*

BOOK 4

Out Of Bounds

BOOK 5

Promises, Promises

BOOK 6

Lake Rescue

"I went to the bookstore and BOOM! I just found the
best book in the world."

~Taryn, 10